THE LAW
OF
THE LAND

EMERSON HOUGH

The Law of the Land

Emerson Hough

© 1st World Library – Literary Society, 2004
PO Box 2211
Fairfield, IA 52556
www.1stworldlibrary.org
First Edition

LCCN: 2005901316

Softcover ISBN: 1-4218-1131-6
Hardcover ISBN: 1-4218-1031-X
eBook ISBN: 1-4218-1231-2

Purchase *"The Law of the Land"*
as a traditional bound book at:
www.1stWorldLibrary.org/purchase.asp?ISBN=1-4218-1131-6

1st World Library Literary Society is a nonprofit
organization dedicated to promoting literacy by:

- Creating a free internet library accessible from any
  computer worldwide.
- Hosting writing competitions and offering book
  publishing scholarships.

Readers interested in supporting literacy
through sponsorship, donations or
membership please contact:
literacy@1stworldlibrary.org
Check us out at: www.1stworldlibrary.ORG
and start downloading free ebooks today.

The Law of the Land
contributed by Tim, Ed & Rodney
in support of
1st World Library Literary Society

CONTENTS

BOOK I

BOOK II

BOOK III

BOOK I

CHAPTER I

MISS LADY

Ah, but it was a sweet and wonderful thing to see Miss Lady dance, a strange and wondrous thing! She was so sweet, so strong, so full of grace, so like a bird in all her motions! Now here, now there, and back again, her feet scarce touching the floor, her loose skirt, held out between her dainty fingers, resembling wings, she swam through the air, up and down the room of the old plantation house, as though she were indeed the creature of an element wherein all was imponderable, light and free of hampering influences. Darting, nodding, beckoning, courtesying to something that she saw - it must have moved you to applause, had you seen Miss Lady dance! You might have been restrained by the feeling that this was almost too unreal, too unusual, this dance of the young girl, all alone, in front of the great mirror which faithfully gave back the passing, flying figure line for line, flush for flush, one bosom-heave for that of the other. Yet the tall white lilies in the corner saw; and the tall white birds, one on each side of the great cheval glass, saw also, but fluttered not; since a lily and a stork and a maiden may each be tall and white, and each may understand the other subtly.

Miss Lady stood at length, tall and white, her cheeks rosy withal, her blown brown hair pushed back a bit, one hand lightly resting on her bosom, looking - looking into the mirror, asking of it some question, getting, indeed, from it some answer - an answer embodying, perhaps, all that youth may mean, all that the morning may bring.

For now the sun of the South came creeping up apace, and saw Miss Lady as it peered in through the rose lattice whereon hung scores of fragrant blossoms. A gentle wind of morning stirred the lace curtains at the windows and touched Miss Lady's hair as she stood there, asking the answer of the mirror. It was morning in the great room, morning for the southern day, morning for the old plantation whose bell now jangled faintly and afar off - morning indeed for Miss Lady, who now had ceased in her self-absorbed dance. At this very moment, as she stood gazing into the mirror, with the sunlight and the roses thus at hand, one might indeed have sworn that it was morning for ever, over all the world!

Miss Lady stood eager, fascinated, before the glass; and in the presence of the tall flowers and the tall birds, saw something which stirred her, felt something which came in at the window out of the blue sky and from the red rose blossoms, on the warm south wind. Impulsively she flung out her arms to the figure in the glass. Perhaps she felt its beauty and its friendliness. And yet, an instant later, her arms relaxed and sank; she sighed, knowing not why she sighed.

Ah, Miss Lady, if only it could be for ever morning for us all! Nay, let us say not so. Let us say rather that this sweet picture of Miss Lady, doubled by the glass, remains to-day imperishably preserved in the old mirror - the picture of Miss Lady dancing as the bird flies, and then standing, plaintive and questioning, before her own image, loving it because it was beautiful and friendly, dreading it because she could not understand.

Miss Lady had forgotten that she was alone, and did not hear the step at the door, nor see the hand which presently pushed back the curtain. There stepped into the room, the tall, somewhat full figure of a lady who stood looking on with eyes at first surprised, then cynically amused. The intruder paused, laughing a low, well-fed, mellow laugh. On the moment she coughed in deprecation. Miss Lady sprang back, as does the wild deer startled in the forest. Her hands went to her cheeks, which burned in swift flame, thence to drop to her bosom, where her heart was beating in a confusion of throbs, struggling with the reversed current of the blood of all her tall young body.

"Mamma!" she cried. "You startled me." "So it seems," said the new-comer. "I beg your pardon. I did not mean to intrude upon your devotions."

She came forward and seated herself-a tall woman, a trifle full of figure now, but still vital of presence. Her figure, deep-chested, rounded and shapely, now began to carry about it a certain air of ease. The mouth, well-bowed and red, had a droop of the same significance. The eyes, deep, dark and shaded by strong brows, held depths not to be fathomed at a glance, but their first message was one of an open and ready self-indulgence. The costume, flowing, loose and easy, carried out the same thought; the piled black hair did not deny it; the smile upon the face, amused, half-cynical, confirmed it. Here was a woman of her own acquaintance with the world, you would have said. And in the next breath you must have asked how she could have been the mother of this tall girl, at whom she now smiled thus mockingly.

"I was just - I was - well, I was dancing, mamma," said Miss Lady. "It is so nice." This somewhat vaguely.

"Yes," said her mother; "why?"

"I do not know," said Miss Lady, frankly, and turning to her with sudden courage. "I was dancing. That is all."

"Yes, I know."

"Well, is it any crime, mamma, I should like to ask?" This with spirit, and with eyes showing themselves able to flash upon occasion.

"Not in the least, my dear. Indeed, I am not at all surprised. I knew it was coming."

"What was coming, mammal? What do you mean?"

"Why, that this was going to happen - that you were going to dance. It was nearly time."

"I do not know what you mean."

"It was always thus with the Ellisons," said the other woman. "All the Ellisons danced this way once in their lives. All the girls do so. They're very strange, these Ellison girls. They dance because they must, I suppose. It's as natural as breathing, for them. You can't help it. It's fate. But listen, child. It is time I took you more in hand. You will be marrying before long -"

"Mamma!" Miss Lady blushed indignantly. "How can you talk so? I don't know - I didn't - I shan't -"

"Tut, tut. Please don't. It is going to be a very warm day. I really can't go into any argument. Take my word, you will marry soon; or if you don't, you will reverse all the known horoscopes of the family. That, too, is the fate of the Ellison girls - certain marriage! Our only hope is in some miracle. It is time for me to take you in hand. Listen, Lady. Let me ask you to sit a trifle farther back upon that chair. So, that is better. Now, draw the skirt a little closer. That is well. Now, sit easily, keep your back from the chair; try to keep your feet concealed. Remember, Lady, you are a woman now, and there are certain rules, certain little things, which will help you so much, so much."

Mrs. Ellison sighed, then yawned, touching her white teeth with the tip of her fan. "Dear me, it certainly is going to be warm," she said at last. "Lady, dear, please run and get my book, won't you? You know your darling mamma is getting so - well, I won't say fat, God forbid! but so - really - well, thank you."

Miss Lady fled gladly and swiftly enough. For an instant she halted, uncertain, on the wide gallery, her face troubled, her attitude undecided. Then, in swift mutiny, she sprang down the steps and was off in open desertion. She fled down the garden walk, and presently was welcomed riotously by a score of dogs and puppies, long since her friends.

Left alone, the elder lady sat for a moment in thought. Her face now seemed harder in outline, more enigmatical. She gazed after the girl who left her, and into her eyes came a look which one must have called strangely unmaternal - a look not tender, but hard, calculating, cold.

"She is pretty," she murmured to herself half-aloud. "She is going to be very pretty - the prettiest of the family in generations, perhaps. Well-handled, that girl could marry anybody. I'll have to be careful she doesn't marry the wrong one. They're headstrong, these Ellisons. Still, I think I can handle this one of them. In fact, I *must*." She smiled gently and settled down into a half-reverie, purring to herself. "Dear me!" she resumed at length, starting up, "how warm it grows! Where has that girl gone? I do believe she has run away. Delphine! Ah-h-h-h, Delphine!"

There came no audible sound of steps, but presently there stood, just within the parted draperies, the figure of the servant thus called upon. Yet that title sat ill upon this tall young woman who now stood awaiting the orders of her mistress. Garbed as a servant she was, yet held herself rather as a queen. Her hair, black and luxuriant, was straight and strong, and, brushed back smoothly from her temples as it was, contrasted sharply with a skin just creamy enough to establish it as otherwise than pure white. Egyptian, or Greek, or of unknown race, this servant, Delphine, might have been; but had it not been for her station and surroundings, one could never have suspected in her the trace of negro blood. She stood now, a mellow-tinted statue of not quite yellow ivory, silent, turning upon her mistress eyes large, dark and inscrutable as those of a sphinx. One looking upon the two, as they thus confronted each other, must have called them a strange couple. Why they should be mistress and servant was not a matter to be determined upon a first light guess. Indeed, they seemed scarcely such. From dark eye to dark eye there seemed to pass a signal of covert understanding, a signal of doubt, or suspicion, or armed neutrality, yet of mutual comprehension.

"Delphine," said Mrs. Ellison, presently, "bring me a glass of wine. And from now on, Delphine, see to it that you watch that girl. Tell me what she does. There's very little restraint of any kind here on the plantation, and she is just the age - well, you must keep me informed. You may bring the decanter, Delphine. I really don't feel fit for breakfast."

CHAPTER II

MULEY

In the warm sun of the southern morning the great plantation lay as though half-asleep, dozing and blinking at the advancing day. The plantation house, known in all the country-side as the Big House, rested calm and self-confident in the middle of a wide sweep of cleared lands, surrounded immediately by dark evergreens and the occasional primeval oaks spared in the original felling of the forest. Wide and rambling galleries of one height or another crawled here and there about the expanses of the building, and again paused, as though weary of the attempt to circumvent it. The strong white pillars, rising from the ground floor straight to the third story, shone white and stately, after that old southern fashion, that Grecian style, simplified and made suitable to provincial purses by those Adams brothers of old England who first set the fashion in early American architecture. White-coated, with wide, cool, green blinds, with ample and wide-doored halls and deep, low windows, the Big House, here in the heart of the warm South-land, was above all things suited to its environment. It was a home taking firm hold upon the soil, its wide roots reaching into traditions of more than one generation. Well toward the head of the vast Yazoo-Mississippi Delta, the richest region on the face of the whole earth, the Big House ruled over these wide acres as of immemorial right. Its owner, Colonel Calvin Blount, was a king, an American king, his right to rule based upon full proof of fitness.

In the heart of the only American part of America, the Big House, careless and confident, could afford to lie blinking at the sun, or at the broad acres which blinked back at it. It was all so safe and sure that there was no need for anxiety. Life here was as it had been for generations, even for the generation following the upheaval of the Civil War. Open-handed, generous, rich, lazily arrogant, kindly always, though upon occasions fiercely savage, this life took hold upon that of a hundred years ago. These strings of blacks, who now, answering the plantation bell, slowly crawled down the lane to the outlying fields, might still have been slaves. This lazy plow, tickling the opulent earth, might have been handled by a slave rather than by this hired servitor, whose quavering, plaintive song, broken mid-bar betimes, now came back across the warm distances which lay trembling in the rays of the advancing sun. These other dark-skinned servants, dawdling along the galleries, or passing here and yonder from the detached quarters of kitchen, and cook-room, and laundry and sleeping-rooms - they also humming musically at their work, too full of the sun and the certainty of comfort to need to hurry even with a song - all these might also have been tenants of an old-time estate, giving slow service in return for a life of carelessness and irresponsibility. This was in the South, in the Delta, the garden of the South, the garden of America; a country crude, primitive, undeveloped in modern ways, as one might say, yet by right entitled to its own assuredness. It asked nothing of all the world.

All this deep rich soil was given to the people of that land by Father Messasebe. Yards deep it lay, anciently rich, kissed by a sun which caused every growing thing to leap into swift fruition. The entire lesson of the scene was one of an absolute fecundity. The grass was deep and green and lush. The sweet peas and the roses and the morning-glories, and the honey-suckles on the lattice, hung ranks deep in blossoms. A hundred flocks of fowl ran clucking and chirping about the yard. Across the lawn a mother swine led her brood of squeaking and squealing young. A half-hundred puppies, toddlers or half-grown, romped about, unused fragments of the great hunting pack of the owner of this kingdom. Life, perhaps short, perhaps rude, perhaps swiftly done, yet after all life - this was the message of it all. The trees grew vast and tall. The corn, where the stalks could still be seen, grew stiff and strong as little trees. The cotton, through which the negroes rode, their black kinky heads level with the old shreds of ungathered bolls, showed plants rank and coarse enough to uphold a man's weight free of the ground. This sun and this soil - what might they not do in brooding fecundity? Growth, reproduction, the multifold - all this was written under that sky which now swept, deep and blue, flecked here and there with soft and fleecy clouds, over these fruitful acres hewn from the primeval forest.

The forest, the deep, vast forest of oak and ash and gum and ghostly sycamore; the forest, tangled with a thousand binding vines and briers, wattled and laced with rank blue cane - sure proof of a soil exhaustlessly rich - this ancient forest still stood, mysterious and forbidding, all about the edges of the great plantation. Here and there a tall white stump, fire-blackened at its foot, stood, even in fields long cultivated, showing how laborious and slow had been the whittling away of this jungle, which even now continually encroached and claimed its own. The rim of the woods, marked white by the deadened trees where the axes of the laborers were reclaiming yet other acres as the years rolled by, now showed in the morning sun distinctly, making a frame for the rich and restful picture of the Big House and its lands. Now and again overhead there swung slowly an occasional great black bird, its shadow not yet falling straight on the sunlit ground, as it would at midday, when the puppies of the pack would begin their daily pastime of chasing it across the fields.

This silent surrounding forest even yet held its ancient creatures - the swift and graceful deer, the soft-footed panther, the shambling black bear, the wild hog, the wolf, all manner of furred creatures, great store of noble wild fowl - all these thriving after the fecund fashion of this brooding land. It was a kingdom, this wild world, a realm in the wilderness; a kingdom fit for a bold man to govern, a man such as might have ruled in days long gone by. And indeed the Big House and its scarcely measured acres kept well their master as they had for many years. The table of this Delta baron was almost exclusively fed from these acres; scarce any item needful in his life required to be imported from the outer world. The government of America might have fallen; anarchy might have prevailed; a dozen states might have been taken over by a foreign foe; a score of states might have been overwhelmed by national calamity, and it all had scarce made a ripple here in this land, apart, rich, self-supporting and content. It had always been thus here.

But if this were a kingdom apart and self-sufficient, what meant this thing which, crossed the head of the plantation - this double line, tenacious and continuous, which shone upon the one hand dark, and upon the other, where the sun touched it, a cold gray in color? What meant this squat little building at the side of these rails which reached out straight as the flight of a bird across the clearing and vanished keenly in the forest wall? This was the road of the iron rails, the white man's perpetual path across the land. It clung close to the ground, at times almost sinking into the embankment now grown scarcely discernible among the concealing grass and weeds, although the track itself had been built but recently. This railroad sought to efface itself, even as the land sought to aid in its effacement, as though neither believed that this was lawful spot for the path of the iron rails. None the less, here was the railroad, ineradicable, epochal, bringing change; and, one might say, it made a blot upon this picture of the morning.

An observer standing upon the broad gallery, looking toward the eastward and the southward, might have seen two figures just emerging from the rim of the forest something like a mile away; and might then have seen them growing slowly more distinct as they plodded up the railway track toward the Big House. Presently these might have been discovered to be a man and a woman; the former tall, thin, dark and stooped; his companion, tall as himself, quite as thin, and almost as bent. The garb of the man was nondescript, neutral, loose; his hat dark and flapping. The woman wore a shapeless calico gown, and on her head was a long, telescopic sunbonnet of faded pink, from which she must perforce peer forward, looking neither to the right nor to the left.

The travelers, indeed, needed not to look to the right or the left, for the path of the iron rails led them directly on. Now and again clods of new-broken earth caused them to stumble as they hobbled loosely along. If the foot of either struck against the rail, its owner sprang aside, as though in fear, toward the middle of the track. Slowly and unevenly, with all the zigzags permissible within the confining inches of the irons, they came on up toward the squat little station-house. Thence they turned aside into the plantation path and, still stumbling and zigzagging, ambled up toward the house. They did not step to the gallery, did not knock at the door, or, indeed, give any evidences of their intentions, but seated themselves deliberately upon a pile of boards that lay near in the broad expanse of the front yard. Here they remained, silent and at rest, fitting well enough into the sleepy scene. No one in the house noticed them for a time, and they, tired by the walk, seemed content to rest under the shade of the evergreens before making known their errand. They sat speechless and content for some moments, until finally a mulatto house-servant, passing from one building to another, cast a look in their direction, and paused uncertainly in curiosity. The man on the board-pile saw her.

"Here, Jinny! Jinny!" he called, just loud enough to be heard, and not turning toward her more than half-way. "Come heah."

"Yassah," said the girl, and slowly approached.

"Get us a little melk, Jinny," said the speaker.

"We're plumb out o' melk down home."

"Yassah," said Jinny; and disappeared leisurely, to be gone perhaps half an hour.

There remained little sign of life on the board-pile, the bonnet tube pointing fixedly toward the railway station, the man now and then slowly shifting one leg across the other, but staring out at nothing, his lower lip drooping laxly. When the servant finally brought back the milk-pail and placed it beside him, he gave no word of thanks. The sunbonnet shifted to include the mulatto girl within its full vision, as the latter stood leaning her weight on one side-bent foot, idly wiping her hands upon her apron.

"Folks all well down to yo' place, Mistah Bowles?" said she, affably.

"Right well."

"Um-h-h." Silence then fell until Jinny again found speech.

"Old Bess, that's the Cunnel's favorite dawg, you-all know, she done have 'leven puppies las' night."

"That so?"

"Yassah. Cunnel, he's off down on the Sun-flowah."

"Um-h-h."

"Yassah; got most all his dawgs wid 'im. We goin' to have b'ah meat now for sho'," - this with a wide grin.

"Reckon so," said the visitor. "When's Cunnel coming back, you reckon?"

"I dunno, suh, but he sho' won't come back lessen he gets a b'ah. If you-all could wait a while, yon-all could take back some b'ah meat, if you wantuh."

"Um-h-h," said the man, and fell again into silence. To all appearances, he was willing to wait here indefinitely, forgetful of the pail of milk, toward which the sun was now creeping ominously close. The way back home seemed long and weary at that moment. His lip drooped still more laxly, as he sat looking out vaguely.

Not so calm seemed his consort, she of the sun-bonnet. Eestored to some extent by her tarrying in the shade, she began to shift and hitch about uneasily upon the board-pile. At length she leaned a bit to one side, reached into a pocket and, taking out a snuff-stick and a parcel of its attendant compound, began to take a dip of snuff, after the habit of certain of the population of that region. This done, she turned with a swift jerk of the head, bringing to bear the tube of her bonnet in full force upon her lord and master.

"Jim Bowles," she said, "this heah is a shame! Hit's a plumb shame!"

There was no answer, save an uneasy hitch on the part of the person so addressed. He seemed to feel the focus of the sun-bonnet boring into his system. The voice in the bonnet went on, shot straight toward him, so that he might not escape.

"Hit's a plumb shame," said Mrs. Bowles, again.

"I know it, I know it," said her husband at length, uneasily. "That is, about us having to walk up heah. That whut you mean?"

"Yassir, that's whut I do mean, an' you know it."

"Well, now, how kin *I* help it? We kain't take the only mewel we got and make the nigger stop wu'k. That ain't reasonable. Besides, you don't think Cunnel Blount is goin' to miss a pail o' melk now and then, do you?"

A snort of indignation greeted this supposition.

"Jim Bowles, you make me sick," replied his wife. "We kin get melk heah as long as we want to, o' co'se; but who wants to keep a-comin' up heah, three mile, for melk? It ain't right."

"Well, now, Sar' Ann, how kin I help it?" said Jim Bowles. "The cow is daid, an' I kain't help it, an' that's all about it. My God, woman!" this with sudden energy, "do you think I kin bring a cow to life that's been kilt by the old railroad kyahs? I ain't no 'vangelist."

"You kain't bring old Muley to life," said Sarah Ann Bowles, "but then -"

"Well, but then! But *whut?* Whut you goin' to do? I reckon you do whut you do, huh! You just walk the track and come heah after melk, I reckon, if you want it. You ought to be mighty glad I come along to keep you company. 'Tain't every man goin' to do that, I want to tell you. Now, it ain't my fault old Muley done got kilt."

"Ain't yo' fault!"

"No, it ain't my *fault.* Whut am I goin' to do? I kain't get no otheh cow right now, an' I done tol' you so. You reckon cows grows on bushes?"

"Grows on bushes!"

"Yes, or that they comes for nuthin'?"

"Comes for nuthin'!"

"Yes, Sar' Ann, that's whut I said. I tell you, it ain't so fur to come, ain't so fur up heah, if you take it easy; only three mile. An' Cunnel Blount'll give us melk as long as we want. I reckon he would give us a cow, too, if I ast him. I s'pose I could pay him out o' the next crop, if they wasn't so many things that has to be paid out'n the crop. It's too blame bad 'bout Muley." He scratched his head thoughtfully.

"Yes," responded his spouse, "Muley was a heap better cow

than you'll ever git ag'in. Why, she give two quo'ts o' melk the very mawnin' she was kilt - two quo'ts. I reckon we didn't have to walk no three mile that mawnin', did we? An' she that kin' and gentle-like - oh, we ain't goin' to git no new cow like Muley, no time right soon, I want to tell you that, Jim Bowles."

"Well, well, I know all that," said her husband, conciliatingly, a trifle easier now that the sunbonnet was for the moment turned aside. "That's all true, mighty true. But what kin you *do*?"

"Do? Why, do *somethin'*! Somebody sho' ought to suffer for this heah. This new fangled railroad a-comin' through heah, a-killin' things, an' a-killin' *folks*! Why, Bud Sowers said just the other week he heard of three darkies gittin' kilt in one bunch down to Allenville. They standin' on the track, jes' talkin' an' visitin' like. Didn't notice nuthin'. Didn't notice the train a-comin'. 'Biff!' says Bud; an' thah was them darkies."

"Yes," said Mr. Bowles, "that's the way it was with Muley. She just walk up out'n the cane, an' stan' thah in the sun on the track, to sort o' look aroun' whah she could see free fer a little ways. Then, 'long comes the railroad train, an' biff! Thah's Muley!"

"Plumb daid!"

"Plumb daid!"

"An' she a good cow for us for fo'teen yeahs! It don't look exactly right, now, does it? It sho' don't"

"It's a outrage, that's whut it is," said Sar' Ann Bowles.

"Well, we got the railroad," said her husband, tentatively.

"Yes, we got the railroad," said Sar' Ann Bowles, savagely, "an' whut yearthly good is it? Who wants any railroad? Whut use have we-all got fer it? It comes through ouah farm, an' scares ouah mewel, an' it kills ouah cow; an' it's got me so's I'm afeared to set foot outsid'n ouah do', lessen it's goin' to kill me, too. Why, all the way up heah this mawnin', I was skeered every foot of the way, a-fear-in' that there ingine was goin' to come along an' kill us both!"

"Sho'! Sar' Ann," said her husband, with superiority. "It ain't time fer the train yit - leastwise I don't think it is." He looked about uneasily.

"That's all right, Jim Bowles. One of them ingines might come along 'most any time. It might creep up behin' you, then, biff! Thah's Jim Bowles! Whut use is the railroad, I'd like to know? I wouldn't be caught a-climbin' in one o' them thah kyars, not fer big money. Supposin' it run off the track?"

"Oh, well, now," said her husband, "maybe it don't, always."

"But supposin' it *did*?" The front of the telescope turned toward him suddenly, and so perfect was the focus this time that Mr. Bowles shifted his seat and took refuge upon another board at the other end of the board-pile, out of range, albeit directly in the ardent sunlight, which, warm as it was, did not seem to him so burning as the black eyes in the bonnet, or so troublous as the tongue which went on with its questions.

"Whut made you vote fer this heah railroad?" said Sarah Ann, following him mercilessly with the bonnet tube. "We didn't want no railroad. We never did have one, an' we never ought to a-had one. You listen to me, that railroad is goin' to ruin this country. Thah ain't a woman in these heah bottoms but would be skeered to have a baby grow up in her house. Supposin' you got a baby; nice little baby, never did harm no one. You a-cookin' or somethin' - out to the smoke-house like enough; baby alone fer about two minutes. Baby crawls out on to the railroad track. Along comes the ingine, an' biff! Thah's yo' baby!"

EMERSON HOUGH

Mrs. Bowles shed tears at this picture which she had conjured up, and even her less imaginative consort became visibly affected, so that for a moment he half straightened up.

"Hit don't look quite right," said he, once more. "But, then, whut you goin' to do? Whut *kin* we do, woman?" he asked fiercely.

"Why, if the men in these heah parts was half men," said his wife, "I tell you whut they'd do. They'd git out and tear up every foot of this heah cussed railroad track, an' throw it back into the cane. That's whut they'd do."

"Sho' now, would you?" said Jim Bowles.

"Shore I would. You got to do it if things keeps on this-away."

"Well, we couldn't, lessen Cunnel Blount said it was all right, you know. The Cunnel was the friend of the road through these heah bottoms. He 'lowed it would help us all."

"Help? Help us? Huh! Like to know how it helps us, killin' ouah cow an' makin' us walk three mile of a hot mornin' to git a pail o' melk to make up some co'hn bread. You call that a help, do you, Jim Bowles? You may, but I don't an' I hain't a-goin' to. I got some sense, I reckon. Railroad! Help! Huh!"

Jim Bowles crept stealthily a little farther away on his own side of the board-pile, whither it seemed his wife could not quite so readily follow him with her transfixing gaze.

"Well, now, Sar' Ann," said he, "the Cunnel done tol' me hit was all right. He said some of ouah stock like enough git kilt, 'cause you know these heah bottoms is growed up so close like, with cane an' all that, that any sort of critters like to git out where it's open, so's they kin sort o' look around like, you know. Why, I done seen four deer trails whils' we was a-comin' up this mawnin', and I seen whah a b'ah had come out an' stood on the track. Now, as fer cows, an' as fer niggers, why, it stands to reason that some of them is shore goin' to git kilt, that's all."

"An' you men is goin' to stand that from the railroad? Why don't you make them pay for whut gits kilt?"

"Well, now, Sar' Ann," said her husband, conciliatorily, "that's just whut I was goin' to say. The time the fust man come down through heah to talk about buildin' the railroad, he done said, like I tol' you Cunnel Blount said, that we might git some stock kilt fer a little while, till things kind o' got used to it, you know; but he 'lowed that the railroad would sort o' pay for anything that got kilt like, you know."

"Pay! The railroad goin' to pay you!" Again the remorseless sunbonnet followed its victim and fixed him with its focus. "Pay you! I didn't notice no money layin' on the track where we come along this mawnin', did you? Yes, I reckon it's goin' to pay you, a whole heap!" The scorn of this utterance was limitless, and Jim Bowles felt his insignificance in the untenable position which he had assumed.

"Well, I dunno," said he, vaguely, and sighed softly; all of which irritated Mrs. Bowles to such an extent that she flounced suddenly around to get a better gaze upon her master. In this movement, her foot struck the pail of milk which had been sitting near, and overturned it.

"Jinny," she called out, "you, Jinny!"

"Yassam," replied Jinny, from some place on the gallery.

"Come heah," said Mrs. Bowles. "Git me another pail o' melk. I done spilled this one."

"Yassam," replied Jinny, and presently returned with the refilled vessel.

"Well, anyway," said Jim Bowles at length, rising and standing with hands in pockets, inside the edge of the shade line of the evergreens, "I heard that thah was a man come down through heah a few days ago. He was sort of takin' count o' the critters that done got kilt by the railroad kyahs."

"That so?" said Sarah Ann, somewhat mollified.

"I reckon so," said Jim Bowles. "I 'lowed I'd ast Cunnel Blount 'bout that sometime. O' co'se it don't bring Muley back, but then -"

"No, hit don't," said Sarah Ann, resuming her original position. "And our little Sim, he just loved that Muley cow, little Sim, he did," she mourned.

"Say, Jim Bowles, do you heah me?" - this with a sudden flirt of the sunbonnet in an agony of actual fear. "Why, Jim Bowles, do you know that ouah little Sim might be a-playin' out thah in front of ouah house, on to that railroad track, at this very minute? S'pose, s'posen - along comes that thah railroad train! Say, man, whut you standin' there in that thah shade fer? We got to go! We got to git home! Come right along this minute, er we may be too late."

And so, smitten by this sudden thought, they gathered themselves together as best they might and started toward the railroad for their return. Even as they did so there appeared upon the northern horizon a wreath of smoke rising above the forest. There was the far-off sound of a whistle, deadened by the heavy intervening vegetation; and presently, there puffed into view one of the railroad trains still new upon this region. Iconoclastic, modern, strenuous, it wabbled unevenly over the new-laid rails up to the station-house, where it paused for a few moments ere it resumed its wheezing way to the south-ward. The two visitors at the Big House gazed at it open-mouthed for a time, until all at once her former thought crossed the woman's mind. She turned upon her husband.

"Thah it goes! Thah it goes!" she cried. "Right on straight to ouah house! It kain't miss it! An' little Sim, he's sho' to be playin' out thah on the track. Oh, he's daid right this minute, he sho'ly is!"

Her speech exercised a certain force upon Jim Bowles. He stepped on the faster, tripped upon a clod and stumbled, spilling half the milk from the pail.

"Thah, now!" said he. "Thah hit goes ag'in. Done spilt the melk. Well, hit's too far back to the house now fer mo'. But, now, mebbe Sim wasn't playin' on the track."

"Mebbe he wasn't!" said Sarah Ann, scornfully. "Why, *o' co'se* he was."

"Well, if he was," said Jim Bowles, philosophically, "why, Sar' Ann, from whut I done notice about this yeah railroad train, why - it's *too late*, now."

He might perhaps have pursued this logical course of thought further, had not there occurred an incident which brought the conversation to a close. Looking up, the two saw approaching them across the lawn, evidently coming from the little railway station, and doubtless descended from this very train, the alert, quick-stepping figure of a man evidently a stranger to the place. Jim and Sarah Ann Bowles stepped to one side as he approached and lifted his hat with a pleasant smile.

"Good morning," said the stranger. "It's a fine day, isn't it? Can you tell me whether or not Colonel Blount is at home this morning?"

"Well, suh," said Jim Bowles, rubbing his chin thoughtfully. "He ah, an' he ain't. He's home, o' co'se; that is, he hain't gone away no whah, to co'te er nothin'. But then ag'in, he's out huntin', gone afteh b'ah. I reckon he's likely to be in 'most any day now."

"'Most any day?"

"Yessah. You better go on up to the house. The Cunnel will be right glad to see you. You're a stranger in these parts, I reckon? I'd be glad to have you stop down to my house, but it's three mile down the track, an' we hatter walk. You'd be mo' comfo'table heah, I reckon. Walk on up, and tell 'em to give you a place to set. My woman an' me, I reckon we got to git home now, suh. It's somethin' might be mighty serious."

"Yas, indeed," murmured Mrs. Bowles, "we got to git along."

"Thank you," said the stranger. "I am very much obliged to you, indeed. I believe I will wait here for just a little while, as you say. Good morning, sir. Good morning, madam."

He turned and walked slowly up the path toward the house, as the others pursued their way to the railroad track, down which they presently were plodding on their homeward journey. There was at least a little milk left in the pail when finally they reached their log cabin, with its yard full of pigs and chickens. Eagerly they scanned the sides of the railway embankment as they drew near, looking for signs of what they feared to see. One need not describe the fierce joy with which Sarah Ann Bowles fell upon little Sim, who was presently discovered, safe and dirty, knocking about upon the kitchen floor in abundant company of puppies, cats and chickens. As to the reproaches which she heaped upon her husband in her happiness, it is likewise unnecessary to dwell thereupon.

"I knowed he would be kilt," said Sarah Ann.

"But he *hain't*," said her husband, triumphantly. And for one time in their married life there seemed to be no possible way in which she might contradict him, which fact for her constituted a situation somewhat difficult.

"Well, 'tain't yo' fault ef he hain't," said she at length. The rest of her revenge she took upon the person of little Sim, whom she alternately chastened and embraced, to the great and grieved surprise of the latter, who remained ignorant of any existing or pending relation upon his part with the methods or the instruments of modern progress.

CHAPTER III

THE VISITOR

The new-comer at the Big House was a well-looking figure as he advanced up the path toward the white-pillared galleries. In height just above middle stature, and of rather spare habit of body, alert, compact and vigorous, he carried himself with a half-military self-respect, redeemed from aggressiveness by an open candor of face and the pleasant, forthright gaze of kindly blue-gray eyes. In spite of a certain gravity of mien, his eyes seemed wont to smile upon occasion, as witnessed divers little wrinkles at the corners. He was smooth-shaven, except for a well-trimmed dark mustache; the latter offering a distinct contrast to the color of his hair, which, apparently not in full keeping with his years, was lightly sprinkled with gray. Yet his carriage was assuredly not that of middle age, and indeed, the total of his personality, neither young nor old, neither callow nor acerb, neither lightly unreserved nor too gravely severe, offered certain problems not capable of instant solution. A hurried observer might have guessed his age within ten years but might have been wrong upon either side, and might have had an equal difficulty in classifying his residence or occupation.

Whatever might be said of this stranger, it was evident that he was not ill at ease in this environment; for as he met coming around the corner an old colored man, who, with a rag in one hand and a bottle in the other, seemed intent upon some errand at the dog kennel beyond, the visitor paused not in query or salutation, but tossed his umbrella to the servant and at the same time handed him his traveling-bag. "Take care of these. Bill," said he.

Bill, for that was indeed his name, placed the bag and umbrella upon the gallery floor, and with the air of owning the place himself, invited the visitor to enter the Big House.

"The Cunnel's not to home, suh," said Bill. "But you bettah come in and seddown. I'll go call the folks."

"Never mind," said the visitor. "I reckon I'll just walk around a little outside. I hear Colonel Blount is off on a bear hunt."

"Yassah," said Bill. "An' when he goes he mostly gits b'ah. I'se right 'spondent dis time, though, 'deed I is, suh."

"What's the matter?"

"Why, you see, suh," replied Bill, leaning comfortably back against a gallery post, "it's dis-away. I'm just goin' out to fix up old Hec's foot. He's ouah bestest b'ah-dog, but he got so blame biggoty, las' time he was out, stuck his foot right intoe a b'ah's mouth. Now, Hec's lef' home, an' me lef home to 'ten' to Hec. How kin Cunnel Blount git ary b'ah 'dout me and Hec along? I'se right 'spondent, dat's whut I is."

"Well, now, that's too bad," said the stranger, with a smile.

"Too bad? I reckon it sho' is. Fer, if Cunnel Blount don't git no b'ah - look out den, *I* kin tell you."

"Gets his dander up, eh?"

"Dandah - dandah! You know him? Th'ain't no better boss, but ef he goes out huntin' b'ah an' don't get no *b'ah* - why, then th' ain't no reason goin' *do* foh him."

"Is Mrs. Blount at home, Bill?"

"Th'ain't no Mrs. Blount, and I don't reckon they neveh will be. Cunnel too busy huntin' b'ah to git married. They's two ladies heah, no relation o' him; they done come heah a yeah er so ago, and they-all keeps house fer the Cunnel. That's Mrs. Ellison and her dahteh, Miss Lady. She's a pow'ful fine gal, Miss Lady."

"I don't know them," said the visitor.

"No, sah," said Bill. "They ain't been heah long. Dese heah low-down niggers liken to steal the Cunnel blin', he away so much. One day, he gits right mad. 'Lows he goin' to advehtize fer a housekeepah-lady. Then Mas' Henry 'Cherd - he's gemman been livin' couple o' yeahs 'er so down to near Vicksburg, some'rs; he's out huntin' now with the Cunnel - why, Mas' 'Cherd he 'lows he knows whah thah's a lady, jus' the thing. Law! Cunnel didn't spec' no real lady, you know, jes' wantin' housekeepah. But long comes this heah lady, Mrs. Ellison, an' brings this heah young lady, too - real quality. 'Miss Lady' we-all calls her, right to once. Orto see Cunnel Cal Blount den! 'Now, I reckon I kin go huntin' peaceful,' says he. So dem two tuk holt. Been heah ever since. Mas' 'Cherd, he has in min' this heah yallah gal, Delpheem. Right soon, heah come Delpheem 'long too. Reckon she runs the kitchen all right. Anyways we's got white folks in the parlah, whah they allus *orto* be white folks."

"Well, you ought to thank your friend - what is his name - Ducherd - Decherd? Seems as though I had heard that name, below somewhere."

"Yas, Mas' Henry 'Cherd. We does thank him. He sut'nly done fix us all up wid women-folks. We couldn't no *mo'* git erlong 'dout Miss Lady now, 'n we could 'dout *me,* er the Cunnel. But, *law!* it don't make no diff'ence to Cunnel Blount who's heah or who ain't heah, he jest gotter hunt *b'ah.* You come 'long wid me, I could show you b'ah hides up stairs, b'ah hides on de roof, b'ah hides on de sheds, b'ah hides on de barn, and a tame b'ah hitched to the cotton-gin ovah thah."

"He seems to make a sort of specialty of bear, doesn't he? Got a pretty good pack, eh?"

"Pack? I should say we has! We got the bestest b'ah pack in Miss'ippi, er in de whole worl'. We sho' is fixed up fer huntin'. But, now, look heah, two three days ago the railroad kyahs done run ovah a fine colt whut de Cunnel was raisin' fer a saddle hoss - kilt it plumb daid. That riled him a heap. 'Damn the railroad kyahs,' sez he. An' den off he goes huntin', sort o' riled like. Now, ef he comes back, and ef he don't git no *b'ah*, why, you won't see old Bill 'round heah fer 'bout fo' days."

"You seem to know him pretty well."

"Know him? I orto. Raised wid him, an' lived heah all my life. Now, when you see Cunnel Blount come home, he'll come up 'long dat lane, him an' de dogs, an' dem no 'count niggers he done took 'long wid him; an' when he gits up to whah de lane crosses de railroad track, ef he come ridin' 'long easy like, now an' den tootin' his hawn to so'ht o' let us know he's a-comin' - ef he do dat-away, dat's all right, - dat's all right." Here the garrulous old servant shook his head. "But ef he don't - well den -"

"That's bad, if he doesn't, eh?"

"Yassah. Ef he don' come a-blowin' an' ef he *do* come *a-singin'*, den look out! I allus did notice, ef Cunnel Blount 'gins to sing 'ligious hymns, somethin's wrong, and somethin' gwine ter drap. He hain't right easy ter git along wid when he's a-singin'. But if you'll 'scuse me, suh, I gotter take care o' old Hec. Jest make yourself to home, suh, - anyways you like."

The visitor contented himself with wandering about the yard, until at length he seated himself on the board-pile beneath the evergreen trees, and so sank into an idle reverie, his chin in his hand, and his eyes staring out across the wide field. His face, now in repose, seemed more meditative; indeed one might have called it almost mournful. The shoulders drooped a trifle, as though their owner for the time forgot to pull himself together. He sat thus for some time, and the sun was beginning to encroach upon his refuge, when suddenly he was aroused by the faint and far-off sound of a hunting horn. That the listener distinguished it at such a distance might have argued that he himself had known hound and saddle in his day; yet he readily caught the note of the short hunting horn universally used by the southern hunters, and recognized the assembly call for the hunting pack. As it came near, all the dogs that remained in the kennel yards heard it and raged to escape from their confinement. Old Bill came hobbling around the corner. Steps were heard on the gallery, and the visitor's face showed a slight uneasiness as he caught a glimpse of a certain spot now suddenly made alive by the flutter of a soft gown and the flash of a bunch of scarlet ribbons. Thither he gazed as directly as he might in these circumstances.

"Dat's her! dat's Miss Lady!" said Bill to his new friend, in a low voice. "Han'somest young lady in de hull Delta. Dey'll all be right glad ter see de Cunnel back. He's got a b'ah sho', fer he's comin' a-blowin'."

Bill's joy was not long-lived, for even as the little cavalcade came in view, a tall figure on a chestnut hunting horse riding well in advance, certain colored stragglers following, and the party-colored pack trotting or limping along on all sides, the music of the summoning horn suddenly ceased. Looking neither to the right nor to the left, the leader of the hunt rode on up the lane, sitting loose and careless in the saddle, his right hand steadying a short rifle across the saddle front. He rode thus until presently those at the Big House heard, softly rising on the morning air, the chant of an old church hymn: "On Jordan's strand I'll *take* my stand, An-n-n -"

"Oh, Lawd!" exclaimed Bill. "Dat's his very wustest chune." Saying which he dodged around the corner of the house.

CHAPTER IV

A QUESTION OP VALUATION

Turning in from the lane at the yard gate, Colonel Calvin Blount and his retinue rode close up to the side door of the plantation house; but even here the master vouchsafed no salutation to those who awaited his coming. He was a tall man, broad-shouldered, lean and muscular; yet so far from being thin and dark, he was spare rather from physical exercise than through gaunt habit of body; his complexion was ruddy and sun-colored, and the long mustache hanging across his jaws showed a deep mahogany-red. Western ranchman one might have called him, rather than southern planter. Scotch-Irish, generations back, perhaps, yet southern always, and by birthright American, he might have been a war-lord of another land and day. No feudal baron ever dismounted with more assuredness at his own hall, to toss careless rein to a retainer. He stood now, tall and straight, a trifle rough-looking in his careless planter's dress, but every inch the master. A slight frown puckered up his forehead, giving to his face an added hint of sternness.

Behind this leading figure of the cavalcade came a younger man. In age perhaps at the mid thirties, tall, slender, with dark hair and eyes and with a dark mustache shading his upper lip, Henry Decherd, formerly of New Orleans, for a few years dweller in the Delta, sometime guest of Colonel Blount at the Big House plantation and companion of the hunt, made now a figure if not wholly eye-filling, at least handsome and distinguished. His dress was neat to the verge of foppishness, nor did it seem much disordered by the hardships of the chase. Upon his clean-cut face there sat a certain arrogance, as of one at least desirous of having his own way in his own sphere. Not an ill-looking man, upon the whole, was Henry Decherd, though his reddish-yellow eyes, a bit oblique in their setting, gave the impression alike of a certain touchiness of temper and an unpleasantly fox-like quality of character. There was an air not barren of self-consciousness as he threw himself out of the saddle, for it might have been seen that under his saddle, and not that of Colonel Blount, there rested the black and glossy hide of the great bear which had been the object of the chase. Decherd stood with his hand resting on the hide and gazed somewhat eagerly, one might have thought, toward the gallery whence came the flash of scarlet ribbons.

Colonel Blount busied himself with directions as to the horses and dogs. The latter came straggling along in groups or pairs or singles, some of them hobbling on three legs, many showing bitter wounds. The chase of the great bear had proved stern pastime for them. Of half a hundred hounds which had started, not two-thirds were back again, and many of these would be unfit for days for the resumption of their savage trade. None the less, as the master sounded again, loud and clear, the call for the assembly, all the dogs about the place, young and old, homekeepers and warriors, came pouring in with heads uplifted, each pealing out his sweet and mournful music. Colonel Blount spoke to dozens of them, calling each by its proper name.

"Here, Bill," he called to that worthy, who had now ventured to return from his hiding-place, "take them out to the yard and fix them up. Now, boys, go around to the kitchen and tell them to give you something to eat."

In the confusion of the disbandment of the hunt, the master of the Big House had as yet hardly found time to look about him, but now, as the conclave scattered, he found himself alone, and turning, discovered the occupant of the board-pile, who arose and advanced, offering his hand.

"This is Colonel Blount, I presume," said he.

"Yes, sir, that's my name. I beg your pardon, I'm sure, but I didn't know you were there. Come right on into the house and sit down, sir. Now, your name is -?"

"Eddring," said the new-comer. "John Eddring. I am just down on the morning train from the city."

"I'm right glad to see you, Mr. Eddring," said Colonel Blount, extending his hand. "It seems to me I ought to know your family. Over round Hillsboro, aren't you? Tell me, you're not the son of old Dan H. Eddring of the Tenth Mississippi in the war?"

"That was an uncle of mine."

"Is that so, is that so? Why, Dan H. Eddring was my father's friend. They slept and fought and ate together for four years, until my father was killed in the Wilderness."

"And my uncle before Richmond; John Eddring, my father, long before, at Ball's Bluff."

"I was in some of that fighting myself," said Colonel Blount, rubbing his chin. "I was a boy, just a boy. Well, it's all over now. Come on in. I'm mighty glad to see you." Yet the two, without plan, had now wandered over toward the shade of the evergreen, and presently they seated themselves on the board-pile.

"Well, Colonel Blount," said the visitor, "I reckon you must have had a good hunt."

"Yes, sir, there ain't a b'ah in the Delta can get away from those dogs. We run this fellow straight on end for ten miles; put him across the river twice, and all around the Black Bayou, but the dogs kept him hot all the time, I'm telling you, for more than five miles through the cane, clean beyond the bayou."

"Who got the shot, Colonel?" asked Eddring - a question apparently most unwelcome.

"Well, I ought to have had it," said Blount, with a frown of displeasure. "The fact is, I did take a flying chance from horseback, when the b'ah ran by in the cane half a mile back of where they killed him. Somehow I must have missed. A little while later I heard another shot, and found that young gentleman there, Mr. Decherd, had beat me in the ride. But man! you ought to have heard that pack for two hours through the woods. It certainly would have raised your hair straight up. You ever hunt b'ah, sir?"

"A little, once in a while, when I have the time."

"Well, you don't go away from here without having a good hunt. You just wait a day or so until my dogs get rested up."

"Thank you, Colonel, but I am afraid I can't stay. You see, I am down here on a matter of business."

"Business, eh?" - Well, a man that'll let business interfere with a b'ah hunt has got something wrong about him."

"Well, you see, a railroad man can't always choose," said his guest.

"Railroad man?" said Colonel Blount. A sudden gloom fell on his ruddy face. "Railroad man, eh? Well, I wish you was something else. Now, I helped get that railroad through this country - if it hadn't been for me, they never could have laid a mile of track through here. But now, do you know what they done did to me the other day, with their damned old railroad?"

"No, sir, I haven't heard."

"Well, I'll tell you - Bill! Oh, *Bill!* Go into the house and get me some ice; and go pick some mint and bring it here to this gentleman and me - Say, do you know what that railroad did? Why, it just killed the best filly on my plantation, my best running stock, too. Now, I was the man to help get that railroad through the Delta, and I -"

"Well, now, Colonel Blount," said the other, "the road isn't a bad sort of thing for you-all down here, after all. It relieves you of the river market and it gives you a double chance to get out your cotton. You don't have to haul your cotton twelve miles back to the boat any more. Here is your station right at your door, and you can load on the cars any day you want to."

"Oh, that's all right, that's all right. But this killing of my stock?"

"Well, that's so," said the other, facing the point and ruminatingly biting a splinter between his teeth. "It does look as if we had killed about everything loose in the whole Delta during the last month or so."

"Are you on this railroad?" asked Blount, suddenly.

"I reckon I'll have to admit that I am," said the other, smiling.

"Passenger agent, or something of that sort, I reckon? Well, let me tell you, you change your road. Say, there was a man down below here last week settling up claims - Bill! Ah-h, *Bill!* Where you gone?"

"Yes," said Eddring, "it certainly did seem that when we built this road every cow and every nigger, not to mention a lot of white folks, made a bee-line straight for our right-of-way. Why, sir, it was a solid line of cows and niggers from Memphis to New Orleans. How could you blame an engineer if he run into something once in a while? He couldn't *help* it."

"Yes. Now, do you know what this claim settler, this claim agent man did? Why, he paid a man down below here two stations - what do you *think* he paid him for as fine a heifer as ever eat cane? Why, fifteen dollars!"

"Fifteen dollars!"

"Yes, fifteen dollars."

"That looks like a heap of money for a heifer, doesn't it, Colonel Blount?"

"A heap of money? Why, no. Heap of *money*? Why, what you mean?"

"Heifers didn't bring that before the road came through. Why, you would have had to drive that heifer twenty-five miles before you could get a market, and then she wouldn't have brought over twelve dollars. Now, fifteen dollars, seems to me, is about right."

"Well, let the heifer go. But there was a cow killed three miles below here the other day. Neighbors of mine. I reckon that claim agent wouldn't want to allow any more than fifteen dollars for Jim Bowles' cow, neither."

"Maybe not."

"Well, never mind about the cow, either; but look here. A nigger lost his wife down there, killed by these steam cars - looks like the niggers get fascinated by them cars. But here's Bill coming at last. Now, Mr. Eddring, we'll just make a little julep. Tell me, how do you make a julep, sir?"

Eddring hitched a little nearer on the board-pile. "Well, Colonel Blount," said he, "in our family we used to have an old silver mug - sort of plain mug, you know, few flowers around the edge of it - been in the family for years. Now, you take a mug like that, and let it lie in the ice-box all the time, and when you take it out, it's sort of got a white frost all over it. Now, my old daddy, he would take this mug and put some fine ice into it, - not too fine. Then he'd take a little cut loaf sugar, in another glass, and he'd mash it up in a little water - not too much water - then he'd pour that in over the ice. Then he would pour some good corn whisky in till all the interstices of that ice were filled plumb up; then he'd put some mint -"

"Didn't smash the mint? Say, he didn't smash the mint, did he?" said Colonel Blount, eagerly, hitching over toward the speaker.

"Smash it? I should say not, sir! Sometimes, at certain seasons of the mint, he might just sort of take a twist at the leaf, to sort of release a little of the flavor, you know. You don't want to be rough with mint. Just twist it gently between the thumb and finger. Then you set it in nicely around the edge of the glass. Sometimes just a little powder of fine sugar around on top of the mint leaves, and then -"

"Sir," said Colonel Blount, gravely rising and taking off his hat, "you are welcome to my home!"

Eddring, with equal courtesy, arose and removed his own hat.

"For my part," resumed Blount, judicially, "I rather lean to a piece of cut glass, for the green and the crystal look mighty fine together. I don't always make them with any sugar on top of the mint. But, you know, just a circle of mint - not crushed - not crushed, mind you - just a green ring of fragrance, so that you can bury your nose in it and forget your troubles. Sir, allow me once more to shake your hand. I think I know a gentleman when I see one."

Oddly enough, this pleasant speech seemed to bring a shade of sadness to Eddring's face. "A gentleman?" said he, smiling slightly. "Well, don't shake hands with me yet, sir. I don't know. You see, I'm a railroad man, and I'm here on business."

"Damn it, sir, if it was only your description of a julep, if it was only your mention of that old family silver mug, devoted to that sacred purpose, sir, that would be your certificate of character here. Forget your business. Come down here and live with me. We'll go hunting b'ah together. Why, man, I'm mighty glad to make your acquaintance."

"But wait," said Eddring, "there may be two ways of looking at this."

"Well, there's only one way of looking at a julep," said Blount, "and that's down the mint. Now, I'll show you how we make them down here in the Sunflower country."

"But, as I was a-saying -" and here Blount set down the glasses midway in his compounding, and went on with his interrupted proposition; "now here was that nigger that lost his wife. Of course he had a whole flock of children. Now, what do you think that claim agent said he would pay that nigger for his wife?"

"Well, I -"

"Well, but what do you *reckon?*"

"Why, I reckon about fifteen dollars."

"That's it, that's it!" said Blount, slapping his hand upon the board until the glasses jingled. "That's just what he did offer; fifteen dollars! Not a damned cent more."

"Well, now, Colonel Blount," said Eddring, "you know there's a heap of mighty trifling niggers loose in this part of the world. You see, that fellow would marry again in a little while, and he might get a heap better woman next time. There's a lot of swapping wives among these niggers at best. Now, here's a man lost his wife decent and respectable, and there's nothing on earth a nigger likes better than a good funeral, even if it has to be his own wife. Now, how many nigger funerals are there that cost fifteen dollars? I'll bet you if that nigger had it to do over again he'd a heap rather be rid of her and have the fifteen dollars. Look at it! Fine funeral for one wife and something left over to get a bonnet for his new wife. I'll bet there isn't a nigger on your place that wouldn't jump at a chance like that."

Colonel Blount scratched his head. "You understand niggers all right, I'll admit," said he. "But, now, supposing it had been a white man?"

"Well, supposing it was?"

"We don't need to suppose. There the same thing happened to a white family. Wife got killed - left three children."

"Oh, you mean that accident down at Shelby?"

"Yes, Mrs. Something-or-other, she was. Well, sir, damn me, if that infernal claim agent didn't have the face to offer fifteen dollars for her, too!"

"Looks almost like he played a fifteen dollar limit all the time, doesn't it?" said Eddring.

"It certainly does. It ain't right."

"Well, now, I heard about that woman. She was a tall, thin creature, with no liver left at all, and her chills came three times a week. She wouldn't work; she was red-headed and had only one straight eye; and as for a tongue - well, I only hope, Colonel Blount, that you and I will never have a chance to meet anything like that. Of course, I know she was killed. Her husband just hated her before she died, but blame *me*, just as soon as she was *dead*, he loved her more than if she was his sweetheart all over again. Now, that's how it goes. Say, I want to tell you, Colonel Blount, this road is plumb beneficent, if only for the fact that it develops human affection in such a way as this. Fifteen dollars! Why, I tell you, sir, fifteen dollars was more than enough for that woman!" He turned indignantly on the board-pile.

"I reckon," said Colonel Blount, "that you would say that about my neighbor Jim Bowles' cow?"

"Certainly. I know about that cow, too. She was twenty years old and on her last legs. Road kills her, and all at once she becomes a dream of heifer loveliness. *I* know."

"I reckon," said Colonel Blount, still more grimly, "I reckon if that damned claim agent was to come here, he would just about say that fifteen dollars was enough for my filly."

"I shouldn't wonder. Now, look here, Colonel Blount. You see, I'm a railroad man, and I'm able to see the other side of these things. We come down here with our railroad. We develop your country. We give you a market and we put two cents a pound on top of your cotton price. We fix it so that you can market your cotton at five dollars a bale cheaper than you used to. We double and treble the price of every acre of land within thirty miles of this road. And yet, if we kill a chance cow, we are held up for it. The sentiment against this road is something awful."

"Oh, well, all right," said Blount, "but that don't bring my filly back. You can't get Himyah blood every day in the week. That filly would have seen Churchill Downs in her day, if she had lived."

"Yes; and if she had, you would have had to back her, wouldn't you? You would have trained that filly and paid a couple of hundred for it. You would have fitted her at the track and paid several hundred more. You would have bet a couple of thousand, anyway, as a matter of principle, and, like enough, you'd have lost it. Now, if this road paid you fifteen dollars for that filly and saved you twenty-five hundred or three thousand into the bargain, how ought you to feel about it? Are you twenty-five hundred behind, or fifteen ahead?"

Colonel Calvin Blount had now feverishly finished his julep, and as the other stopped, he placed his glass beside him on the board-pile and swung a long leg across so that he sat directly facing his enigmatical guest. The latter, in the enthusiasm of his argument, swung into a similar position, and so they sat, both hammering on the board between them.

"Well, I would like to *see* that damned claim agent offer me fifteen dollars for that filly," said Blount. "I might take fifty, for the sake of the road; but fifteen - why, you see, it's not the money; I don't care fifteen cents for the fifteen dollars, but it's the principle of the thing. T'aint right."

"Well, what would you do?"

"Well, by God, sir, if I saw that claim agent -"

"Well, by God, sir, *I'm* that claim agent; and I *do* offer you fifteen dollars for that filly, right now!"

"What! You -"

"Yes, me!"

"Fifteen dollars!"

"Yes, sir, fifteen dollars."

Colonel Blount burst into a sudden song - "On *Jor*-dan's strand I'll *take* my stand!" he began.

"It's all she's worth," interrupted the claim agent.

Blount fairly gasped. "Do you mean to tell me," said he, in forced calm, "that you are this claim agent?"

"I have told you. That's the way I make my living. That's my duty."

"Your duty to give me fifteen dollars for a Himyah filly!"

"I said fifteen."

"And I said fifty."

"You don't get it."

"I don't, eh? Say, my friend," - Blount pushed the glasses away, his choler rising at the temerity of this, the only man who in many a year had dared to confront him. "You look here. Write me a check for fifty; and write it now."

"I've heard about that filly," said the claim agent, "and I've come here ready to pay you for it. Here you are."

Blount glanced at the check. "Why, it's fifteen dollars," said he, "and I said fifty."

"But I said fifteen."

"Look here," said Blount, his calm becoming still more menacing, as with a sudden whip of his hand he reached behind him. Like a flash he pulled a long revolver from its holster. Eddring gazed into the round aperture of the muzzle and certain surrounding apertures of the cylinder. "Write me a check," said Blount, slowly, "and write it for fifty. I'll tear it up when I get it if I feel like it, but no man shall ever tell me that I took fifteen dollars for a Himyah filly. Now you write it."

He spoke slowly. His pistol hand rested on his knee, now suddenly drawn up. Both voice and pistol barrel were steady.

The eyes of the two met, and which was the braver man it had been hard to tell. Neither flinched. Eddring returned a gaze as direct as that which he received. The florid face back of the barrel held a gleam of half-admiration at witnessing his deliberation. The claim agent's eye did not falter.

"You said fifty dollars, Colonel Blount," said he, just a suggestion of a smile at the corner of his mouth. "Don't you think there has been a slight misunderstanding between us two? If you are so blamed particular, and really *want* a check for fifty, why, here it is." He busied himself a moment, and passed over a strip of paper. Even as he did so, the ire of Colonel Blount cooled as suddenly as it had gained warmth. A sudden contrition sat on his face, and he crowded the paper into his pocket with an air half shamefaced.

"Sir - Mr. Eddring," he began falteringly.

"Well, what do you want? You've got your check, and you've got the railroad. We've paid our little debt to you."

"Sir," said Blount. "My friend - why, sir, here is your julep."

"To hell with your julep, sir!"

"My friend," said Blount, flushing, "you serve me right. I am forgetting my duties as a gentleman. I ask you into my house."

"I'll see you damned first," said Eddring, hotly.

"Right!" cried Blount, exultingly. "You're right. You're one of the fighting Eddrings, just like your daddy and your uncle, sure as you're born! Why, sir, come on in. You wouldn't punish the son of your uncle's friend, your own daddy's friend, would you?"

But the ire of Eddring was now aroused. A certain smoldering fire, long with difficulty suppressed, began to flame in spite of him.

"Bring me out a plate," said he, bitterly, "and let me eat on the gallery. As you say, I am only a claim agent. Good God, man!" and then of a sudden his wrath arose still higher. His own hand made a swift motion. "Give me back that check," he said, and his extended hand presented a weapon held steady as though supported by the limb of a tree. "You didn't give me a fair show."

"Well, by the eternal!" half whispered Colonel Calvin Blount to himself. "Ain't he a fighting chicken?"

"Give it to me," demanded Eddring; and the other, astounded, humbled, reached into his pocket.

"I will give it to you, boy," said he, soberly, "and twenty like it, if you'll forget all this and come into my house. I'm mighty sorry. I don't want the money. You know that. I want *you.* Come on in, man." He handed back the slip of paper. "Come on in," he repeated.

"I will not, sir," said Eddring. "This was business, and you made it personal."

"Oh, business!" said Blount.

"Sir," said John Eddring, "the world never understands when a man has to choose between being a business man and a gentleman. It does not always come to just that, but you. see, a man has to do what he is paid to do. Can't you see it is a matter of duty? I can't afford to be a gentleman -"

"And you are so much one, my son," said Calvin Blount, grimly, "that you won't do anything but what you know is right. My friend, I won't ask you in again, not any more, right now. But when you can, come again, sir, some day. When you can come right easy and pleasant, my son, why, you know I want you."

John Eddring's hard-set jaw relaxed, trembled, and he dared not commit himself to speech. With a straight look into Colonel Blount's eyes, he turned away, and passed on down the path, Blount looking after him more than half-yearningly.

So intent, indeed, was the latter in his gaze upon the receding figure that he did not hear the swift rush of light feet on the gallery, nor turn until Miss Lady stood before him. The girl swept him a deep courtesy, spreading out the skirt of her biscuit-colored gown in mocking deference of posture.

"Please, Colonel Cal," said she, "since he can't hear the dinner bell, would he be good enough to tell whether or not he will come in and eat? Everything is growing cold; and I made the biscuits."

Calvin Blount put out his hand, and a softer shade came upon his face. "Oh, it's you, Miss Lady, is it?" said he. "Yes, I'm back home again. And you made the biscuits, eh?"

"You are back home," said Miss Lady, "all but your mind. I called to you several times. Who is that gentleman you are staring at? Why doesn't he come in and eat with us?"

Colonel Blount turned slowly as Miss Lady tugged at his arm. "Who is he?" he replied half-musingly. "Who is he? You tell me. He refused to eat in Calvin Blount's house; that's why he didn't come in, Miss Lady. He says he's the cow coroner on the Y. V. road, but I want to tell you, he's the finest fellow, and the nearest to a gentleman, that ever struck this country. That's what he is. I'm mighty troubled over his going away, Miss Lady, mighty troubled." And indeed his face gave warrant to these words, as with slow footsteps and frowning brow, he yielded to the pressure of the light hand on his arm, and turned toward the gallery steps.

CHAPTER V

CERTAIN PROBLEMS

After his midday meal, Colonel Calvin Blount, wandering aimlessly and none too well content about the yard, came across one of his servants, who was in the act of unrolling the fresh bear hide and spreading it out to dry. He kicked idly at a fold in the hide.

"Look here, Jim," he said suddenly, "Mr. Decherd killed this b'ah, didn't he?"

"Yassah," said Jim.

"And he shoots a rifle; and here are three holes - buckshot holes - in the hide. And you had a gun loaded with buckshot. Did you lend it to Mr. Decherd?"

"No, sah," said Jim, turning his head away.

"Look here, boy," said Blount. "There is no liar, black or white, can go out with my dogs; because my dogs don't lie and I don't. Now, tell me about this."

"Well, Cunnel," said the boy, half ready to blubber, "the b'ah was faihly a-chawin' ol' Fly up. He wus right at me, an' I ran up close so's not to hurt ol' Fly, and I done shot him."

"That's all right," said Colonel Blount. "How about the rest?"

"Well, sah, I had the b'ah mos' skinned, when up comes Mr.

'Cherd. 'That's my b'ah,' said he. 'Co'se it is,' says I. Then he 'lowed he'd give me two dollahs ef I said he was de man dat killed de b'ah."

Blount stared reflectively at a knot-hole in the side of the barn.

"Jim," said he, at length, "give me the two dollars. I'll take care of that." So saying, he swung on his heel and turned away.

The day was now far advanced, and the great white house had grown silent. As Blount entered, he met no one at first, but finally at the door of a half-darkened room midway of the hall, he heard the rustle of a gown and saw approaching him the not uncomely figure of the quasi-head of the menage, Mrs. Ellison. The latter moved slowly and easily forward, pausing at the doorway, where, so framed, she presented a picture attractive enough to arrest the attention of even a bear-hunting bachelor.

"I am glad to see you back, Colonel," said she. "I am always so uneasy when you are away;" she sighed.

Blount felt himself vaguely uncomfortable, but was not quite able to turn away.

"I was just in my room," said Mrs. Ellison, "as I heard you passing by. I had a little headache."

"That's too bad," said Colonel Blount, and turned again to go. The unspoken invitation of the other still restrained him. She leaned against the door, soft-eyed, her white hand waving an effective fan, an attractive, a seductive picture.

"Why don't you ever come in and sit down and talk to me for a minute?" said she, at length. "I scarcely see you at all any more."

Blount gathered an uneasy hint of something, he knew not what; yet he followed her back into the half-darkened room, and presently, seated near her, and wrapped in his own enthusiasms, forgot all but the bear chase, whose incidents he began eagerly to relate. His vis-a-vis sat looking at him with eyes which took in fully the careless strength of his tall and strong figure. For some time now her eyes had rested on this same figure, this man who had to do with work and the chase, with hardship and adventure, and never anything more gentle - this man who could not see!

"You must be more careful," said Mrs. Ellison. "But still, you are safely back, and I'm glad you had good luck."

"Well, I don't know what you would call good luck," said Blount. "The fact is, I had a little trouble, coming in."

"Trouble? In what way?"

"Well, it happened this way," said he, with a quick glance about him. "I don't like to mention such things, but I suppose you ought to know. This was about a couple of negroes back in the country a way. You know, I am a sort of deputy sheriff, and I was called on to do a little work with those same negroes. I suppose you know, ma'am, that those negroes used to run this whole state a few years ago, though they ain't studying so much about politics to-day."

"I know something of that," said Mrs. Ellison. "That was soon after the war, they tell me. But they gave that up long ago. They don't bother with politics now."

"No," resumed Blount. "They're not studying so much as they used to. Not long ago I had a number of northern philanthropists down here, who came down to look into the "conditions in this district." I said I'd show them everything they wanted; so I sent out for some of my field hands. I said to one of them, "Bill," said I, "these gentlemen want to ask you some questions. I suppose your name is William Henry Arnold, isn't it?" "Yassah," said Bill. "You was county supervisor here some years ago, wasn't you, Bill?' 'Yassah,' said Bill. I said, 'I beg your pardon, Mr. William Henry Arnold, but will you please step up here to my desk and write your name for these gentlemen?' 'Why, sho'! boss,' said he, 'you know I kain't write mah name.' 'That's all,' said I.

"'Now, gentlemen,' said I, 'exhibit number two is Mr. George Washington Sims. 'George,' said I, 'you used to be our county treasurer, didn't you?' He said he did. 'Who paid the taxes, then, George?' said I. 'Why, boss, you white folks paid most of 'um.' 'All right, Mr. George Washington Sims,' said I, 'you step up here and write your name for these gentlemen.' He just laughed. 'That'll do,' said I.

"'Exhibit number three,' said I to these northern philan-thropists, 'is our late distinguished fellow citizen, Abednego Shadrach Jones. He was our county clerk down here a while back. 'Nego, who paid the taxes, time you was clerk?' He was right uncomfortable. 'Why, boss,' said he, 'you paid most of 'um, you an' the white folks in heah. No niggah man had nothin' to pay taxes on.'

"'You know that we white folks had to pay for the schools and bridges, and the county buildings - had to pay salaries - had to pay the county clerk and the janitor - had to pay everything?' I said to him. 'Yassah,' said Nego.

"'You were elected legally, and we white folks couldn't out-vote you, nohow?' 'Yassah,' said he. 'I s'pose we wus all 'lected legal 'nough. I dunno rightly, but dey all done tol' me dat wuz so.'

"'Nego,' said I, 'step up here to your boss' desk and write your name, just like you do when I give you credit for a bale of cotton.' Nego he steps up and he makes a mark, and a mighty poor mark at that. 'You can go,' I said to him.

"'Now, gentlemen,' said I to them, 'do you want exhibits number four and five and six?' And they allowed they didn't.

"There was one fellow in the lot who stepped up to me and

took my hand. He was a Federal colonel in the war, but he said to me, 'Colonel Blount, I beg your pardon. You have made this plainer to me than I ever saw it before. It would be the ruin of this country if you gave over the control of your homes and property and let them be run by people like these. You have solved this problem for yourselves, and you ought to be left to solve it all the time. As for us folks from the North, we are a lot of ignorant meddlers; and as for me, I'm going home.'"

Blount fell silent, musing for a time. "Some folks say, 'Educate the negro,'" he resumed finally, "they say 'Uplift him.' They say 'Give him a chance.' So do I. I will give him more than a chance. I will let the negroes do all they can to help themselves, and I'll do the balance myself. But they can't rule me, until they are better than I am; and that's going to be a long while yet. Constitution or no constitution, government or no government, the black rule can't and don't go in the Delta! It wouldn't be *right*.

"Now, I'll tell you about those two poor fellows to-day," he continued. "There was Tom Sands, who works on a plantation about twelve miles from here. He has been getting drunk and beating his wife and scaring his children for about three months. Judge Williams had him up not long ago and bound him over to keep the peace, and when I last saw the judge he told me to take this negro up, if I was going by there any time, and bring him up and put him in jail for a while, until he got to behaving himself again. You know we have to do these things right along, to keep this country quiet.

"Well, when we were coming in from the hunt, we passed within a few miles of his cotton patch, and I rode over to see him. He was out in the field, and I found him and told him he had to come along. He refused to come. He swore at me - and he was not even a county surveyor in the old days! Then I ordered him in the name of the law to come along. He picked up a piece of fence rail and started at me. I had to get down off my horse to meet him. I own I struck him right hard. There was another boy, a big black negro, that must have come in here lately from some other part of the country, a big, stoop-shouldered fellow - well, he started for me, too. I took up the same piece of fence rail and knocked him down.

"I ought not to have told you this, ma'am," said Blount, rising. "But then, maybe it's just as well that I did. You never can tell what will come out of these things. We live over a black volcano in this country all the time. Now, I didn't bring in either one of my prisoners. I hoped that maybe they would take this fence rail argument as a sort of temporary equivalent to a term in jail. But to-morrow I'm going down in there and bring that Sands boy in. We never dare give an inch in a matter of this kind."

"Do you think they will make any trouble?" said Mrs. Ellison.

"Never you mind about the *trouble* part of it," said Blount, quietly. "I reckon he'll come in. I'm going to take a *wagon* this time. So that's the kind of luck we had on this b'ah hunt."

He arose to go, and left Mrs. Ellison sitting still in the shaded room, her fan now at rest, her eyes bent down thoughtfully, but her foot tapping at the floor. The incidents just related passed quickly from her mind. She remembered only that, as they talked, this man's eye had wandered from her own. He was occupied with problems of politics, of business, of sport, and was letting go that great game for a strong man, the game of love! She could scarce tell at the moment whether she most felt for him contempt or hatred - or something far different from either.

At length she arose and paced the room, swiftly as the press of strange events which were hurrying her along. Indeed, she might, without any great shrewdness, have found warning in certain things happening of late in and around the Big House; but Alice Ellison ever most loved her own fancy as counsel. The blacks might rise if they liked; Miss Lady might do as she listed, after all. Delphine and young Decherd might go their several ways; but as for her, and as for this man Calvin Blount - ah, well!

She yawned and stretched out her arms, feline, easy, graceful, and so at length sank into her easy chair, half purring as she shifted now and again to a more comfortable position.

CHAPTER VI

THE DRUM

John Eddring, the heat of his late encounter past, sat moodily staring out from the platform of the little station to which he had returned. He was angry with all the world, and angry with himself most of all. It had been his duty to deal amicably with a man of the position of Colonel Calvin Blount, yet how had he comported himself? Like a school-boy! But for that he might have been the accepted guest now, there at the Big House, instead of being the only man ever known to turn back upon its door. But for his sudden choler, he reflected, he might perhaps at this very moment be within seeing and speaking distance of this tall girl of the scarlet ribbons, the very same whose presence he had vaguely felt about the place all that morning, in the occasional sound of a distant song, or the rush of feet upon the gallery, or the whisk of skirts frequently heard. The memory of that picture clung fast and would not vanish. She was so very beautiful, he reflected. It had been pleasanter to sit at table in such company than thus here alone, hungry, like an outcast.

He felt his gaze, like that of a love-sick boy, turning again and again toward the spot where he had seen her last. The realization of this angered him. He rebuked himself sternly, as having been unworthy of himself, as having been light, as having been unmanly, in thus allowing himself to be influenced by a mere irrational fancy. He summoned his strength to banish this chimera, and then with sudden horror which sent his brow half-moist, he realized that his faculties did not obey, that he was thinking of the same picture, that his eyes were still coveting it, his heart - ah, could there be truth in these stories of sudden and uncontrollable impulses of the heart? The very whisper of it gave him terror. His brow grew moister. For him, John Eddring - what could the world hold for him but this one thing of duty?

Duty! He laughed at the thought. These two iron bands before his eyes irked his soul, binding him, as they did, hard and fast to another world full of unwelcome things. There came again and again to his mind this picture of the maid with the bright ribbons. He gazed at the distant spot beneath the evergreens where he had seen her. He could picture so distinctly her high-headed carriage, the straight gaze of her eyes, the glow on her cheeks; could restore so clearly the very sweep of the dark hair tumbled about her brow. Smitten of this sight, he would fain have had view again. Alas! it was as when, upon a crowded street, one gazes at the passing figure of him whose presence smites with the swift call of friendship - and turns, only to see this unknown friend swallowed up in the crowd for ever. Thus had passed the view of this young girl of the Big House; and there remained no sort of footing upon which he could base a hope of a better fortune. Henceforth he must count himself apart from all Big House affairs. He was an outcast, a pariah. Disgusted, he rose from his rude seat at the window ledge and walked up the platform. He found it too sunny, and returned to take a seat again upon a broken truck near by.

There was a little country store close to the platform, so built that it almost adjoined the ware-room of the railway station; this being the place where the colored folk of the neighbor-hood purchased their supplies. At the present moment, this building seemed to lack much of its usual occupancy, yet there arose, now and again, sounds of low conversation partly audible through the open window. The voices were those of negroes, and they spoke guardedly, but eagerly, with some peculiar quality in their speech which caught the sixth sense of the Southerner, accustomed always to living upon the verge of a certain danger. The fact that they were speaking thus in so public a place, and at the mid-hour of the working day, was of itself enough to attract the attention of any white dweller of that region.

"I tell yuh," said one, "it's gone fah 'nough. Who runs de fahms, who makes de cotton, who does de wu'k for all dis heah lan'? Who used to run de gov'ment, and who orter now, if it ain't us black folks? Dey throw us out, an' dey won't let us vote, an' we-all know we gotter right to vote. Dey say a nigger ain't fitten ter do nothin' but wu'k, wu'k, wu'k. Nigger got good a right to live de way he want ter as de white man is. Now it's time fer change. De Queen, you-all knows, she done say de time come fer a change."

A low growl, as from the throats of feeding beasts, greeted this comment. Footfalls, shuffling, approached the speaker.

"Tom Sands is daid, dat's whut he is," resumed the first speaker, "leastways as good as daid, 'cause he's just a-layin' thah an' kain't move er speak. An' look at me, look at my haid. De ol' man hit him pow'ful hahd, an' ef he didn't hit me jest de same, it wasn't no fault o' his'n, I tell you. He jes' soon killed bof of us niggers thah as not. Whaffor? He want we-all to come inter town an' git fined, git into jail ag'in." More growls than one greeted this, and then there came silence for a while.

"My ol' daddy done tol' me twenty-five yeah ago," said the first speaker, "dat de time was a-goin' ter come. Dey wus onct a white man f'om up Norf come all over dis country, fifty yeah ago, an' he preached it ter de niggers befo' de wah dat some day de time gwine come. We wus ter raise up all over the Souf an' kill all de white folks, an' den all de white women -

"We wus ter kill all de white men," at length resumed the same voice. "De white men f'om de Norf wus ter ride intoe de towns den an' rob all de banks an' divide de money wid we-all, an' dey wus to open de sto's and give ebery nigger all de goods he want wifout paying nuthin' fer 'em; and den nigger ain't gwine to wu'k no mo'.

"Dat white man and his folks, my ol' daddy said, fifty yeah ago, dey wu'k secret all over the Souf, from Tenn'ssee ter Louisian'. Dat was fifty yeah ago, but my ol' daddy say when he was a piccaninny, dis heah thing got out somehow an' de white folks down Souf dey cotch dis white man f'om de Norf, an' done hang him, an' dey done hang and burn a heap o' niggers all over de Souf.

"Dat wus long time befo' de wah. Dey tol' us-all dat de time wuz sho' comin' den; but den de preachers and de doctors dey tol' us-all it mightn't be come den, but it would come some day. Den 'long come de wah, an' de preachers an' de doctors an' de white folks up Norf dey done tol' us, nigger gwine ter be free, not to have ter wu'k no mo'. Huh! Now look at us! We wu'k jest as hard as we ever did, an' we git no mo' fer it dan whut we eat an' weah. We kain't vote. Dey done robbed us outen dat. We kain't be nobody. We kain't git 'long. We hatter wu'k jest same, wu'k, wu'k, wu'k, all de time. Nigger jest as well be daid as hatter wu'k all de time - got no vote, ner nuthin'. Dat's whut de Queen she done tol' me right plain las' meetin' we had. She say white folks up Norf gwine to help nigger now, right erlong. Things gwine be different now, right soon."

Murmurs, singularly stirring, peculiarly ominous, answered this extended speech. Encouraged, the orator went on. "We ain't good as slaves, we-all ain't. We wu'k jest ez hahd. Dey gin us a taste o' de white bread, an' den dey done snatch it 'way f'om us. We want ter be like white folks. Up Norf dey tell us we gwine ter be, but down heah dey won't let us."

Now suddenly the voice broke into a wail and rose again in a half-chant. Evidently the storekeeper was absent, perhaps across the way for his dinner. The building was left to the blacks. Without premeditation, those present had dropped into one of those "meetings" which white men of that region never encourage.

"Dey brung us heah in chains, O Lord!" shouted the orator.

"Yea, in chains dey done weigh us down! O Lord, make us delivery. O Lord, smite down ouah oppressohs."

"Lord! Lord! yea, O Lord, smite down!" responded the ready chorus. And there were sobs and strange savage gutterals which no white ear may ever fully understand. The white listener on the station platform understood enough, and his eager face grew tense and grave. A meeting of the blacks, thus bold at such a time, meant nothing but danger, perhaps danger immediate and most serious.

The wild chant rose and fell in a sudden gust, and then the voice went on. "De time is heah; I seen it in a dream, I seen it in a vision f'om de Lord. De Lord done tell it to de Queen, and done say ter me, 'Rise, rise and slay mightily. Take de land o' de oppressoh, take his women away f'om him an' lay de oppressoh in de dus'! Cease dy labors, Gideon, cease an' take dy rest! Enter into de lan', O Gideon, an' take it foh dyself! O, Lord, give us de arm of de Avengeh. I seen it, I seen it on de sky! I done seen it foh yeahs, an' now I seen it plain! De moon have it writ on her face las' night, de birds sing it in de trees, de chicken act it in his talk dis vehy mawnin'. De dog he howl it out las' night. De sun he show it plain dis vehy day. De trees say it, now weeks an' weeks. All de worl' say to nigger now, jes' like he heah it fifty yeah ago, jes' like he heah it in de wah we made - 'De Time, de Time!' I heah it in my ears. I kain't heah nuthin' else but dat - 'De Time, de Time am heah!' Nuthin' but jes' dis heah, 'De Time, de Time am heah!'"

And now there ensued a yet stranger thing. There was no further voice of the orator; but thee arose a wild, plaintive sound of chanting, a song which none but those who sang it might have understood. Its savage unison rose and fell for just one bar or so, and then sank to sudden silence. There came a quick shuffling of feet in separation. The group fell apart. The store was empty! Out in the open air, under the warm summons of the sun, there passed a merry, laughing group of negroes, happy, care-free, each humming the burden of some simple song, each slouching across the road, as though ease and the warm sun filled all his soul! Dissimulation and secretiveness, seeded in savagery, nourished in oppression, ingrained in the soul for generations, are part of a nature as opaque to the average Caucasian eye as is the sable skin of Africa itself.

They scattered, but a keen eye followed them. Eddring saw that they began to come together again at different points, group joining group, and all bending their steps toward the edge of the surrounding forest. Had the owner of the Big House, or any planter thereabout, seen this gathering at the midday hour, when the people should have been at their work, he would assuredly have stopped them and made sharp questioning. But at the moment the storekeeper was at home asleep in his noonday nap; the owner of the Big House had problems of his own, and, as it chanced, none of the neighboring planters was at the railroad station. John Eddring, now fully alert, looked sharply about him, then slipped down from the railway platform. He crossed a little field by a faint path, and hurried off to the shadow of the woods, his course paralleling the forest road as nearly as might be.

At half-past three that afternoon, at a point five miles from the railway station, there was enacted a scene which might more properly have claimed as its home a country far distant from this. Yet there was something fitting in this environment. All around swept the heavy, solemn forest, its giant oaks draped here and there with the funereal Spanish moss. A ghostly sycamore, a mammoth gum-tree now and then thrust up a giant head above the lesser growth. Smaller trees, the ash, the rough hickory, the hack-berry, the mulberry, and in the open glades the slender persimmon and the stringy southern birches crowded close together. Over all swept the masses of thick cane growth, interlaced with tough vines of grape and creeping, thorned briers. It was the jungle. This might have been Africa itself!

And it might have been Africa itself which produced the sound that now broke upon the ear - a deep, single, booming note which caused the brooding air of the ancient wood to shiver as though in apprehension. There had been faint forest sounds before that note broke out: the small birds running up and down the tree-trunks had chirped and chattered faintly; the squirrels on the nut trees had dropped some bits of bark which rustled faintly as they fell from leaf to leaf; a rabbit ambling across the way had left a vine a-tremble as it disappeared, and a far-off crow had uttered its hoarse note as it alighted on a naked limb. But as this deep, reverberant, single note boomed out across the jungle, there came a sudden hush of all nature. It was as though each living thing caught terror at the sound. Only far above, as though they heard a summons, the black-winged buzzards idly circled over.

The note came again, single, deep, vibrant, smiting a world gone silent. There had been the interval of a full minute between the two echoes of the giant drum. A minute followed before it spoke again. And thus there boomed out across the jungle, deep, solemn, ominous, miles-wide in its far-reaching quality, this note of the savage drum; the drum never made by white hands, never seen by the eyes of white men; the drum whose note has never yet been heard in the North, but which some day, perhaps, may be; whose note is not yet understood by those of the North, over-wise, arrogant in the arrogance of an utter ignorance, who may yet one day hear its strange and frenzied summons!

The drum spoke on - the drum of the savage people, of the ancient savage tribes. The rolling vibration of its speech swung and extended, causing the leaves to shiver in its strange power. The sound could have been heard for miles - was heard for miles. Slipping down the little leafy paths in the cane, pushing along the edges of the highway for a time, ready to step out of sight upon the instant did occasion arise for concealment; coming down the paths made by deer and bear and panther; moving slowly but speedily and with confidence through this cover of vine and jungle, to which the black man takes by instinct, but which is never really understood by the white man; knowing the secrets of this savage wilderness, yielding to its summons and to this summons of the compelling drum, whose note shivered and throbbed through all the heavy air of the afternoon - these people, these inhabitants of the jungle, slipped and slunk and hesitated and came on, until at last this little, secret, unknown building which served as their hidden temple was fairly packed with them; and a circle, open-eared, alert for any sudden danger, made a human framing half-hidden in the shrouding of the mighty canes.

One blast of the horn of white hunter or of chance traveler, and the spot had been deserted on the instant, its peopling vanished beyond discovery. But there was no horn of hunter, no sound even of tinkling cow-bell, no voice of youth in song or conversation. Only the sound of the great drum, the drum made years ago and hidden in a spot known to few, spoke out its sullen summons, slowly, in savage deliberation. Its sound had a carrying quality of its own, unknown in white men's instruments. It was heard at the Big House, five miles away, though it was not recognized as an actual and distinct sound, white ears not being attuned to it. Even here at the hidden temple it seemed not more than the whisper of a sound, scarce louder than it appeared miles away. It was bell and drum in one, and trump of doom as well.

The drum spoke on, the drum of the jungle. It whispered of revenge to those who crept up to the dusky drummer and stood waiting to drink in at each long interval this deep intoxicating stimulus, the note of the priestly drum. And each deep throb of the drum carried a greater frenzy, a frenzy still suppressed, yet mysteriously growing. The riot of the ominous clanging sank into the blood of these people, though still it only caused them to shiver and now and then to sob - to sob! these giants, these tremendous human beings, these black or bronze Titans of the field, transplanted - in time, perhaps, to have their vengeance of the ages! They stood, their eyes rolling, their mouths slavering slightly, the muscles of their shoulders now and again rolling or relaxing, their hands coming tight together, palm smitten to palm, jaw clenched hard upon its fellow.

The drum spoke on. Inside the low log building certain preparations progressed, mummeries peculiar to the tribesmen, not to be described, strange, grotesque, sickening, horrible. A few donned fantastic uniforms cut out from colored oil-cloths. They placed upon their heads plumed hats of shapes such as white men do not create. They buckled about their bodies belts spangled with bits of shining things such as white men do not wear. They drew slowly together and passed apart. They seated themselves now, in long rows, upon logs hewn out as benches, on either side of the long room; but restless of this, they rose again and again to pace, walking, walking, uneasy, anxious. Now and then an arm was flung up. Outside, where ranks of eyes gazed unwinking, hypnotized, upon the door of the temple, there rose no sound save now and then this strange sobbing.

And still the drum throbbed on, the drum of the jungle, whose sound not all white men have heard as yet. The forest shivered across its miles of matted growth, as it heard the growling voice which called, "The Time! The Time!" Relentless, measured, so spoke the savage drum.

CHAPTER VII

THE BELL

Meanwhile at the Big House there was no suspicion of what was going forward in the forest beyond; indeed the occupants had certain problems of their own to absorb them. A strange unrest seemed in possession of the place. Decherd had disappeared for a time. Mrs. Ellison, in her own room, rang and called in vain for Delphine. The master himself, moody and aloof, took saddle and rode across the fields; but if there were fewer hands at labor than there should have been, he did not notice the fact as he rode on, his hat pulled down over his face, and his mind busy with many things, not all of which were pleasing to him.

As for Miss Lady, she occupied herself during the afternoon much after the fashion of any young girl of seventeen left thus, without companions of her own sex and age. She strolled about the yard, finding fellowship with the hounds, with the horses in the neighboring pasture. She looked up in pensive question at the clouds, feeling the soft wind, the hot kiss of the sun on her cheek. Upon her soul sat the melancholy of youth. In her heart arose unanswered queries of young womanhood.

Now, as to this young man, Henry Decherd, thought Miss Lady, why should he trouble her by being continually about when she did not care for him? Why had he been so eager, even from the first day when he met her at the Big House? What had he to do with her coming to the Big House? Why did her mother now leave her with him, and, then again, capriciously call her away from him? And why should she herself avoid him, dismiss him, and then wonder whither he had gone?

Miss Lady, with one vague thought or another in her mind, wandered idly back to the great drawing-room where but an hour ago she had last seen Henry Decherd. He was not there as she peered in at the door; wherefore she needed no excuse, but stepped in and dropped into a chair which offered invitation in the depths of the half-darkened room.

A beautiful girl was Miss Lady, round of throat and arm, already stately, quite past the days of flat immaturity. A veritable young goddess one might have called her, with her high, short mouth and upright head, and her shoulders carried back with a certain haughtiness. Yet only a gracious, pensive goddess might have had this wistfulness in the deep eyes, this little pensive droop of the mouth corners, this piteous quality of the eye which left one saying that here, after all, was a maiden most like to the wild deer of the forest, strong, beautiful, yet timid; ready to flee, yet anxious to confide.

As she sat thus, the idle gaze of Miss Lady chanced upon an object lying on the floor, fallen apparently by accident from the near-by table. She stooped to pick it up, examining it at first carelessly and then with greater interest. It was a book, a little old-fashioned book, in the French language, the covers now broken and faded, though once of brave red morocco. The type was old and quaint, and the paper yellow with age. Miss Lady had never seen this book before, and now, failing better occupation, fell to reading in it. Presently she became so absorbed that once more she was surprised by the quiet approach of Mrs. Ellison. The latter paused at the door, looked in and coughed a second time. Miss Lady started in surprise.

"You frightened me, mamma," said she, "coming up so close. You are always frightening me that way. Do you think I need watching all the time?"

"Well, you know, my child, we must not keep Colonel Blount

waiting for his dinner."

"But tell me, what book is this, mamma?" said Miss Lady to her. "It's French. See, I can read some of it. It is about people in St. Louis years and years ago. It tells about a Louise Loisson - isn't that a pretty name! - who was a captive among the Indians, or something of that sort. She was an heiress, like enough, too, I can't make out just what, but certainly well-born. I think her father was a count, or something. Mamma, you should have insisted upon my taking up French more thoroughly when I was at the Sisters'. Now, this is the strangest thing."

"Nonsense, child. Can't you spend your time better than fooling with such trash?"

"It isn't trash, mamma. The girl went to France, to Paris, and she danced - she was famous."

Mrs. Ellison shifted uneasily. "You are old enough to begin reading books of proper sort. I don't know how you pick up such notions as this," said she.

"Is not the book yours, mamma?"

"Why, no, of course not. I don't know whose it is."

How much it might have saved Mrs. Ellison later had she now simply picked up this book, admitted its ownership and so concealed it for ever! How much, too, that had meant in the life of Miss Lady, its chance finder! Yet this was not to be. Fate sometimes teaches a woman to say the thing which at the instant relieves, though it later damns. It was Mrs. Ellison's fate to deny all knowledge of this little volume.

"Come, we must hurry, my child," she repeated. Miss Lady resolved to come back after dinner and look further into this interesting book. Mrs. Ellison resolved the same. Her interest in the little volume was far greater than she cared to evince.

She hesitated. Her eyes turned to it again and again, her hands longed to clutch it. Once more in her possession, she resolved that never in the future should it be left lying carelessly about, to fall into precisely the wrong hands. She hurried Miss Lady away from the place.

"Go and get ready for dinner," she commanded, "and try to look your best to-night; you know we've Mr. Decherd, and perhaps other company. That girl Delphine has run away, and I had to look after things myself; I don't want you to disgrace me -"

"I'll try not," said Miss Lady, coolly, and swept her a mocking courtesy.

Mrs. Ellison gazed after her with ill-veiled hostility, but turned away presently, quite as anxious as she was angry. This girl was a problem, and a dangerous one as well.

Things were not going smoothly at the Big House. Sam, the curly-headed, embryonic butler, who gazed out over Colonel Blount's dinner-table each evening in solemn dignity, knew that something was wrong with his people that evening, though he could not tell what. Some of them talked too much. Miss Lady laughed too much. The boss was too thoughtful, and young Massa Decherd - whom Sam had never learned to like - was too scowling. Little Sam was almost relieved when a knock summoned him without, and he betook his ten years of dignity from Colonel Blount's right hand, to learn what might be wanted at the door.

"What is it, Sam?" asked Colonel Blount.

"M-m-m-m-man outside, sah, h-h-h-he wants to see you, sah."

"Well, Sam, if there is a gentleman outside, why don't you ask him to come in and eat with us? Don't you know your manners, Sam? Why do I give you this place to run if you can't ask a gentleman to come in and sit at your table when we are having dinner?"

"D-d-did as-s-s-sk him, sah," said Sam, "b-b-but he wouldn't c-c-c-*come* in; n-n-n-no, sah, wouldn't c-c-c-*come* in."

"What, wouldn't come in, eh?"

"No, sah, s-s-s-says you must come out, sah. W-w-w-wants to see you, sah. H-h-h-he won't wait."

It was the claim agent of the Y. V. railroad who stood on the gallery awaiting the appearance of Colonel Blount. The latter looked at him quietly for a moment, and held out his hand.

"Come in," said he, "you are just in time for dinner. I'm glad to see you back."

"Colonel Blount," said Eddring, in spite of himself grown again swiftly choleric, "damn your dinner! I have come back because as a white man I've got to tell you what you ought to know." There was an eagerness in his tone whose import was recognized by Blount.

"What's up?" said he, shortly. "Niggers?"

"Yes, down below there."

"Down towards the Sands' place?"

"Yes, they've been holding a meeting all the afternoon; they've got a regular church over there in the cane. They've got a leader this time, of some sort; I can't find out who it is, but it all means trouble. There has been a plot going on for a long time. They think you have been too rough with them, and, in fact, I reckon they are just generally right desperate and dangerous. They've heard a lot of this political and educational talk from up North, and it's done what might have been expected all along. The niggers are up. They are going to march on your house to-night. Why, haven't you heard their infernal drum going all the evening! This is insurrection, I tell you!"

"Come in," said Blount, simply. "I thank you."

"I don't want any thanks," said Eddring, "I am telling you this because you are a white man and so am I. It is my duty."

Blount reached out his hand again. "Not necessary," said Eddring; but the older man threw a long arm over his shoulders, so that for an instant they looked into each other's eyes; then quickly Eddring turned and caught Blount by the hand.

"I can't come in," said he, "until you take back this infernal voucher we were wrangling over."

"Oh, well," said Blount, "I will take it, if that will please you, or you may keep it, if that will please you better. There's no time for that sort of thing now. Come in and sit down at my table - and now you, Sam, run and tell Mollie to ring the big plantation bell, and keep it ringing until I tell her to stop."

John Eddring thus came back to the Big House which lately he had left in anger; and as he entered the great dining-room he saw once more his coveted picture, the image of the morning, the tall young girl with the brown ruff of hair rolling back from the smooth brow, above the clear-seeing dark eyes. Here again, by miracle, had come his friend, to meet him in the smother of the grimy way of life! Yet he thought the girl looked at him but coldly as he stood wearily apart. He felt himself unaccredited, a man of no station. Again there swept over him the feeling of his own insufficiency, his own failure of all life's things worth having. It seemed to him that in this young girl's gaze there called out to him the cool, insolent tone of pitiless youth, saying: "I know you not; you are not my friend."

Himself simple and direct in good masculine sort, he knew

little of such thing as coquetry, nor knew that the soul feminine might hide much curiosity, if not interest, behind a glance indifferently turned, a word calmly or coolly spoken. And so he raged, unhappy in his own ignorance, and most of all unhappy for that, now disobedient to all his mandates, there surged up in his heart a great and dangerous longing, the mutiny of a soul too long crushed down by the iron hand of the commonplace, - the iron hand of this thing called Duty.

Out of this sudden conflict, and out of this sudden misery, he could formulate no better course of action to set him straight; and in the uneasy silence, tense, overstrung, he almost longed for that physical action which he knew must presently follow.

But now there pealed out suddenly upon the air of evening the mighty clangor of the great bell, the one used only in time of stress at the Big House, which soon sent all else silent. High and clear arose the note, ringing out for a moment and then silent, only to resume. The dinner in the great hall passed with few explanations vouchsafed, and presently Mrs. Ellison hurried Miss Lady away. Eddring, dimly aware that now in spite of himself he was established on some sort of footing in the Big House, none the less reflected that the occasion counted for but little from a social standpoint. He caught himself looking at the door where the tall young woman had disappeared. For the time he forgot his own station, and his own errand in that place. He forgot no more than an instant, for there came to him the swift feeling that a grave peril impended for this girl, for all the white women of the house. From that moment his problems became savagely impersonal. He was simply one of a few men called upon to defend a home, and the women of that home. He asked his soul as to his fitness for the task, and rejoiced grimly that he found himself calm and ready for this thing which was now his duty.

Colonel Calvin Blount scarcely spoke, yet he gladly welcomed his neighbor, the storekeeper, Ben Buckner, who now came strolling up to the gallery steps; and he smiled with yet greater pleasure when he peered out of the window into the twilight and saw riding up to the gate his other neighbor, Jim Bowles, who carried across the saddle in front of him a long rifle. Behind Bowles, on the family mule, sat his wife, Sarah Ann, dipping snuff vigorously.

"Good even', Cunnel," said Bowles, alighting, "I heah you-all got a b'ah this mawnin'. I just brung my own gun 'long heah, 'lowin' I might see somethin' 'long the road, even if it is gittin' a little dark." Blount smiled grimly. No mention was made of the ringing of the bell until Blount himself explained.

"You-all know something is up," said he.

"Yas, sah," said Buckner, evincing no great curiosity.

"Well, there's trouble enough on hand right now. We need every white man we can get. Bowles, take your wife inside to get something to eat, and you, Ben, go back and get your women-folks; and don't forget your Winchester."

The bell spoke on. The plantation paths now began to blacken with slowly moving figures, but within the Big House there was no confusion. Colonel Blount paced slowly up and down the gallery. Hearing footfalls, he turned.

"Oh, it's you, Decherd, is it? I'm right glad you're going home to-morrow morning, and not to-night. We need men who can shoot. I will give you something for every black head you can make a hole in to-night. What would you like? Say about two dollars?" Decherd gulped and reddened, and made such shamefaced defense as he could. There was an ugly look of ill temper on his face, but he found Calvin Blount a hard man to approach with any masculine asperities.

"The next time," said Blount to him, quietly, "if I were you, Mr. Decherd, and I heard the Blount pack going out, I don't believe I would ride along." He was away before Decherd could frame reply. At that instant Eddring appeared on the gallery calling out to him.

"Listen, listen to it," cried Eddring, "don't you hear it? That's their drum; it's coming closer."

The little party of white men faced toward the sound.

"Here, Bill," cried Blount. "Call the ladies here to me at once." He turned to them, as presently they appeared, questioning him.

"Never mind," he said, "there's going to be a little trouble, but we can handle it. It's out of the difficulty with that Sands nigger that I was telling you about, Mrs. Ellison. Now, here, you and Miss Lady take these two pistols, and go into Miss Lady's room. No matter what happens, you stay there until you are called. If any one tries to get into the room, wait until he gets almost in, then shoot, and shoot straight. Don't be scared, and keep quiet; well take care of you, these gentlemen and myself. I must tell you that it was my friend Mr. Eddring here who brought the news and warned us. You ought to thank him, but not now; get on into that room."

The women took the weapons, and Eddring noticed that of the two Mrs. Ellison seemed the more frightened. The younger one was pale, but her eye did not flicker or falter. She looked straight at each man, at Bowles and Buckner, both impassive, at Calvin Blount, now beginning to flush under his fighting choler; yes, and at last at him, John Eddring, pale and serious, but steady as the door-jamb against which he leaned.

"It was fortunate for us, sir, that you came," she said in a voice that did not tremble as much as did his in stammering a reply. So she passed on within, and the eyes of those silent men followed her.

"Now then, Bill," cried Calvin Blount, sharply, "get the hands into line so we can count them. Here, into the kitchen there, all you people, every one of you. If I see a head out of the window this night it will get a hole put through it. Do you hear? Get under cover and stay there. Ring that bell, Bill, louder, louder! Keep it going! We'll show these people what we think, and what we'll do."

So, high over the droning sounds of sleeping evening-tide, there arose the challenge of the white man's bell, calling out to the savage drum its answer and its defiance.

CHAPTER VIII

THE VOLCANO

At length the sound of bell and drum alike ceased. The great house went grim and silent. The sound of the flying night-jars died away, and the chorus of crickets and katydids began as the dusk settled down. Inside the kitchen, a detached building in which the plantation forces were now practically confined, there arose occasional sounds of half-hysterical laughter, snatches of excited talk, now and then the quavering of a hymn. In the kennel yards a hound, prescient, raised his voice, and was joined by another, until the whole pack, stirred by some tense feeling in the air, lifted up in tremulous unison a far-reaching wail.

After a time even the mingled calling of the pack droned away, and silence came once more, a silence hard to endure, since now each occupant of the Big House knew that the assailants must be close about. Each man had a window assigned to his care, and so all settled for the task ahead. An hour passed that seemed a score of hours. Then, over toward the railroad track, there came a confused sound of muffled footfalls in ragged unison, and presently a sort of chant, broken now and then by shoutings. Suddenly there boomed out once more, full and unmistakable, the voice of the great drum of Africa. The beating was now rapid and sonorous, and the sound of the drum was accompanied by a savage volume of cries. A mass of shadow appeared at the end of the lane, soon lapping over into the yard in front of the Big House.

There arose near at hand answering calls, containing a scarcely concealed note of encouragement. At a window in the kitchen there appeared a head and arm thrust out. Eddring saw it and pointed. "Why don't you shoot, man?" said the slow voice of Bowles at his elbow.

"I can't; it's murder!" said Eddring, drawing away. Yet even as he did so he saw the long brown barrel of the squirrel rifle rise level and hang motionless. There came a sharp, thin, inadequate report, and at the kitchen window the shoulders of the unfortunate flung upward and fell hanging. Eddring felt sick with horror, but Bowles lowered his rifle calmly, as if this were but target practice. Not a hand in the kitchen dared pull back into the room the body of the dead negro.

And now there came a sudden rush of feet; a medley of deep-throated callings came almost from the gallery edge. The assault, savage, useless, almost hopeless, had begun. Eddring remembered always that it seemed to him that this young gentleman, Henry Decherd, was a trifle pale; that Bowles was at least a dozen feet tall; that Colonel Calvin Blount was quite turned to stone; and that he himself was not there personally, but merely witnessing some fierce and fearful nightmare in which others were concerned. Once he heard Mrs. Ellison call repeatedly to Delphine, and was dimly conscious that there was no answer. Once, too, he saw, standing at the door, the tall figure of the young girl, Miss Lady - the white girl, the prototype of civilization; woman, sweet, to be shielded, to be cared for, to be protected - yea, though it were with a man's heart-blood. And after this spectacle John Eddring looked about him no more, but cherished his rifle and used it.

About him were vague and confused sounds of a conflict of which he saw little save that directly in front of his own window. He was conscious of a second insignificant rifle-crack at his right, and heard other shots from Blount's window at the left. His own work he did methodically, feeling that his duty was plain to him. He was a rifleman. His firing was not aimless, but exact, careful, pitilessly unagitated.

The black mass in front broke and scattered, and drew together again and came on. The assailants reached every portion of the front yard, hiding behind buildings, trees, anything they could find. At the rear of the house, among the barns, there arose the yelping of dogs cut down at the kennels, and screams rang out where the maddened blacks, no longer human, were stabbing horses and cattle and leaving them half dead. Then there arose a sudden flicker of flame. Some voice cried out that they had fired the cotton-gin. From other buildings closer at hand there also arose flames. From the kitchen came cries and lamentations. Here and there over the ground, plain in the moonlight, or huddled blackly in the shadows, there lay long blurs where the rifles had done their work. Yet from a point not far from the corner of the gallery there came continual firing.

"That's from behind that board-pile out there," cried Blount, stepping back from his window. "We've got to get them out." Eddring, not pausing for speech, plunged out of the window, rushed across the gallery and over the narrow space to the shelter whence was coming this close firing. His weapon spoke once and was lowered. Then he fled back as swiftly as he had gone.

"Get back in here, you fool!" cried Blount, pulling him in at the window as he returned. "How many were there?"

"Two," said Eddring, breathless. "One was a woman."

"Woman!" cried Blount; "what woman?"

There was no time to ponder as to this, for now shouts sounded behind them. The crashing of glass and cries of fear came from the room where the women had been left. The men hurried thither, and as they gained the door, a black face appeared at the broken pane. Once more Eddring felt hesitation at what seemed simple murder, yet still his rifle was rising when he felt a sudden dizziness assail him. A long arm pushed him away. He saw the brown barrel of the squirrel rifle rising into line once more. The black at the window fell back, shot through the forehead. Sarah Ann handed Jim Bowles another bullet. "I always did love you, ol' man," said Sarah Ann, as he blew the smoke from the long barrel of his rifle before reloading.

Eddring saw and heard thus much, but presently he sank half-unconscious, not knowing the puzzle of the shot which had struck him here so far toward the interior of the house. After a time the horror of it all drew to its climax and passed on. Buckner, the storekeeper, slipped down to the railroad station and set going an imperative clicking on the wire. Two hours later there came a special train, whose appearance put an end to the conflict. Dawn found the engine fuming at the station-house, and dawn saw the Big House still standing, charred a little at one corner, near which lay the body of the unfortunate who had sought to apply the brand. Eddring, still faint and dizzy, but not seriously hurt, sat at a little table opposite Colonel Blount, who, himself gray and gaunt, had paused for a time in his uneasy walk about the premises. A mocking-bird on the trellis without the door trilled its song high and sweet, as though the coming sunshine could reveal nothing of that which had been there.

CHAPTER IX

ON ITS MAJESTY'S SERVICE

John Eddring, one morning, a month, or so after the Big House battle, sat in the offices devoted to the use of the division claim agent of the Y. Y. lines, whose headquarters were situated in a squat building around which went on the scattered industries of the city known as the industrial capital of a certain region of the South. Beyond these dingy confines might have been seen other structures yet more squat and dreary, from which issued the lines of iron rails which led out into the South, rails which even here paralleled the shores of the great river, as though dependent upon it for maintenance and guidance. The mighty flood, unmindful, swept toward the South, its tawny mane far out in midstream wrinkled by the breath of an up-stream air.

Beyond the nearest bend there arose, above the cover of the gray forest, the dense smoke of a steamer, and near at hand there came now and again the coughing roar of the whistles of yet other river boats. Slow smoke issued also from steamers tied up at the levee, where, under low wooden canopies, lay piles and rows of brown-cased cotton bales, continually increased in number by other bales brought up in long drays, each drawn by a single mule. Above the hot wharves rose the slope of close stone riprapping, fence against Father Messasebe, who now and then, in spirit of sport or of forgetfulness, reached out for his immemorial tribute of the soil. The sun was reflected from this wall down on the depot building and the wharf floor beyond. Across the water came the strumming of a banjo, and the low note of singing also arose from the rooms where workmen shuffled about with truck and hook, shifting the cotton bales. An inspector, almost the only white man at the wharf, moved slowly from bale to bale, ripping the covers with his knife and probing with his cotton auger into the middle of each bale to test its quality. Mules dozed about with lopping ears. Nowhere was there haste; neither here nor on the street; nor in the railway offices beyond, where sat John Eddring, agent of the personal injury department of this southern railway.

The room was not attractive, with its few chairs, its rows of letter files, its desks and copying presses. The table at which Eddring sat was worn and lacking in polish. Upon the wall hung a map showing the divers lines of the Y. V. railroad; a chart depicting the street crossings in the city of New Orleans; an engineer's elevation of a bridge somewhere on the line. Severely professional were these surroundings; as was indeed the central figure in the room, who now sat at his desk opening the morning mail. He looked up presently as there came a knock at the door, and soon was on his feet, hat in hand; for the first caller of the day proved to be a lady. Apparently she was an acquaintance of the claim agent, who addressed her by name.

"Come in, Mrs. Wilson," he said pleasantly.

Mrs. Wilson, just arrived from a small town down the railroad, had brought with her her sister, her mother and four children, not to mention a neighbor who had come along to do a little shopping. Eddring employed himself in getting a sufficient number of chairs for this little body of visitors. Inquiries as to the health of himself and his family ensued, reciprocated politely by Eddring, who asked after Mrs. Wilson's kith and kin and the leading citizens of her town. These preliminaries were long, but the claim agent was apparently well acquainted with them and regarded them as necessary.

"Well, now, Mr. Eddring," said Mrs. Wilson, "I've come in heah this mawnin' to see you about ouah hawse. You know ouah Molly hawse got kilt down at the depot two weeks ago by the railroad kyahs. I declare, I felt so bad I sat down and cried; I couldn't get supper that day. We was so much attached to Molly - why, Mr. Eddring, you don't know how bad we-all did feel about that hawse. It don't seem right to us nohow."

"No, things do go wrong sometimes, Mrs. Wilson," said Eddring, soothingly. "Now, I know that horse. Mr. Wilson drove me behind her the other day when I was down at your town. Good horse. A little old and a trifle lame, if I remember right." He smiled pleasantly.

"Lame! Why, Molly never was lame a day in her whole life. She never did have no lameness at all, unless it was a sort of hitch now and then like, but you couldn't call it right lame. Now, Mr. Wilson didn't come up. I tol' him you was a mighty nice man and you wouldn't let a lady get the worst of a business deal. I thought we could talk it over and you would do about what was right. Now, two hundred dollars -"

"Two hundred dollars! Why, my dear madam, you know I can get you another horse -"

"Get us another hawse like Molly! I'd like to know where you can get a hawse that's been in ouah family twenty years for any two hundred dollars! Why, Mr. Eddring, I always thought you was a fair-minded gentleman."

"Don't call me that, don't call me a gentleman," said Eddring, "and don't you call *me* fair-minded! But now, just look here. We didn't ask that Molly horse to get on our track. We didn't want to kill her, now, did we? All we wanted was to steam up there to the platform, and put off some groceries and let off a few passengers. We didn't want to kill *anybody's* horse. Now, I know Molly has been in your family a long time; a good horse, I don't deny it. We couldn't make it right with you if we paid you a *thousand* dollars; so just let's forget it and try to be friends. Let me give you a check for forty dollars."

"Forty dollars!"

"Now, then, Mrs. Wilson, this is not to be for Molly, it's just trying to be friendly. I want to feel free to come down and sit at your table and look you all in the face."

"I don't see how you could do that, and only pay me forty dollars, Mr. Eddring." A grieved look sat on the lady's face.

"Well, now, I reckon I could, if I just saw you dressed up in a new gown that I saw in the window down at the store this morning. I reckon I could, if I saw hanging in your hall that hat that I saw this morning, down on the street."

"Do you think forty dollars would buy them, Mr. Eddring?" asked Mrs. Wilson.

"Surely it would, and leave you enough to pay for your whole trip up here, and buy some things for the children besides. Now, look here, I don't want you to think I'm offering that to *pay* you for Molly. I ain't paying for any horses for Mr. Wilson. He is a gentleman that don't need ask favors of anybody, and he's going to pick out his own horses. You tell him I said he was a good judge of a horse. I want you to tell him I scorn to offer you money for this here Molly horse of yours - I scorn to do so. Mr. Wilson will make more than two hundred dollars in a day or so, the way cotton is going up this week. I just throw in this forty dollars - here is the voucher for it - so as to show you I am your friend. Now, if you ever want any shopping done up here any time; Mrs. Wilson, just write to me and I'll do the best I can. I'd go right down to the store with you to look at that dress, if it wasn't that I have to be right busy here for a while. Good-by, Mrs. Wilson, good-by, madam. Good-by to you all. I am glad you all came in. Good-by, little folks; here's something;" and each, small hand received a silver piece from the claim agent.

Mrs. Wilson passed out with a puzzled expression on her face. On the stairway she sighed. "Well, he is a nice man, anyhow," said she, to her companion.

This little party had scarce disappeared before there came another visitor, this time a fat colored woman of middle age, who labored up the stair and halted at the door.

"Come in, auntie," called the claim agent, from Ms desk, "what's the matter?"

"You know whut's the matter, Mr. Edd'ron," said the caller. "You 'membehs me?"

"Yes," said the claim agent, "you had a baby run down at the street crossing yesterday. We sent it to the hospital. How is it getting along?"

"Hit's daid, Mr. Edd'ron. Yas sah, my lil' Gawge is daid."

"What? Oh, pshaw!"

"Yas sah, lil' Gawge done die six o'clock dis maw-nin'." She shook with sobs. The claim agent dropped his own face into his hands. The weary look came back again into his eyes. At last he turned and went up to the black woman where she stood sobbing, and extended his hand.

"There, there, auntie," he said, "I'm sorry, mighty sorry. Now, listen. I can't settle this thing this morning. Here is ten dollars of my own money to help bury the boy decently. As soon as I can, I will take up the matter, and I will settle it the best I can for you. Now, go away; please, go away."

The negro woman ceased her sobbing as she took the bill.

"Ten dollahs," said she, "ten dollahs for dat baby! Dat'll buhy him right fine, it sho' will, Mr. Edd'ron. You'se a fine man, Mr. Edd'ron, 'deed you is."

Eddring smiled bitterly. He paced up and down the room, his

head bent down. Presently he turned to his assistant.

"Go on over to the depot," said he, "and see if there is any more mail. I don't think I will do any letters just now."

Left alone, he continued to pace up and down, until at length he heard steps and again a knock at the door, after the custom in business in that region. This time there entered the tall form of his whilom friend, Colonel Calvin Blount, from his plantation down the road. Him he saluted right gladly and asked eagerly regarding his health.

"I am well, right well," said Blount, "Just came up to see about a little cotton. It looks like twelve cents before long."

"Well, with cotton at twelve cents you ought not to have any quarrel with the world, Colonel Blount."

"Well, now," replied Blount, "I need about everything I can get to put my place in order again. It's some months now since we had our little war down there, and I haven't got together half the hands I need yet. Some of my people cleaned out and we never did hear anything more of them. We've got plenty of niggers in jail down there yet; but that ain't the way we want it. We want 'em to get out of jail and into the fields at work. They'd rather stay in jail. They get as much to eat, and more time to rest."

"Well, they did raise trouble that time, didn't they?" said Eddring. "What do you suppose started them, Colonel? Who was it put them up to do it?" Blount shook his head.

"That's the puzzle," said he. "It was some one with brains; and not the kind of brains that grows under kinky hair, either."

The two men sat silent for a time. "Oh, by the way," said Blount, at length, "I was just going to say I brought up Mrs. Ellison and Miss Lady with me this morning. I left them over at the hotel right now. Do you know, Eddring, that girl has grown up to be a plumb beauty! She's handsome enough to just scare you. Why, I never did know there was so many young men in this whole town before that were acquainted with me. Looks like she was a public menace to business on the streets. Pine girl. And just as good as she's handsome!"

Eddring felt the blood surge up into his face, but he made no comment. He knew that the one unsafe thing for him to do was to see again this same Miss Lady, and yet against this decision all the riotous blood of his heart surged out in protest. He took a swift turn to the window.

"By Jove, Colonel," he cried, "out there goes that fellow Jim Hargis, from over near Jewelville. He's got that brag dog of his along."

"Dog? What dog?" cried Blount.

"There, that's the one," said Eddring, pointing out a man passing by, who was accompanied by a pepper-and-salt foxhound. "Do you see that dog? Well, Jim Hargis says that's the coldest-nosed hound ever run a trail, and he's got five hundred dollars to bet his equal don't live in the South."

"Humph," sneered Blount, "I reckon he never did see my old Hec."

"Hec! Why, he says he'd make Hec look like a pot-licker if he ever got mixed up with his dog."

"What! My old Hec! Five hundred dollars! Say, you just holler to him, while I run down stairs." And away went the irate Colonel, his hands fumbling in his pockets.

Eddring did not stay to see the result of his stratagem. Instead, as he found himself alone, he walked up in front of the little mirror which hung upon the wall. He gazed straight into it, examining with frowning face the reflection which he witnessed. He ran a hand across the gray-tinged hair, turned up a corner of the mustache with a reflective finger, man-fashion, and looked eagerly, searchingly, at the face which confronted him. It was a face slightly lined, a trifle tired. He stood there thinking, questioning this image. As he turned away he sighed.

The wind rustled the dingy curtains at the dingy window, as he flung himself discontentedly into a chair, A bar of sunlight lay across the floor; at the window there came the sound of a song bird from a near-by tree; but these signs and sounds of an outdoor world John Eddring did not note. He felt nothing but the grim imprisonment of these dusty walls. In his soul was revolt, rebellion. He smote his hand hard upon the papers which, lay before him on the desk.

"This, this," he exclaimed aloud, "this is all my life! Good God! It is to buy life, human life, human sufferings, and to buy them cheap! I swear, I can see blood on every voucher that I sign! That's my business. I must buy these things cheap; and they say I don't buy them cheap enough - they want me to put in my whole heart, and honor, and principles. Here is my salary for the month." Pie drew the slip of paper toward him and sat looking at it. "And here is the last correspondence from the superintendent. Complaints, all of it. Once I thought I should succeed. Success-yes, I have succeeded - in being absolutely wretched every day of my life. God! God! Is this all?"

He pushed the papers from him and half rose, leaning over the desk, resting on his hands.

"Success," he muttered again to himself. "What is it? I gave up the law and I took the salary." He paused and sighed. "At any rate," he resumed, musing still aloud, "my old mother has had a roof over her head, and has had three meals a day. Well, it's made me old. I suppose I oughtn't to mind, but oh, damn everything! Damn everything, I say!" He scattered the papers with a blow of his hand, and whirling, stood once more before the mirror, which seemed to have some unusual interest for him. He did not at first hear the step of the visitor who now entered the door and came gently up behind him.

"Confound you!" cried he, suddenly, as at length he caught the footfall. "What do you mean by coming in like that?"

The frail and gray-haired lady who halted at this salutation was as much startled as himself. "Why, John!" said she. "Why, John!"

Turning, Eddring caught her by the hand, his face flushed.

"Mother!" he cried, "I thought it was the clerk."

"Why, John," repeated Mrs. Eddring, "I didn't know that you ever swore."

"I don't, mother, except sometimes. The fact is - well, today I just had to."

"You were thinking of something else."

"Well, yes. I beg your pardon. I was just feeling pretty good over the way business matters were going, and - well, the truth is, I was just a little - well, a little exuberant, you know."

Mrs. Eddring seated herself and looked about her at the dingy little office, which ever seemed to her poor housing for one who, in her belief, was the greatest man in all the world.

"I beg your pardon, John," said she, "for intruding in your business hours, but I was down-town to-day, and I thought I would just drop in to see you." She gazed at him keenly, noting with a mother's eye the worn look on his face.

"I don't think you've been looking well lately, John," said she. "Does your arm still trouble you?"

"Why, of course not, it's all well. Why, I'm feeling fine, fine!

You and I ought to be feeling well these days, for you know we have just finished paying for our house, and everything is looking perfectly splendid all around. You didn't know I had a raise in my salary last month, did you?" He turned his back, as he said this last, that his mother might not discover on his face so palpable a falsehood.

"Is that so, John?" she said. "Why, I'm so glad!" A faint spot of color came into the faded cheeks, and the old eyes brightened. "Well, I'm sure you deserved it. They couldn't pay you more than you're worth."

"No," said Eddring, grimly, "they are not apt to." His mother caught no hidden meaning, but went on.

"You're a good business man, John, I know," said she, "and I know you have always been a gentleman in your work." Here spoke the old South, its pride visible in the lift of the white crowned head, and the flash of an eye not yet dimmed in spite of the gentleness of the pale, thin face.

Eddring gulped a bit. "Well, you know, in business," said he, "a fellow pretty near has to choose -"

"And you have always chosen to be a gentleman."

"As near as I could, mother," said he, gravely. "I have just done the best I could. Now, as I was saying, I am feeling mighty fine to-day. Everything coming out so well - the truth is -"

"John," said his mother, sharply, "why do you say 'the fact is,' and 'the truth is'? You don't usually do that."

He did not answer, and there went on the subtle self-communings of the mother-brain, exceedingly difficult to lead astray. For the time she did not voice her thought, but approaching him, placed a hand upon his shoulder, and brushed back a lock of hair from his forehead.

"Pretty gray, isn't it, mother?" said he, smiling at her.

"Nonsense! Is that what you were thinking about?"

"Well, you see, I'm getting -"

"No, you're not! You don't look a day over twenty-five."

"That's right. That's right," said he, blithely. "I am twenty-five, exactly twenty-five; and they're raising my salary right along. What'll it be when I'm fifty?"

"You ought to have a new necktie, John," said his mother, smoothing down the lapel of his coat. "A rising man, like you, my son, must always remember little things."

"That's right," said he. "That's right. You know I'm so careless. The truth is -"

"There you go again, John! Now why are you so particular to tell me that what you are saying to me is the truth? Just as if you ever in your life said anything which wasn't true."

He did not answer, but hurriedly turned away, that the keen eyes might not examine his face too closely. She followed him.

"John," said she, sharply, "tell me, what's the trouble? Tell me the truth."

"I have," said he. The words choked him, and she knew it. He evaded once more the attack of her eyes, but again she followed him, her face now very pale, her lips trembling.

"Boy," said she, "tell me, what is it? Is there a woman? Is there anybody?"

"Nobody in all the world but you," he declared bravely. It was of no avail, and he knew it, as the keen eyes finally found his own.

"John!" said his mother, "you have *not* been telling me the truth."

"Well, I know it," said he, calmly, and with far greater happiness. "Of *course* I haven't. Who said I was? O, Lord! you can't fool a woman any way on earth. Now here -"

"Who is this girl?" asked his mother, with a certain sternness as she gazed at him directly; "for of course I knew very well what was the matter. I suppose I shall have to face this some day, though it has been so long -"

Eddring looked her straight in the face in return, and this time without flinching.

"The dearest girl in the world," said he. "But I reckon she's not for me."

"Who is she? Where is she? Where did you meet her? Have you a picture?"

"I don't need one."

"What's her name - her family? Of course -"

"She hasn't any family. I don't know where she came from."

"*John!*"

"Well, it's true."

"But you could not expect -"

"I expect nothing!" cried he, again striking his clenched hand upon the table. "Here is my world. Oh, well, you know now if I ever swear, and why."

Her lip trembled. "I never knew you did," said she. "John, tell me, have you ever spoken to her?"

"Good God! no, never. How could I? What have I to offer a girl like her? Who am I? What am I?"

She caught his head in her arms and drew his face down to her bosom. "There, there," said she. "There, there, now."

But presently he broke from her, and swung out into the room, erect and active once more, a sudden triumph in his carriage, a brighter glance in the eye for a time grown dull.

"Pshaw! Here," said he, "here I am, pitying myself! That isn't a good thing for a man to do. A man oughtn't to complain. He ought to take his medicine."

"Look," he cried, coming to her again, "maybe the world is just loving me, that's all, and doesn't know. Maybe it's the same as it was when I scratched my face on your breast-pin when I was a baby, when your arms were around my neck. You did not mean it. Maybe life does not mean it. Maybe it's just *loving* us all the time.

"Come, now, you shall see this girl who is of no family. Come with me. She is here, right in town, this very day."

"Where is she, John?"

"Why, Colonel Blount told me that she and her mother were over at the hotel. Could we call? Wouldn't it be all right if we did?"

"If the ladies are strangers in town," said Mrs. Eddring, slowly, "and if they are friends of yours, then I will call on them with you."

"Come!" said he, feverishly. "Come!" - then suddenly: "Tell me, mammy, does my hair look so awfully gray?"

"John," said she, "there isn't a gray hair in it. Come on, what are you waiting for?"

Eddring had turned, and was fumbling at a drawer in his desk. He raised a face flushed and conscious-looking. "The fact is, mother, I've got a new necktie right here, and - and I want to put it on."

EMERSON HOUGH

CHAPTER X

MISS LADY OF THE STAIR

"I have always told you, Lady," said Mrs. Ellison, "how a girl who hasn't any fortune can best achieve things. Of course, it's a question of a man. When she has found the man, it rests with her. She must let herself out and yet keep herself in hand. Emotion, but not too much, and at the right time - that's the scheme for a girl who wants to succeed."

"How you preach, mamma!" said Miss Lady, petulantly. "You are always talking to me about the men. As if I cared a straw!"

"You ought to care, Lady. Men! Why, there's nothing in the world for a woman except the men."

Miss Lady said nothing, but went on adjusting a pin which she took from among several others held in her mouth. At length she patted down her gown, and frowned with a sigh of satisfaction, as she looked down over her long and adequate curves. Discovering a wrinkle in the skirt of her gown, she smoothed it out deftly with both hands.

"There are not very many gentlemen to bother about down at the Big House now, mamma," said she; "at least, not since Mr. Decherd left. But then, he's coming back. Did you know that?"

Mrs. Ellison's face showed a swift gleam of satisfaction. "I hope he will," said she. "But, after all, we must sometime go somewhere else. Now, New Orleans, or New York perhaps.

You are almost pretty sometimes, Lady. We could do things with you, in the right place."

Miss Lady stamped her foot upon the floor in sudden fury. "Mamma," cried she, "when you talk this way I fairly hate you!"

"You talk like all the foolish Ellisons," said the other, slowly. "Now, I could tell you things, when the time came. But, meantime, you forget that you and I have absolutely no resources."

"Excepting me!" This with white scorn.

"Excepting you." This with frank cynicism.

Miss Lady controlled herself with difficulty. "At least," said she, "we have a home with Colonel Blount. He has always said he wanted us to stay, and that he couldn't do without us. Now" - and she laughed gaily - "if Colonel Blount didn't have a red mustache, I might marry him, mightn't I?"

"Be done with such talk," said Mrs. Ellison, sharply, "You'd much better think about Mr. Decherd. And yet," - she frowned and nervously bit her finger-tips as she turned away. Miss Lady made no answer except to go over again to stand before the mirror, where she executed certain further pattings and smoothings of her apparel.

The two were occupied, in these somewhat dingy quarters in the hotel, in preparing for their sallying out upon a shopping expedition in the city, an event of a certain interest to plantation dwellers. Mrs. Ellison paused in her own operations to extract from a hand-bag a flask, wherefrom she helped herself to a generous draft. Miss Lady caught the flask from her.

"You disgust me, mamma," said she. "How often have I told you!"

"You were not quick enough, my dear," said Mrs. Ellison, calmly. "Now, I was saying that you were born for lace and satins. Promise me, Lady, no matter what happens, that if you ever get them, you will give me a few things for myself, won't you? Sometimes - sometimes I am not certain." She smiled as she spoke. There might have been politic overture, or beseeching, or threat, or deadly sarcasm in her speech. Miss Lady could not tell; and it had taken, indeed, a keen student to define the real meaning of the enigmatical face of Alice Ellison, woman not yet forty, ease-loving, sensuous, yet for this time almost timorous.

"Now, a good, liberal man," began Mrs. Ellison presently, however, "is the best ambition for any young woman. For some reasons, we might do better than remain at the Big House longer. We will see, my dear, we'll see." And so they stepped out into the hall.

It was a vision when Miss Lady came down the stair. Young men who saw her removed their hats, and old men thanked God that the day of miracles was not gone; so fair was Miss Lady as, with head high, and body slow and stately beyond her years, and foot light and firm, she came down the little stairway, and glorified it with youth and the spirit of the morning.

Miss Lady had indeed, within the last few months, rapidly grown up into compellingly beautiful young womanhood. Much of the girlishness was gone and the firmer roundness of full femininity had taken its place. Her neck, a column of white above its frill of laces, rose strong and fine. Her hair, unlighted by the sun, was dark and full of velvet shadows. Her eyes, with long lashes softly falling, offered the shadows and the mysteries of the dawn. Her figure asked small aid, and, needing none, carried, and was not made by, the well-cut gown of light silken weave, dotted here and there with small red fleur-de-lis. A maze of long scarlet ribbons hung from Miss Lady's waist, after a fashion of her own, and for purposes perhaps remotely connected with a tiny fan which now appeared, and now again was lost. A cool, sweet ripeness was reflected in the spot of color here and there upon the fawn-colored wide brim of the hat, upon the smooth cheek, on the lips of the short and high curved mouth. As she walked, there was heard the whispering rustle of the Feminine; that sound indefinable, which creeps upon man's unwitting senses and enslaves him, he knows not how or when or why.

Well enough all this served to set in tumult the pulses of at least one who saw Miss Lady, fresh as a little white cloud, warm as a tiny spot of yellow sunlight, cool and mysterious as the morning, thus framed as a picture on the stair.

John Eddring and his mother, unannounced by reason of the slothfulness of a negro messenger, sat in the hotel waiting-room, which served as the "ladies' parlor," opening out near the foot of the stairway. And so it chanced that they saw Miss Lady and her companion as they descended. It seemed to Eddring that this vision on the stair was the most beautiful thing in all the world. He was smitten at once dumb and motionless. He felt his mother's hand on his arm.

"John," said she, "did you see that girl? She was *perfectly* beautiful!" The touch aroused him. She saw it all written in his face.

"She?" he murmured. "Miss Lady!" and presently sprang after, to return a moment later with the two ere they had left the hall. Whereupon followed all manner of helpless, hopeless, banal and inadequate commonplaces, out of which Eddring blankly remembered only that the visit of Miss Lady to the city was to terminate that evening, at the departure of the down train. And so, after all, little remained for him but a present parting, though all his soul cried out for speech with Miss Lady alone, for the sight of her face only. It was as though within the moment all the energies of his life had been directed into a new channel, whose insufficient walls were threatened with destruction by the flooding torrent. The primeval man arose, exulting, sure; and so, in a moment, John Eddring knew why the world was made, and by what tremendous enginery of imperious desire it is driven on its way. Work, riches, art, music, architecture, the vast industrialism of an age, all this thing called progress - all, all were for this alone, this thing of love! The atmosphere about him thrilled, vibrant with this message of the universe. The interspaces of all things seemed lambent, and therein fixed centrally was this ineffaceable and ineffable picture. He gazed, and as he gazed there came to him but one thought: For ever.

"John," said Mrs. Eddring, when they were again alone, "that's a sweet girl, a *very* sweet girl. Did you notice how she thanked me - as being the elder lady, you know - for our call? I think -" Eddring started, only half-hearing her.

"But that lady, her mother," went on Mrs. Eddring, "I can't tell, yet for some reason I do not fully understand her. But -" and here she gained conviction, "you need not tell *me!* There is *family* somewhere back of that girl, my son. She's good enough. She's -"

"Good enough!" cried John Eddring. "Good enough! What do you mean?"

"Ah, my boy," said Mrs. Eddring, sighing, "I know. I presume, I hope, that you feel quite as the general did, when I was a girl. Sometimes I have thought the world was changing in such matters. I shall want to see this young lady again, and often. We must inquire - but here I am, talking with you, when of course you must be back at your work. I'll leave you now."

"Work!" cried John Eddring. "Work!"

CHAPTER XI.

COLONEL CALVIN BLOUNT'S PROPOSAL.

The mild winter of the Delta region wore itself gradually away, and now again the sun was high in the mid-arc of the sky, glowing so warm that the earth, rich and teeming, seemed once more to quiver under its ardor. The sloth of ease and comfort was in the air. The big bees droned among the flowers at the lattice, and out in the glaring sunlight the lusty cocks led their bands betimes, crowing each his loud defiance. In the pastures, under the wide-armed oaks, the cattle and horses stood dozing. Life on the old plantation seemed, after all, to have set on again much in its former quiet channels. If within the year there had been insubordination, violence, death hereabout, the scene no longer showed it. The Delta, less than a quarter white, more than three-quarters black, was once more at rest, and waiting.

This was the scene over which Miss Lady looked out one day as she sat in a big rocking-chair in the shade, in a favorite spot of the wide gallery, feeling dreamily, if not definitely, the spirit of the idle landscape which lay shimmering in the sun. Her gaze gained directness and comprehension at last.

This, thought Miss Lady, was the world! It was all the world for her. This, so far as she could see, was to be her fate - to sit and look out over the wide reaches of the cotton fields, to hear the negroes sing their melodies, to watch the lazy life of an inland farm. This was to be the boundary of her world, this white and black rim of the forest hedging all about. This lattice was to shut in her life for ever. She might meet no white woman but her mother, no white man. Things were not quite clear to Miss Lady's mind to-day. She sank back in the chair, and all the world again seemed vague, confused, shimmering, like this scene over which she gazed. She sighed, her foot tapping at the gallery floor. Sometimes it seemed to Miss Lady that she must break out into cries of impatience, that she must fly, that she must indeed seek out a wider world. What was that world, she wondered, the world out there beyond the rim of the ancient forest that hedged her in? What did it hold for a girl? Was there life in it? Was there love in it? Was there answer in it?

The old bear-dog, Hec, came around the corner of the house from his napping in the shade, and sat looking up in adoration at his divinity, inquiring mutely whether that divinity would permit a common warrior like himself to come and kiss her hand. She saw him finally and extended one hand idly; at which Hec dropped his ears, wagged his tail uncertainly, and came on slowly up the stair. He nozzled his head tentatively against her knee; and so, receiving sanction, went into delighted waggings, licking tenderly the soft white hand which stroked his head.

"Oh, Hec, dear old Hec," said Miss Lady, "I am *so* lonesome!" And Hec, understanding vaguely that all was not quite well with his divinity, uplifted his voice in deep regret. "I am so *lonesome,*" repeated Miss Lady, softly, to herself.

A step on the gallery caused her to turn. Colonel Blount crossed the length of the gallery and paused at her side. "Miss Lady," said he, "you just literally honey my b'ah-dogs up so all the time, that after a while I'll be ashamed to call the pack my own. I'm almost afraid now to take them out hunting, for fear some of them will get hurt; and you always make such a fuss about it."

"You get them all bitten and cut up," said Miss Lady. "How do you think that feels?"

"I know how it feels," said Blount, slowly. "As to dogs, I think there are times when it's a sort of relief to them. You can't change the way the world is made, Miss Lady. How'd you like to sit here for ever and never get a chance to see anything outside of this here yard?"

Unconsciously, he had come close to a certain mark. "I should die," said Miss Lady, simply. "I was just thinking -"

"What were you thinking?" said Blount, suddenly.

"I don't blame Hec, after all. I should die if I had to stay here for ever, with just nothing to do - nothing - nobody -"

Blount suddenly pulled up his chair and sat down close at hand.

"Tell me, Miss Lady, what do you mean?" said he. "Tell me, child. Ain't you happy here?"

"Well, I don't know."

"Yes, you do know; and I asked you if you weren't happy."

"Maybe you don't understand all about girls, Colonel Calvin," said Miss Lady.

"I don't reckon I do. I don't reckon God A'mighty does, either, hardly. I thought you and your mother were contented here. You've made it a sort of heaven for me. I 'lowed it would run along for ever that-away."

Silence fell between them. "Miss Lady," said Blount, finally, "I came out here this morning on purpose to hunt you up. Now, listen. You say you're not happy here. I have been nothing but happy ever since you came. For a long time I didn't know why. I didn't know why I kept on asking where was Miss Lady at, where was Miss Lady gone to. 'Now, where is Miss Lady?' I found myself asking this very morning. About an hour ago I found myself asking that mighty strong. Then I just set myself down, right out there on the board-pile, and done reasoned it all out. Then I found out why I was asking that question so much. I found out why I never did get married, Miss Lady. The reason was, I never wanted to, till now."

Miss Lady was looking far away now, out across the fields. Her face was pale, save for a small red spot in either cheek. She moved as though she would have turned to face this man whose eyes she felt, yet this she was unable to do. She heard the voice go on, softer than she had ever known it before.

"Miss Lady," said Calvin Blount, "now listen to me. I've grown up down here like any savage. I haven't been much better than my old daddy, nor much different; and every man ought to grow better than his dad, if he can. I have driven the niggers to work, and I have been comfortable on what they raised. I can see it's right rough down here, though. I never used to think so. All I wanted in the world was rain enough to make the cotton sure, and mast enough to make the b'ahs come. I was happy, or thought I was, until you came, though I reckon I never really knew what that word meant before. I never did see a woman I liked as well as my pack of dogs. This place was good enough for me. Now, listen. I was fool enough to think for one minute, Miss Lady, for just one minute, that it was good enough for you. I thought maybe you and I could understand a heap of things together. Now, I hear you say that you're lonesome, that you're not happy here. Happy? Why, I tell you, Miss Lady, I am half-dying of lonesomeness right now, right here in my own home, on my own ground, in the only place in God A'mighty's world where I am fit to live."

"You must not," said Miss Lady, and turned toward him eyes in which stood sudden tears. "I must go. I must go away."

"Listen, I tell you," said Blount again, sternly, and put out a hand as she would have risen. "You go away? Where would you go? What would you do? Now, wait till I get done. Here," he cried almost savagely, "stand up here like I tell you, and listen to what I've got to say! Stand right there!" He drew in one grasp from his pocket his handkerchief and his gauntlet gloves, and swept a place clean upon the gallery floor before her.

"Stand right there, Miss Lady," said he, with all his old imperiousness. "Stand in that place where I done made it clean and easy for you, like I want to make the whole world clean and easy for you always. I'd like to smooth it that-away for you, always. Now, look at me, Miss Lady. I ain't a coward, at least I never was till now, and maybe not now; for I came here as soon as I knew how this thing was, though God knows I wanted to get on my horse and ride the other way as fast as I could. I came here because I wouldn't have been a man if I hadn't come, if I hadn't said this to the first woman I ever thought twice about."

"Don't, don't, please! please!" cried Miss Lady, pushing out her hands, but he commanded her again, sternly.

"Stop," said he. "There's one time when a man has a right to say his say, and say it all. I've got to tell you this. I've got to offer myself to you in marriage, Miss Lady. I've got to ask that of you; and, God pity me, I've got to give myself my own answer. Listen! Stop! It ain't for you to answer. It's for me.

"Now, look at me. I'm strong. I'm not afraid of any living thing, except you. I'm old, but there's younger men that's no better. I'm rich enough. I've got two thousand acres of the best land in the Delta, and that's the best on earth. There's money enough here to take you anywhere you want to go in all the world. I couldn't be mean to no woman. It's in my nature to feel that a woman is a thing to be took care of, for ever and for ever - that oughtn't to work, that oughtn't to worry, that ought to just *be!* I don't know much about women, but I always did feel that-away. You'd never have to worry about that. I wouldn't lie to you, not for any reason. No man should ever raise a breath against you. If" - he swept a hand over his face, but still went on.

"Listen," he said, "Miss Lady Ellison, I, Calvin Blount, old Calvin Blount, this sort of man like I told you, I offer myself to you, and all I have, for your own. I offer you that -" The girl's eyes looked up at him, swimming now all the more in tears. His face was distorted, but he went on. "Don't," said he, "please don't! Listen, here's the answer. By the Eternal, you *can't* and you *shan't* marry old Cal Blount! It wouldn't be right. It wouldn't be right, Miss Lady," said he again, presently. "It's right for me to tell you that I never thought twice of any other woman, that in my soul I love you, that I never shall know a happy day without you; but it's right, too, for me to give myself the answer, and I do. And it's No, Miss Lady, it's No!" He turned away. Miss Lady felt about her blindly and dropped her head on the rail of the chair, sobbing.

"I can't help it. I can't help things, Colonel Cal," said she, "but then, but then -"

"Yes, child; yes, Miss Lady," said Calvin Blount, gently, "but then, but then! I never did know much, but I'm learnin'. I'm man enough now to know all about what you mean when you say 'but then.' Come, it's all over. But I can't bear to see you cry. Please stop, Miss Lady. Don't do that."

Miss Lady could not stop. She buried her face in her hands. She half felt the touch of a hand, very light, upon her head, a touch given but once, and swiftly withdrawn. She heard him continue. "This home is yours," said he, "and you can stay here, I'll go out into the woods again. You need not fret and you need not fear. We couldn't, maybe, both stay here together now. Or, it may be there's a bigger world for you somewhere, and you want to go there. I won't stand in your way, and I'll help you all I can. I'm done talking about this, now and for ever. But if you don't stop crying, I'll get on my horse right now, and I'll ride out in the woods and I never will come back again."

Miss Lady put out her hand to him.

"Sir," said she, half-whispering, "I didn't know that men were this way. It's different from what I thought. But you must remember," and she smiled wanly, "you must remember always only that it was you who refused yourself. Please think of it that way, Mr. Cal."

Old Hec ventured up the steps again and stood looking dumbly from one to the other of these two. At last he deserted his master and went over and laid his big head on Miss Lady's lap, looking up at her with questioning eyes.

CHAPTER XII

A WOMAN SCORNED

As Colonel Blount passed from the gallery into the house he came under the gaze of a close observer. Mrs. Ellison, for reasons of her own watchful and suspicious, had heard these agitated voices on the gallery, and, had it been possible without detection, would not have been in the least above eavesdropping. This being impossible, she was forced to draw her own conclusions, based in part upon her own suspicions. The droop of this man's shoulders, the drawn look of his face, spoke plainly enough for her. Hardly had the sound of his footsteps died away before she was out of the door of her room and by the side of Miss Lady, who still sat, pensive and downcast, in her rocking-chair on the gallery.

Miss Lady was not prepared for the spectacle which thus met her gaze, this woman with clenched hands and distorted face, and attitude which spoke only of antagonism and threat. There came a swift catch at her heart, for this was the woman to whom of natural right she should now have fled in search of consolation. It seemed to her now as though all her world had known a sudden change. It was as when some tender creature, fresh risen from the earth, ventures into the strange, new world of the air, to flutter its brief day. Eternity seems to stretch before it, an eternity of joy hinted in the first glance at this new universe which it attains. Yet comes the sun, the sudden, blighting sun, the same influence which has broken the brooding envelope of another world and brought this gentle being into its new life, and this cruel sun withers at once the tender creature in all its hope and youthfulness and beauty, ending its bright day ere it as yet is noon. Thus seemed the universe to Miss Lady, no longer young, care-free, joyous, but now suddenly grown old. One look, one sudden flash of her inner comprehension, and she knew it to be for ever established that this woman, her mother, was her mother no more! Why, she knew not, yet this was sure, she was not her mother, but her enemy. How dubiously swam all the world about poor Miss Lady at that instant! She knew, even before the enraged woman at her side had formulated her emotion into speech.

"So now, you treacherous little cat," said Mrs. Ellison, between her shut teeth, "you've been at work, have you? Oh, I might have known it all along. You've been trying to undermine me, have you? Why, do you think I'll let a little minx, a little half-baked brat like you, keep me out of getting the man I want? I'll show you, Miss Lady girl!"

"Stop! Wait! What are you saying?" cried Miss Lady.

"You'll listen to what I am saying," cried Mrs. Ellison. "You've been leading him on, and now you presume to reject him - to reject the roof over your head and the bread in your mouth. Why, I never thought of him seriously for you! You've ruined us both in every way, yourself and me. Why, can't you see that if we stayed here he had to be for one or the other of us? And could you not know that I wanted him for myself? Oh, don't say 'wait' - don't speak to me! I know it all as well as if I had seen it. Now, you've got to walk, that's all."

"Oh, mamma, mamma," cried Miss Lady, "do not!"

"'Oh, mamma, mamma!'" mocked the other; "stop your tongue, girl, and don't you dare to call me 'mamma' again. I am not your mother, and never was!"

Miss Lady gasped and went pale, but the cruel voice went on. "You don't know what you are, or who you are. You're nothing, you're nobody! You had no chance except what I could give you, and you'll never know now what a chance that was! I would have made you, girl. I would have done something with you, something for us both - but not now, ah, no, not now! You, to cut me out from the only man I ever really did want!"

Miss Lady rose, suddenly aflame with resentment, and feeling a courage which came she knew not whence.

"Madam," said she, with calmness in spite of her anger, "I don't know what you mean by this, but I am certain you are telling the truth. I will not talk to you at all. You degrade us both. As to Colonel Blount, I never said a word, I never did the first thing - I didn't - I didn't tell him anything - I could not help -"

"You could not help! You could not help! Of course you could not help! Neither can I help. But the main thing, after all, is that you have thrown away a home for both of us -"

"Madam," said Miss Lady, now very quiet and calm, "there is only one thing certain in all the world to me at this moment, and that is that you do not love me, that you never will, and that I don't feel toward you as I should. It is as you say. I could not stay here now; I shall have to go somewhere. Colonel Blount himself knows that. He said so."

"Your mother!" resumed Mrs. Ellison, laughing shrilly, "I am about as much your mother" - she began, but caught herself up; "you are nobody, I say, and you'll have to go take care of yourself as best you can. You don't know what you're throwing away, young woman. If you had left things to me there would have been none of this trouble. Now I shall have to go too, for I would die rather than stay here now. I hate that man!"

Miss Lady for a moment saw the naked soul of this woman whom she had called her mother, even as at that moment she saw her own soul; and between this which she saw and that which remained in her own bosom, she recognized no kinship.

Problems there were for her, but this was not one of them.

"Madam," said she at length, with a dignity beyond her years, "you are right. We must go, both of us; but we shall not go together."

She turned to leave the gallery, and as she passed, gazed straight into the face of Mrs. Ellison. She saw there a swift change. The red rage, the anger, the jealousy were gone. Haggard, with eyes shifting as though in search of refuge, the woman showed now nothing so much as a pale terror! Miss Lady unconsciously followed her gaze. There, near a door at the farther end of the gallery, quiet, impassive, stood the girl Delphine. She did not speak, but gazed at Mrs. Ellison with eyes wherein there might have been seen a certain somber fire.

"I - I did not call, Delphine," stammered Mrs. Ellison. "No, no, I did not call."

Silent as before, Delphine turned back. With swift intuition Miss Lady caught the conviction that some relationship existed between these two which she herself did not understand. A sudden sense of insecurity possessed her, mingled with the reflection that the master of the Big House was ignorant of what arrested drama was here going on under his own roof. If she dared but tell the master what she suspected - ah! then perhaps this comfortable landscape, which but lately she had found monotonous, might again enfold her sweetly and safely; and never again would she call it aught but satisfying. Yet every instinct told her that to the master of the Big House she could go no more. Thus she pondered, and as she pondered her panic fear increased to a blind terror, overwhelming every other emotion. But one resolve remained - as soon as might be, she must fly, and find a hiding spot unknown to any of those who had been her associates in this place which for a time she had called home.

CHAPTER XIII

JOHN DOE VERSUS Y.V.R.R.

There are but few of the humble who are untrustworthy. Continually we discover the great truth that faithfulness and loyalty are general human traits, nowhere more so than among those from whom they should not be expected; nowhere more so than among those who are debarred from hope. The great captains of industry so-called, themselves blown full of pride of circumstance, prate often of the inefficiencies of human cattle; yet continually the wonder remains that these same cattle continue to do that which their conscience tells them is right for them to do, and to do it for the sake of the doing. The lives of all of us are daily put in charge of beings entitled fully to an Iago-like hatred, who might hate for the very sake of hating; yet these are the faithful ones, who do right for the sake of its doing. When one of these forsakes his own creed - then it is that danger exists for all. It is the unfaithfulness of the humble which is the unusual, the fateful, the tremendous thing.

There was small active harm in the somewhat passive soul of John Eddring's assistant, William Carson, the large-handed young man who acted as clerk and stenographer and rendered more or less blundering service about the office. Perhaps there was more of curiosity than evil in his nature. It was curiosity in the first place which gave him personal knowledge of a certain list of judgment claims against the Y.V. railway, which the chief agent of that road had recently cautioned Eddring, division agent, to keep revised up to date and to hold close under cover as a matter of absolute secrecy. These things were more or less familiar to William Carson through his acquaintance with the correspondence of the office. This very injunction of secrecy inflamed his curiosity to the point of action. In the absence of his chief, he rummaged through the office papers until he unearthed these lists, and to these latter he gave a more careful scrutiny than he had accorded many other matters under his immediate charge. He figured up the totals of the unpaid claims, and the figures startled him. He reflected that so much money in one sum would represent very many things to him personally. This established, he reflected further that it was in the first place most unrighteous to withhold these sums from the lawful claimants, and in the second place, to withhold them from himself. He was sure that the company did not need, and ought not to have, this money. If only, thought William Carson, these judgments might be collected, and if only - but beyond this thought his brain was not shrewd enough to travel.

It needed a bolder mind, and this, as it chanced, was at hand, after the devil's fashion in such affairs. Henry Decherd had known Carson in the community where he had lived before his removal to the city. The two had since then met by chance now and again on the street or elsewhere. Once, when Eddring chanced to be out of town, they happened to meet and paused for a conversation longer than usual. There came a hint from Carson, a word of quick inquiry from Decherd, a flush of timorous guilt upon the face of the unfaithful humble one; and presently these two repaired to the office of the claim agent, locked the door behind them, and soon were absorbed in certain lines and columns of figures which had been prepared by Carson.

"This ain't for ten years, nor half of it," said the latter, at length. "But you can see it runs up to a good lot of money. Look here." Decherd gave a long whistle as he looked at the footings of the columns of figures.

"And they're all unpaid claims," he said. "Judgments from one end of the line to the other, it looks like. By Jove, it does seem that the road had to pay for about everything in the Delta, doesn't it?"

"Oh, it don't have to pay *these* things, don't you worry," said Carson. "It don't need no sympathy, *this* road don't. It will take care of itself, all right. These ain't claims that's going to be *paid,* but ones that *ain't* going to be paid. They're ones that's in judgment and can be collected; but the owners of these judgments don't seem to know their rights. They don't collect. Maybe they're dead or moved away, or maybe they've forgotten all about it, or maybe their lawyers haven't taken pains to tell them - you can't tell about all these things. Every big accident that happens on the road, there's a lot of judgments taken against the road; but they don't all get paid, as you see. That is one of the secrets of our business."

"A pretty situation of affairs, isn't it?" said Decherd. "Looks like the road would have to pay, if these claims were fought."

"I should say so. These judgments are on the court records all the way from here to New Orleans, and they're all as good as gold. The company can't dodge out of one of them, if a fellow takes enough. interest to get around and collect. Most of them are air-tight. Some have gone on appeal to upper courts, but we don't bother to appeal these little ones. And, you know, there ain't a court in the Delta that wouldn't cinch the road if it got a chance."

"How much do they foot up?" said Decherd again, reaching out his hand for the papers.

"About eighty thousand dollars, or something like that. Why, if a fellow -"

"A fellow couldn't push the whole thing at once, you know; he would be discovered the first thing," said Decherd. The other pricked up his ears eagerly.

"Suppose he was caught," said he, "what could they do? If I want to go down to John Jones' cabin, down somewhere in the cane-brakes, and give him five dollars for a judgment that he has forgot about, or is scared to try to collect, why, I get the judgment, and it's legal, ain't it? Or suppose I just poke him up to collect it and he gives me half? That's legal, ain't it? And who can help it, even if anybody knew? Why, say, if I was Mr. Eddring there, knowing what he does about these claims, do you reckon I'd be working very long? I reckon not. I'd go in along this line of road and I'd get some fellow to hunt up these claims, a few at a time, and I'd see that the company *paid* these judgments!" He swelled up at the thought of his own daring. "Why, Mr. Eddring," he went on, "he could stand in on both *sides* - draw a salary from the company, an' divide with the niggers and the white folks that has claims against the road. It's easy, especially with the niggers, because they never do know what's going on, anyhow."

Decherd puckered up his lips, and paused for a time in thought. Carson went on. "I wouldn't ask anything better than this," said he, "to get plumb rich in about two or three years."

Decherd walked up and down slowly, his finger pressed to his chin in thought. His face was worn and haggard. His clothing had taken on a seedy cast not formerly common to him. Apparently things might have been better with him in a financial way. Perhaps he saw a way to mend matters. "Halves?" said he at length, suddenly looking straight into Carson's face.

The clerk flushed a dull red. The conspiracy was formed. "Why, yes," said he, his voice half-trembling. "I reckon that would be about right."

"Well, then, give me the lists," said Decherd. "I'm up and down the road in the Delta now and then. I'll take care of these things. As for you, whatever you see or hear, keep your mouth shut, or it'll be the worse for you."

"Sure," said Carson, and endeavored to laugh.

CHAPTER XIV

NUMBER 4

One day not long subsequent to the little meeting of Decherd and Carson in Eddring's office, there chanced to be in the same southern city one James Thompson, traveling representative of a furnishing house in the North, he being then engaged in completing his regular business trip through that part of the country. Mr. Thompson, it seemed, found himself in need of a traveling-bag, and, fancying the merchandising possibilities of the place, stepped into a prominent shop on the main street at a late hour of the afternoon, and proceeded to satisfy his somewhat exacting personal taste. He selected a bag of alligator leather, of what seemed to him suitable dimensions and trimmings.

"This will do me, I think," said he, "about as long as I need one. I'm going to quit the road and settle down before long."

"You better haf your name-cart put on it, anyvays," said the salesman. "It's more stylish."

But Mr. Thompson was in a hurry and could not wait for that. He was obliged to leave the city that night on train Number 4, the New Orleans Limited on the Y. V. railroad. Presently, he chuckled to himself, he would not be taking train Number 4 any more, but would be sleeping at home in his own bed, and not obliged to get up in the morning until he felt like it. His season's work was nearly over, and after that he intended to retire from the house and start up in a business of his own; all of which are very comforting reflections to one who is past fifty, and who has been "on the road" for many years.

In due time Mr. Thompson, smoking a comfortable cigar, ambled up to the gate beyond which stood Number 4 in the railway station. He tossed his alligator bag to the porter at the car step, who placed it among others on the platform of the car. Mr. Thompson then ambled into the car and sought out the smoking-compartment, heaving a sigh of content as he settled down to the enjoyment of his cigar.

The conductor of Number 4 looked at his watch, raised his hand and cried out "All aboard!" shortly and sharply. In the waiting-room of the station a negro train-caller sang out, "All abo-o-oh-d!" in a long-drawn minor, which sounded rather as warning than as invitation. The caller, as he completed his last round, sprang aside to escape the rush of a young man who ran through the gate just in time to catch the moving train. He threw his own hand-bag up on the platform for the porter's care, and also passed back into the train. This late-comer was Henry Decherd.

As Number 4 rolled out to the southward, the usual little comedy of a railway train at night-time began. An old lady asked the porter a dozen times what time the "kyars would get to N'Yawlns." Two florid gentlemen leaned together in one seat and discussed cotton, cotton, cotton. In yet another berth two young farmers were having their first experience in high life, and were eager to try the experience of actually going to sleep upon the cars while the same continued their forward progress - a thing which had seemed impossible to them. Not removing their clothing, they venturesomely pulled off their shoes, and thereafter, in some fashion, managed to squeeze together into the same berth. "Why, I'm a-layin' mighty comf'table now," exclaimed one presently, to his own evident surprise and gratification.

"So'm I," exclaimed the other. Silence then for a little while, when again the first voice was heard: "Why, my feet's right wahm!"

"So's mine!" replied his friend, in equal delight and surprise.

"I reckon I'll take my shoes inside," said the first speaker, presently.

"So'll I," said the second; after which there came silence.

In another part of the car was a lady with a little child, which jumped and squirmed about, and made eyes at all mankind, including James Thompson. The latter made eyes in turn, and waggled his fingers at the youngster, which trilled and gurgled as it danced up and down, now hiding its face, again springing up into view above the back of the plush-covered seat.

"I have three of my own back home, madam," said Mr. Thompson, going up to the mother of the child. "Come here, baby, and give me a kiss; because I'm a poor man who can't be kissed by his own little girl." The child kissed him gleefully and sweetly a dozen times; and perhaps, after all, that was shriving and absolution for James Thompson. Not all of us go down into the valley of the shadow with the kiss of innocence on our lips.

Number 4 steamed on to the southward. She crossed the flat bottoms where the great river was hedged out by the levees; edged off again toward the red clay hills and finally, leaving this fringe of little eminences, plunged straight and deep into the ancient forests of the Delta, whose flat floor lay out ahead for many miles. Number 4 was now in the wilderness. Panther, and fox, and owl went silent when the wild scream of Number 4 was heard; of Number 4, carrying its burden of the ancient comedy and tragedy of life, its hates, and loves, and mysteries, its sordid, its little and its tremendous things.

Later in the night Number 4 groaned and creaked and protested at the stop for the little siding of the Big House plantation, eighty miles from the point where she had begun her flight. Her brake shoes ground so sternly that the heavy oaken beams whined at the strain put on them; yet obedient to the hand of man, she did stop, though it was but to discharge a single passenger.

Henry Decherd hurried out into the darkness like some creature hard pursued. Number 4 swept on, clacking, rumbling, screaming. The shriek of her whistle, heard now and again, was loud, careless, imperious, self-assured.

But what meant this hoarse and swiftly broken note, as though Number 4 were caught in sudden mortal fear? What meant this broken, quavering wail, as though the monster were suddenly arrested by an utter agony? What, sounding far across the sullen forest, was this rending and crashing roar? Number 4 had been here, hurrying onward. But now - now where and what was Number 4?

Meeting her fate, Number 4 plunged, ground, shivered, shortened and then fell apart, shattered like a house of toys. For an instant the wilderness heard no sound, until there arose, terrible in its volume, the wail of a general human agony. There was no answer save that, borne far upon the humid air of the night, there came the solemn calling of the deep-throated hunting pack of the Big House kennels. Each night the pack called out their defiance to Number 4 as she swept by with her roar and rattle and the imperious challenge of her whistle. She was their enemy. But now they knew that evil had been done, that life was in jeopardy; even as they knew that the mighty at last had fallen.

CHAPTER XV

THE PURSUIT

It was a strange party that took breakfast at the Big House table on the morning after the railway wreck. All these guests, injured or well, crippled or whole, were gay and talkative. Gestures, hysterical smiles marked their conduct. Their faces showed no spell of horror. Men had looked at the long row of dead on the platform at the station. "That is my father," said one; and another, "This is my sister," but they spoke impersonally, and only to satisfy the curiosity of others. There was no room for an individual terror. A woman with both arms broken and her head heavily bound sat laughing, and again raised her voice in a hymn of thanksgiving.

The broken-hearted search, the frenzied efforts at relief occupied all comers far into the morning. It was long before any one thought of asking the cause of the disaster; yet presently reason sufficient was discovered. The broken railway train covered with its wreckage the immediate cause of the accident: a pile of timbers erected carefully and solidly between the rails. Seeing this, after a time, there began to mount in the jarred and dazed senses of these human beings a sullen desire for justice or revenge.

Among the first to seek the head of the train where the wrecking timbers lay was John Eddring, who arrived on the early train from the city. By virtue of his office as agent of the personal injury department, he at once began to possess himself of such facts as might be of use later on. With face pale, but steady, he traversed the entire length of the shattered train, examining, inquiring, making a record of the dead and injured, and in some cases examining papers and effects for purposes of identification.

There was in particular one victim, a large, well-looking man, who had been killed in the forward compartment of one of the sleeping cars, he being the only one who suffered death or extreme injury in that car. Close by was his hand-bag, but this bore no card and offered no distinguishing mark serving to identify its owner. The porter could remember only that this gentleman had got on at the city and had not yet been "checked up." The porter was sure that this was his valise, for he had himself brought it in from the platform.

"Thompson, James Thompson," said a newspaper worker, one of those who mysteriously appeared before the accident was many hours old. "Here's his accident insurance card. Got it in his pocketbook. It's twelve thousand to his wife, anyhow, I reckon. Davenport, Iowa; that's his home."

Eddring felt it his duty to examine more thoroughly the effects of this victim. The hand-bag held absolutely no items of personal equipment. Its sole contents were a small and curiously bound little volume, printed in the French language, and a bundle of papers of legal size, typewritten and backed in the form of railway documents. Eddring could not conceal a start as he glanced at these papers. Hurriedly he thrust into his pocket papers, book and all.

He had reason for surprise. Here, in this nameless package in the care of this stranger, James Thompson of Davenport, Iowa, was a full list of the outstanding judgment claims against the Y. V. railway throughout his own division; a list of whose existence he supposed no one except himself had any knowledge whatever! Attached to the package of papers there was a letter written in a woman's hand. Hasty and professional as was his glance, and much disturbed as he was by the discovery which accompanied his finding of the letter, the words which met his eyes carried a shock such as he had not known in all the years of service in his eventful calling.

"Dearest," ran the communication, not wholly ill written: "Dearest, you said you would come last week, but you did not. I am uneasy. Are you forgetting me? Does that girl mean more to you than I do - does either of them? Why, they don't know how to love. You know I would do anything for you if you kept on in the old way, but you shall not leave me. You say you have to 'keep things in careful shape.' I have wished a thousand times that girl had been out of the way long ago. Then you would have to depend on me now for everything, love and all. You say you will divide it all with me when we get it. What do I care about that? Let it all go, and let us go and live somewhere together and be happy as we were.

"Now if you are not telling me the truth, you are getting yourself into trouble, and you will have enough of that anyhow. As for madam, it's not you she wants any more. Yet she can't bear to have you look at the girl. You don't know women very much. Now she has forgotten her part, let her make it up with old man Blount and let the girl go. You and I can fight it out the way we started to before they ever came down here. I say one string to a bow is better than two. You will have to choose between these strings.

"If I ever feel certain that you are lying to me, I'll do what ought to have been done, and then I won't care. You can have all the money if you ever get it, but I am going to have all of you, and no dividing with anybody. I have no place in the world here, and am standing everything and waiting and hoping. Sometime people will hear from me. Sometimes I hate myself and you, and all the world. I would do big things if I once started. The best thing you can do is to come down here to me right soon. We must have a talk, and, besides, I want to see you."

The letter bore no signature, save a scrawled mark or sign, which Eddring did not pause to examine at the moment. Indeed he had no time to ponder or to speculate, for even as he folded the letter and placed it in his pocket with the other articles taken from the valise, he heard a sudden cry, and, going forward, joined again the group that had formed about the pile of fatal timbers at the head of the wreck. Some one showed him a handkerchief, a sodden bit of linen which had been taken from under the heap of logs. It was a woman's handkerchief, and as Eddring spread it out on his hand he noted in one corner a curious embroidered mark. At this he gazed intently, with a vague feeling that somewhere he had seen a similar mark before. It was like some rude monogram or crest.

"If you don't mind," said he, quietly, "I should like to have that handkerchief. It might be useful with other evidence which I have in my possession." None offered objections, and Eddring presently moved away. He felt a certain mental uneasiness which he could not fully formulate; but presently all speculation was carried from his mind by the crowding of events about him.

There had by this time appeared the sheriff of Tullahoma County, who brought with him the most practical agencies of justice possible for that peculiar country, three dogs known widely as skilled followers of human trails. To the sheriff Eddring now offered the newly discovered handkerchief. The latter held it out to the dogs, which sniffed at it gravely, and sniffed also at the place where it had been found under the derailing timbers. The sheriff went about his duties methodically, now moving back all the spectators so that the dogs might have full opportunity in their work.

The tail of the lead dog at length began to move slowly from side to side. He walked a pace or so down the bank and paused, the other two coming to him. The sheriff pointed silently. Distinctly marked in the soil was the print of a shoe - a woman's shoe, long, narrow. All three of the dogs now moved toward a gap in the row of stumps which formed a rude hedge for the cleared right of way. At this little gap the narrow footprint was seen again, with others made by bare feet. At the edge of the wood, there came a long, low, sobbing call from the lead dog, and presently the others wailed their confirmation; so that the trail was now steadily begun.

They followed the dogs for miles, across glade and ridge and opening, through jungles of vines and matted cane; and presently they came upon paths which converged, separated and converged again, as might have been in the jungle about a village of the Black Continent. They went on and on, and finally they came out, as John Eddring in his heart knew they presently would, at the edge of a little hidden opening, surrounded by a wall of deep green cane. There before them stood a long, low, log structure, which he himself could have described in advance. Upon the door, done in the blind, morbid egotism of crime, which so often leaves open sign and signal for its own undoing, there showed, cut deep in the jamb, a rude sign, cabalistic, mysterious, fetish-like. To Eddring it seemed for the instant to be the same mark as that upon the handkerchief. He could not explain these things in his own mind. Others of the party were more interested in pointing out once more, in the confusion of footprints before the building, the imprint of the same narrow shoe. Eddring was striving to connect this imprint with the mark on the handkerchief and on the door, with certain things which he had heard on this very spot long before; and with that glimpse of a woman's garb in the darkness at the time of the night attack on the Big House.

There was no time to ponder upon these things. The dogs passed over the trampled ground in front of the building, sniffed at the door, circled the building, sniffed at the windows, passed slowly into the empty room when the door was opened for them. Then they drew apart again, and, wailing once more solemnly, headed back along a path which presently brought all into the plain road to the railway station. The procession moved more rapidly now, and presently it had crossed the railway track and turned into the lane which led up to the Big House, the dogs threading without hesitation the maze of footprints which covered all the ground thereabout.

They came on with heads down and tails slowly moving, now and again giving utterance to their long and mournful note, until presently they and those who followed them were met at the yard gate by Colonel Blount, who came down to greet the sheriff of the county, whom he knew very well.

"Jim," said he, "I know you and your dogs, and I know what you're doing. It's all right, but I want to warn you to be mighty careful about my own dogs. They won't run with any other pack, and they'll kill a strange dog just as sure as they can get to him."

The sheriff looked at him and shook his head, as if to say that justice must have its course. Blount made no further objection, and the three trailing dogs, entering the gate, now crossed the lawn and passed around the corner of the house toward the quarters of the servants, beyond which lay the kennels of the fighting Big House pack. The baying of these dogs, penned up, had been incessant. They could tolerate no thought of intelligence other than their own at this work. They were born and trained to fight, and knew no kinship with their species. It had been better for Jim Peters, sheriff of Tullahoma, had he taken the advice of the master of the Big House; for as he turned into the yard at the rear of the house, the prediction of the latter came true, and so swiftly that none saw how it chanced.

Who loosed the gate no one ever knew; but certainly it was opened, and the fighting bear-pack came boiling out, eager for any foe. There was ineffectual shouting over a mass of writhing, snarling creatures of many colors. In a moment the solemn-faced emissaries of justice lay dead and mangled on an unfinished trail. Blount caught the sheriff's hand as it moved toward his revolver.

"It's no use shooting the dogs, Jim," said he. "You've run the trail fair to here, and you know I'll help you run it to the end. I don't know what to say. Hell's broke loose in the Delta."

CHAPTER XVI

THE TRAVELING-BAG

The sheriff turned upon Blount his grave face, and for a time made no answer. "You're right, Cal," said he, at length. "Things are bad down here. It's no nigger planned this thing. But if it wasn't, then who did?"

"I don't know," said Blount. "Some day, my friend, we'll find out, and then we'll see whether or not there's any law left in the Delta for people who do things like that." He pointed toward the spot where a long line of men were now busily engaged in removing from the rails the fragments of what had been train Number 4.

"Come into the house, men," said Blount, presently. "Let's get something to eat." There had been more than a hundred persons taken in as guests at the Big House that day, but even yet the hospitality of the old planter's home was not quite exhausted. The two ladies of the house had abundance to do in caring for the injured, but the servant, Delphine, had become the presiding spirit of the household in these hours of stress. In some way Delphine brought partial order out of the chaos, and the great table still was served.

By this time there had begun the pitiful procession which was to empty the Big House of its company. The tracks were nearly cleared by the wrecking crew, and long rows of fires were consuming the broken evidences of the ruin that had been wrought. The injured had been cared for as best might be by the physicians of the relief train, and this train, with its burden of the living and the dead, now started on its journey northward. The day of Number 4 was done. The iron way would soon again have its own. Another Number 4, screaming, exultant, defiant, would again pursue its course across the wilderness.

Naturally, in hours so crowded with perplexities, the master of the Big House had had small time to specialize his hospitality. The demands of the living, the needs of the suffering, the eagerness of all in the search for the author of this disaster, kept him, as well as others, so occupied that he scarce knew what was going forward. He had not known that Henry Decherd was about the place until he saw him seated at his own table. He made no inquiries, supposing that Decherd might have been a passenger on the train; yet he greeted this uninvited guest none too warmly, even in that sanctuary. Deeherd thought best later to explain his presence. He had been on the wrecked train, he said to Colonel Blount, but had by some miracle escaped. He was on his way to New Orleans, and wished to take the first train down as soon as traffic was resumed. He hoped that he was not intruding too much if he once more dropped in on his old friend. To this Colonel Blount listened grimly and said no word, only sweeping his hand toward the table. "Eat," said he, and so turned away. He would have done as much for a strange hound in his yard, and Decherd knew it.

It was well on in the afternoon when John Eddring, still busy with his confused mass of papers, was in turn approached at the table where he sat by this same Henry Decherd. The latter carried in his hand a traveling-bag which he extended toward the claim agent. "Mr. Eddring." said he, "I found this bag in my room, but it isn't mine. They tell me you've got track of a lot of things. Did you see anything of an alligator bag about like this?"

"Why do you ask?" said Eddring, quietly.

"Well, I know you're claim agent on the road," said Decherd.

"You seem to be getting ready for a lot of trouble later on. I didn't know but you might have seen my bag among others. Nothing in it much - a few collars and brushes, you know; things I could use now if I had them."

"Would you let me see this bag?" said Eddring. Decherd, somewhat uneasily, as it seemed to Eddring, opened the valise and displayed its contents. "This seemed to belong to some fellow by the name of Thompson," said he, as he rummaged among the articles. "Maybe he has gone back to the city - maybe he's got my bag. See, here's a letter addressed to him, 'James Thompson, Davenport' -" Eddring glanced at the handwriting. It bore no resemblance to that of another letter which at that moment rested in his own pocket. His face half-flushed. He begged the dead man's pardon. This, he felt assured, was from James Thompson's wife. The other letter, he felt with swift conviction, was from a woman different. Yes, and to a different man. Yet he held his own counsel as to this.

"I shouldn't wonder if it were your bag that I've got in my own room, Mr. Decherd," said he. He rose and led the way, and Decherd, perforce, must follow. "Is this yours?" He held up to Decherd's view the valise which had once contained the book and papers earlier mentioned. Eddring looked narrowly into Decherd's face. He saw it suddenly change color, going from pale to sallow.

Decherd made a distinct effort at recovering himself. "Y-yes, that's it - it looks like it, anyhow," said he.

Eddring handed him the valise. Decherd pressed the spring of the lock and looked into the interior.

"Why, it's empty!" cried he. "What in -"

"Yes," said Eddring, simply, "it's empty." Decherd cast at him one swift, veiled look, under which Eddring saw all the covert venom of a dangerous serpent that is aroused. "It's not my bag, anyhow," said Decherd, regaining his composure. "I thought it was, but mine had my name on the plate."

"Yes?" said Eddring. "I am sorry I can't help you. Well, if the bag isn't yours, I'll just keep it. I don't doubt the owner will be found in time." The eyes of the two met fairly now; and from that instant there was issue joined between them.

CHAPTER XVII

MISS LADY AND HENRY DECHERD

Why Henry Decherd should have remained so long at the Big House at this particular time might have found plausible answer in any of a dozen ways. There were reasons indeed why Decherd should be covertly pleased at matters as he now found them. Colonel Blount touched his pride keenly enough by practically ignoring his presence, yet he made amends by continuing moody and aloof, spending little time about the house. John Eddring had long since taken his departure for the city. Mrs. Ellison was rarely visible about the house. There was an atmosphere of uneasiness, an unsettled discontent over all things. Yet, for the oblique purposes of Henry Decherd, matters could not have been better arranged. So much being established, he played his chosen part at least with boldness. In spite of all this recent stress and strain, in spite of this continuing trace of sadness and anxiety which lay over all, Henry Decherd none the less knew very well that there was now at hand the best and perhaps the last opportunity which, he might expect for the carrying out of a certain intention which, above all other purposes, worthy or unworthy, had long possessed his soul. At times he was absent from the Big House, none knew where; for in the careless bigness of that place there were no locks upon the doors and no hours for the spreading of the table. Each came and went as he pleased. In no other situation could Decherd have found things shaped better to his plan.

That plan, the sole motive which could have kept him at that time in that certain locality, was to speak alone with Miss

Lady. Even thus favored by circumstances, he found this purpose difficult to accomplish. Now it was Colonel Blount who passed moodily across the yard; or it was Mrs. Ellison who accosted him just as he started to follow the young girl down the hall or out on the gallery. Once or twice the girl Delphine stopped him in some such errand and held him on one pretext or another in some corner of the place. Yet Decherd, involved as was the game he played, persisted and at length had his more immediate wish.

He came upon Miss Lady at last in the twilight on the big gallery, when the birds were chirping all about and the insects were attuning their nightly orchestra. He walked directly up to her.

"Miss Lady," he said suddenly, without parley or preface, "ah, Miss Lady, how glad I am to find you at last!"

The girl drew back from him, at once divining the import of his air and tone; but he went on.

"I've waited so long," said he. "There's always been some one about. Couldn't you see - don't you see what it is that brings me to you!" He would have caught her hand in his own feverish one, but again she drew away, looking at him with startled eyes.

"Dearest," he went on, "listen. I can't do without you. I have loved you ever since first I saw you. Come, tell me -"

Even the icy silence of the girl scarce served to check him. There was, indeed, evident on his face the existence of an emotion as genuine as could be conceived in a soul like his. It was, moreover, the very devil's instant for approaching this poor girl, hopeless, outcast, overstrung, altogether and piteously in need of comfort. At that time Miss Lady could count upon no friend in all the world. She had no confidante, no counselor. That, of all possible moments, was the most fortunate time for a man like Henry Decherd, even had the sweet beauty and helplessness of this girl not wrung from him respect as well as an unrestrained and passionate regard. What was it, then, which at that moment intervened between these two? What was the hidden guidance that came to Miss Lady at that time? She herself could not explain. She could not have told what caused her to tremble as though of an ague - could not have told why, though she sought to see clearly the face of this man who came to her with the words of a lover, there seemed to fall between them some interposing veil, rendering his features uncertain, indistinct. Craving and needing a friend at this hour of her life, none the less she saw not now that friend.

"No," she called out, frightened. "No! Do not!" And that was all that she could think, as all that she could do was to move yet farther away.

He would not accept repulse, but followed on with eager and impassioned words. "I love you!" he whispered. "Come, what is this place to you? There's a big world full of things to see and do! We'll be married, we'll travel, we shall see the world. You shall know what love can mean - what life really is! Miss Lady, dearest -"

After all, by the will of the immortal gods, who sometimes have in care the welfare of the Miss Ladys of this earth, Henry Decherd erred in these very proofs of a passion sincere as he was capable of feeling. A too hasty ardor failed where a calmer friendship had gone further toward winning a heart-sore, helpless girl. The balance of the issue, for a moment trembling in his favor, was, within the instant, quite destroyed.

"Sir," said Miss Lady, and he paused as she freed her hand and stepped back from him, strangely cold and calm, "I have given you no possible right -"

"But you don't understand. Listen, I tell you," he began again.

"I can not listen; it is not right for me to listen. I am too troubled with many things to listen to you now. You don't know who I am. I do not know, myself, who I am. You've been deceived by her - you don't know. I have no mother, as I thought I had. I am going away from here to-morrow. I don't know where I shall go, but I know I shall not stay here. It's wrong for me to stay. It's wrong for me to listen to yon. I can't tell you all I've heard." Miss Lady's lip trembled.

"Did she tell you? Has Mrs. Ellison -" cried Decherd, suddenly flushing. But Miss Lady was too much disturbed to notice his speech or his changed expression. She could only reiterate, "I am going away."

"Oh, come now," said he, his voice again gaining confidence and his face showing relief as he glanced about him. "Come, you are only tired. I ought not to have troubled you this way, this evening, but I could not help it - I could not wait. I was afraid - but then to-morrow - I'll see you to-morrow. Think, Miss Lady, think -"

"I have thought," said Miss Lady, with sudden decision. "I have thought; and as for to-morrow, there'll be none for me at this place. I'm going away at once. I must begin life all over again. It has been wrong for me to live here at all. Why did you ask us to come here? We would have been better off where we were, even if we were poor and helpless."

"It's been heaven here since you came."

"Oh, it was kind of you to get mamma and me a home here. It has been home. It has been so sweet. I love it - I shall always love it. It is big and free here for everybody. One can live here - one could live here if it were right. Colonel Blount is a splendid man, a grand man -"

"Yes?"

"Yes, yes, a splendid man."

"But you'll not stay here?" There was well-nigh as much eagerness as regret in his tone. She did not note it.

"No, I can not," she replied. "I can't tell you everything - I don't want to tell you everything. No one is to blame, I suppose. It's all because I have just grown up, and find I'm in the wrong place. I have been living along here just - just like one of the blacks out there in the fields - without - without taking thought. If it were honest, if I could do anything, if I belonged to any one and could feel that in some way I earned the right to - to - not take thought, then it would be different."

"That's what I say! That's as I want to have it," he began; but she would not listen.

"But it isn't right," she went on. "I can't tell you everything. I can't even tell you about Mrs. Ellison. Perhaps you have been deceived. Ask her. Go ask Colonel Blount, and he may tell you what he likes. But for me, just forget me. I couldn't love you - I couldn't love any one now. I am cold, all through."

The plaintiveness of her speech touched even this man. He held out his arms. "No, no," she cried, as she drew back. "I tell you, the world has gone to pieces. I must find a new one. I am not myself, I am lost; I don't know what I am." Again for a half-instant, touched as he was, Decherd went near to forgetting the lover. There was almost exultation on his face as he saw how fortune was now favoring him in his plans. There was nothing he wished so much as that Miss Lady might leave the Big House at once and for ever.

"I can't tell who I am!" the girl repeated, as though in an agony of entreaty. "I'm some one else! It's so strange. I must go -"

"But where would you go?" said he.

"I do not know; somewhere."

"But then? Why, what could you do, alone? Think - here am I

offering you all you need, a home in some other place, comfort, safety, some one to care for you - why, perhaps it might mean riches before long - I will tell you - you'll find it hard enough alone."

"Yes, it will be new and hard," said Miss Lady, with a wan smile. "I have never thought very much for myself. Some one has always seemed ready to do things for me. I can't do very much. But then, you know, sometimes the things you can't do show you the way to things that you can."

"You are obstinate," cried Decherd, angry now, as only a weak man would have been. "I'll follow you, wherever you go! The time will come when you will be glad enough to see me."

"Mr. Decherd," said Miss Lady, straightening into a quick aloofness, "you said you loved me. That sounds to me as if in some way you were threatening me."

"Well, I will," he reiterated sullenly. "You'd better think."

Miss Lady shook her head slowly from side to side. "I am frightened," she said. "Perhaps some girls would not be. But, in some way, though I am easy to frighten, I don't seem easy to frighten from things that I think I ought to do."

Knowing now that he had found obstacle in this girl's will not thus to be overcome, Decherd allowed his anger to get the better of him.

"Go, then!" he cried brutally.

"Sir," said Miss Lady, "you yourself may go now, if you please;" and she stood so unagitated, so composed and certain of herself, certain as well of his obedience, that Decherd knew here was a woman different from any with whom he had hitherto had to do. Flinging out his hands in anger at his own mistake, his own folly, he turned and strode away. Miss Lady, sinking into the chair, gazed out at a world now grown indistinct and shadowy, full of the terrors of uncertainty.

Decherd knew himself beaten for the time, when he left her. But though he promised it to himself, he did not follow Miss Lady at that time; for before another moon had lit the mysterious realm of the forest beyond which lay an unknown world, Miss Lady was indeed gone. Carrying with her not even a clear knowledge of her own past, doubting her own parentage, doubting almost her own identity; helpless, unprepared, and all too ignorant of the world from which such as she should for ever be shielded and protected, she had left the only spot on earth she knew as home, the only place where she could claim a friend, and fared out into the unknown! It was as if some evil harpy of the air had swooped down and borne her into the pathless sky, as though the earth or the waters had closed over her and left no trace. The simple and the sincere, those most direct and frank, ofttimes are most difficult to follow in their actions when they take counsel wholly of themselves. Miss Lady had no involved motive, none but the one direct and imperative, no means except the one immediately at hand. Hence, so impelled, so guided, she disappeared completely, impossible as that might have seemed. Not even in the piteous little note which Colonel Calvin Blount later crushed in his hand, did she give any clue to her destination.

Henry Decherd did not take the down train on that day. Had he taken Miss Lady's declarations seriously, and suspected a deliberate intention on her part, he might have watched the only avenue of escape possible for her. But this he did not do.

In truth the plans of Henry Decherd himself, *quasi* guest at the Big House, guest tolerated, guest under suspicion, were at that time of a nature singularly intricate, and demanding all his skill and resources. It was certain that Decherd did not disappear with Miss Lady - so much was left to comfort Colonel Calvin Blount. It was certain also that he said no adieus to his long-time host, nor gave any hint as to his own departure. Yet it was clearly proved by many of the servants about the Big House that Decherd was seen mounted and riding to the westward at an early hour of the same morning in which Miss Lady was thought to have left the place.

This fact, indeed Decherd himself, was well-nigh forgotten in the grief which now came to the master of the Big House. Troubled as Colonel Calvin Blount was, there was born, and there remained, in his mind the unshakable belief that Miss Lady had not of her own will gone with Henry Decherd.

EMERSON HOUGH

CHAPTER XVIII

MISFORTUNE

How narrow and inefficient are sometimes all the ways of fate and life! By how small a margin, passing upon the crowded ways of life, do we ofttimes miss the friend who comes with running feet to meet us! The very train which bore Miss Lady from the Big House brought down from the northward John Eddring, eagerly bent upon an errand of his own - John Eddring, for weeks restless, harried and driven of his own heart, and now fully committed to a purpose whereon depended all his future happiness. He must find Miss Lady, must see her once more; must tell her this one thing indisputably sure, that the paths of earth had been shaped solely that they two might walk therein for ever! He must tell her of his loneliness, of his ambitions; and of this, his greatest hope. Desperately in haste, he scarce could wait until the train pulled up at the little station. He sprang off on the side opposite from the station, and ran up the lane.

Ah! blind one, not to see, not to feel, not to know that the dearest dweller of the Big House was here, directly at hand upon the platform, unseen, but upon the point of stepping aboard the train which had brought him, and which was now to carry her away. Miss Lady, laying her plans well, had practically concealed herself until the very moment of the arrival of the train. And so now these two passed, their feet thereafter running far apart.

Colonel Blount received his guest with a strikingly haggard look upon his face; yet at first he made no explanations. He saw Eddring glancing round, and knew whom he sought.

"She isn't here," the planter said very quietly, and handed him the note which he had but a few moments earlier discovered. Eddring's face went as bloodless as his own as he read the few simple lines.

"What's the reason of this?" he cried fiercely. "When did she go?"

"I don't know," said Blount, "unless it was right now. She may have been right by you - right there at the train for all I know; and I reckon like enough that's just how it happened."

"Where's Decherd?"

"I don't know - gone somewhere. He didn't go with her."

"But Mrs. Ellison?"

"She's not gone," said Blount, grimly, "but she's going. I don't count her in any more. Here's the key to Mrs. Ellison's room. It's better she shouldn't see any one this morning."

"But Blount - why, Cal, my friend - what does all this mean?"

"I don't know. All I can say is, hell's broke loose down here."

They passed down the hall together toward Blount's office room.

"By the way," said the latter, "here's a telegram that got here just before you did. It's come from the city on a repeat order and must have passed you on your way. It's railroad business, I reckon."

Eddring tore open the sleazy gray envelope and read the message. His face was hardened into deep lines as he looked up at his friend, and without comment handed over the bit of paper. The message read as follows:

"Eddring, Division Superintendent Personal Injury Department, - : You are temporarily relieved duties your office by Allen, of Hillsboro, pending investigation irregularities charged your division. Strong developments of claims long considered abated. Letter. Dix, Agent."

The two men looked at each other for a moment. Blount extended his hand, and Eddring, gulping, took it.

"God!" he gasped, as he looked at the two bits of paper in his hand. "Did more wrong and misery ever come to a fellow all at once than I've got here in these?"

"I know what this telegram means," he said, "and it's all a mistake. In a week or so I'd have put the whole thing before them. But now, they suspect me of being a thief, and I'll never work another day for them, exonerated or unexonerated."

"Well, what of that?" Blount speke hotly. "You're lucky to lose that job - I've been hoping for a long time that cussed railroad would fire you. There's bigger things in the world for you than drudging along on a salary. You just go ahead and set up office for yourself - fight 'em every chance you get; give 'em hell; I'll stake you till you get on your feet. But damn it, boy, that's not what's bothering me - it's that girl - she's *got* to be found."

"She's got to be found," Eddring repeated. Even Calvin Blount, little used as he was to searching beneath the surface, knew that Eddring had ceased to give the railroad a thought.

Blount looked at him keenly.

BOOK II

CHAPTER I

THE MAKING OP THE WILDERNESS

In the northern pine-lands Father Messasebe murmured to himself, whispering among his rush-environed shores.

"You have taken from me my own," murmured Father Messasebe. "You have swept away my children. You have made child's roads for yourselves along my courses. You have had freedom with me, the Father of the Waters. You, small, have had your liberties with me - with me, who am great, ancient, abiding. But now, since you have taken away my red wilderness, I shall make for myself a black wilderness. In time between these two there shall lie a wilderness of that which once was white!"

And so Father Messasebe, the mighty, the ancient, the abiding, called upon the spirits of the air, which are his kin, and upon the spirits of the earth, which are his friends, and these made cause. The small drop of dew, which hung upon the green beard of the wild rice-plant, dropped down into the hands of Father Messasebe. It did not tarry, as had once been its wont, upon the mossy floor of the wilderness, but hastened on. It met rain-drops shaken from the trees, these drops also hastening. The fountains, once slow and deliberate among the roots of the ancient forest floor, tarried not now upon their beds, but hurried on to join the dew and the rain in a great journeying. The ravaged forest gave up its springs. The brooks ran dry, and left barren the penetralia of the tamaracks and

EMERSON HOUGH

cedars. All these hurried on, little flow meeting little flow, and they joining yet others; and so finally a great flood joined itself to others great, and this volume coursed on through lake and channel, and surged along all the root-shot banks of the great upper water-ways.

The floods passed on, making a merriment which grew more savage and exultant. The scarred and whitening trees stood silent, watching the waters pass; and the round hills smiled not as their feet were washed high with the hurrying floods. And when Father Messasebe at length came into the country where tall hills stood, neither did these hills protest, but joined in that which was now forward, and sent down red and gray and brown trickles of their own to augment the tawny waters. And then the country of low hills, which had no trees, sent out its sluggish streams also, across the deep loam-lands, to stain still further the once clean stream of Messasebe. And word went abroad that Father Messasebe had rebelled - word that reached the white-topped mountains far in the West; and these mountains, loyal, sent their white waters down until they, too, grew red, but still tarried not, and rolled on to meet the general stream. And the green mountains in the East, also loyal, sent their floods as well; until Father Messasebe, hating gathered all his armies, marched on and on, to make anew a wilderness of his own.

Thus the floods came at length to a wide land covered with great trees, a land deep and rich, filled with all manner of growing and brooding things; a land of fat soil carried thither no one knows whence; a land apart and prepared. So Messasebe, having traveled many miles, came to a country inhabited by the slow snake, by the otter, and the beaver, the panther, the deer, the bear - many children whom he long had loved.

Along the edge of this lower land there ran low earthen fences made by the white man, who had laid claim upon the kingdom of the Father of the Floods - vainly-built fences of earth, hopelessly seeking to hedge out the imperious flow of

Messasebe, the ancient, the enduring. Father Messasebe, seeing these things, called back to the following legions of his children that here was time for sport. And all the waters laughed loud and long, dallying with their prey.

"In the North they have robbed me," said Father Messasebe to his legions. "Here in the South they would bind me. Ho! now for the game of letting in the floods, of making anew my wilderness.

"For a wilderness," said Father Messasebe, "the world has ever had. And whether gentle overpower barbarian, or barbarian in turn overcast the gentle, always there will be a wilderness, and out of it will come combat.

"But the World is ancient and abiding," said Father Messasebe to his children, "and the World cares no whit for those things sometimes called good and new. In the years, that which is new becomes old. Only the World and its children endure. Only the old prevails. Only the wilderness, and the combat of weak and strong, remain for ever.

"And at all combat," said Father Messasebe to his children, "the World smiles, knowing that the strong must win; and knowing that in time the strong will become weak. Wherefore let us build our wilderness for a time, like to that which will one day rise again along all my shores, great trees growing where cities are to-day.

"Only in the ages," said Father Messasebe to his children, "do the weak come to be the strong. Wherefore must the strong prevail, each in his own day. It is the Law!"

BOOK III

CHAPTER I

EDDRING, AGENT OP CLAIMS

Some three years subsequent to that mysterious departure of Miss Lady in search of a world beyond the rim of the confining forest, there sat in his office, one fine morning in June, no less a person than John Eddring, formerly claim agent of the Y.V. railway. Eddring looked older, more wearied. He seemed disappointed in his years of fruitless search, in the following of false clues, in the death of new hopes. And yet from the man's clear eye there shone a certain grim comfort of accomplishment.

He was now surrounded, as before, with the customary paraphernalia of a business office. A few desks, a cabinet letter-file, a typewriter stand or two, a chart, a picture askew upon the wall - this might still have been the office of the Y.V. railway. Indeed, there was printed upon the office door the modest sign, "John Eddring, Agent of Claims."

Yet this was no longer the office of Eddring, claim agent of the railway. There had been change. Eddring, agent of claims, was in business for himself, and upon the other side of the pretty game of cross purposes. That which he had taken for calamity had proved good fortune. The world had loved him, even as it tried him. The advice of his old mother he had discovered to be almost prophetic. At last he found himself making use of that legal profession which had formerly been but one of the adjuncts of his earlier occupation. He had opened office for himself, and now paid service to no man.

Eddring had made it his especial care, from the beginning of this work, to undertake that less esteemed branch of the law which has to do with the collection of claims, and, naturally or by choice, he found himself concerned more commonly with the claims of the weak against the strong. Collection law is little esteemed as against the better paid and vaster practice of the corporation law; yet Eddring had succeeded. To his own surprise, and that of others, he began to find his humble way of life pleasant and desirable. His business had widened rapidly, and, to his own wonder, now began to offer him a view into wide avenues of employment. Occupied not only with many minor matters, but with more considerable prose-cutions, John Eddring, agent of claims, was possessor of a business yielding him four-fold the yearly value of his former salary on the Y.V. road.

As to the latter, it had promptly withdrawn charges which presently it found impossible to prove. The head men of the railway were keen enough, after all. They studied the growing list of judgments collected against the road throughout the Delta country, but they could find no trace of John Eddring behind these claims. No system of detectives, no hired espionage could belie the truth. Finally convinced, they did the unusual and somewhat handsome thing of writing their former claim agent a full letter of apology and of asking his return to his late employment, at a salary precisely double that which he had resigned. Eddring had replied to this that, though agent of claims, he could not find it in his heart to serve as a corpo-ration claim agent. So, he had labored on, prosperous to a just extent, and happy as only that man can be who finds work which gives him delight in the doing, and which offers a future built upon the honest accomplishment of the present.

On this morning Eddring, humming contentedly as he went about his work at the humble desk before him, heard a knock and a shuffling tread which by instinct he knew belonged to some member of the colored race. "Come in," said he, without looking up.

"Good mawnin', Mas' Edd'ern," said the newcomer.

"Oh, it's you, is it, Jack?" said Eddring. "Well, come in."

Jack by profession was a local expressman, owner of a rickety wagon and a tumble-down mule. He was coffee-colored in complexion. His feet projected quaintly behind as well as in front. His lips projected also, as did his eyes, wide-rimmed and bulging. His trousers were too long for him, and his coat hung limp from his stooped shoulders. His speech was low and soft. Not an heroic figure, you would have said, yet, as it seemed, a person possessed of a certain history.

"Where did you come from, Jack?" said Eddring. "I thought you were in jail up at Jackson."

"No, sah, Mas' Edd'ern," replied Jack. "Dem folks up thah never did put me in jail at all. I got tired of it, an' at las' I jest walked on home."

As to the case of Jack, there had recently been enacted, on the public square of this southern city, a tawdry little tragedy in brown and coffee color, having to do with the fascinations of a certain damsel known in her own circles as the "gold-tooth girl." The latter had, in her earlier days, drifted northward, where she had learned many things, among these the fact that the white race is exceedingly difficult to imitate, desirable though such imitation may seem. The mistress of Sally chanced to be the possessor of a gold-crowned tooth, and nothing would do Sally herself except the same ornament. Having persuaded a dentist to sacrifice one of her splendid bits of ivory, she became so enamored of her own dazzling smile that perforce she must return again to the South, where such radiance would in all likelihood meet with a better reception. To such charms it was small wonder that Jack, a man of certain solidity and stability of business among his kind, should have fallen victim. Jack and Sally had lived together some six months before Jack had come into Mr. Eddring's office and asked for the loan of a six-shooter. This latter he had returned a couple of hours later, with the calm remark that he had just shot a "yaller nigger" who had been "pesterin' 'round his wife." Jack's arrest and trial followed quickly. Eddring, out of friendship, took his case, and promptly lost it, it being the argument of the prosecuting attorney that "we can't have shooting here on the streets by niggers." Pending the argument for a new trial, Jack had been sent to Jackson jail, where he met with the difficulty of one for whom there seems to be no place in the social system.

"Dem white folks up thah never would let me in jail at all," said he, complainingly. "When I got thah, de jailah man and his wife wuz right sick, and dey warn't no one to take care o' things. I ain't bad at nussin' folks, so I jest turned in an' nussed dat jailah man an' his folks fer 'bout six weeks. I soht o' run dat jail, up dah, fer a while, myself. De jailah was too po'ly to enjoy wu'kkin' vehy hahd, so I tuk de keys, an' when dey didn't need me at nights, ovah at his house, I allus locked myse'f in reg'lar every night, so's to feel I wuz doin' right, you know. In de mawnin', right early, I made breakfast foh dem, an' fix dem up like. Fin'lly, dey got well, an' I giye de keys to de jailah er de she'iff, er whoever he wuz, and I sez I reckon he bettah lock me up now, and he sez to me, 'Go long, you damn nigger, I ain't a-goin' to lock you up at *all*. I *couldn't*,' says he to me. It looks like dere ain't no place fer a nigger."

"Well, Jack," suggested Eddring, trying not to smile, "why don't you walk across the bridge there, over into Arkansas, and get clear of this whole thing for good?"

"Now, Mas' Edd'ern, whut makes you talk like dat? You know I wouldn' do dat an' leave you heah, 'sponsible fer me."

"Well," said Eddring, "in some ways your case does seem a little irregular, but perhaps the court would fix it up now and let you stay right where you are. You go and get your mule and wagon, if you can find them, and go to work again. I'll see

Judge Baines this evening, and tell him just what you have told me. Go on, now. I suppose you are going to take that woman back to live with you?"

"Oh, yessah. I kain't help dat nohow. I done licked her dis mawnin', fust thing I done. She's a heap more humble and con-*trite* now."

At this Eddring grumbled and turned back to his work. Still Jack hesitated. A certain gravity sat on his face.

"Mas' Edd'ern," said he, finally, "kin you tell me why de rivah is out all ovah de lan' down below, and why dere's so many people wu'kkin' tryin' to stop de breaks?"

"No," said Eddring. "I know there's a big overflow, and it's getting worse."

"Mas' Edd'ern," said Jack, stepping close to him, "dar's been a heap of devil-*ment* to wu'k down dah."

"What do you know about it?"

"I knows a heap about it. De niggers all over in dah is gittin' mighty bad. Now, my wife she done tol' me dat dis mawnin', - she's a-feelin' mighty con-*trite.* "

"What did she tell you about it?"

"Well, Mas' Edd'ern, you know, sah, dere's a heap o' things about black folks dat white folks kain't understand an' nevah will. You know fer ovah fifty yeahs black folks has been thinkin' sometime dey'd run dis country. All de time dere's some 'ligious doctah, or preacheh or other, tellin' dem dat. Now, dat sort o' thing been goin' on down dah fer long while. Dere's a sort o' woman, conjuh woman, 'mongst dem. Dey call her de Queen now.

"Now, while I wuz up at Jackson, my wife she done had a heap o' truck wid dem niggers f'om down in dah. My wife tol' me all about dis yer Queen. She tol' me all about the devil-*ment* dat's been goin' on and is a-gwine to go on down in dat country. Hit's right in whah Cunnel Blount lives. I've knowed for yeahs, o' co'se, how frien'ly you two is to each otheh. Now, Mas' Edd'ern, you've been right good to me. I dess thought - seein' dat I couldn't pay you nohow - I'd tell you dis heah, and you could do whut you liked. De trufe is, niggers down heah been gittin' mighty biggoty lately, dey get so much 'couragement f'om up Norf. Massa Edd'ern, dey sho'ly do think dey gwine ter run dis country atter while. O' co'se every nigger whut's got any sense knows diff'rent f'om dat, but it seem like dey allus wuz a heap o' triflin' niggers whut ain't willin' to wu'k, but *is* willin' to make trouble. I dess thought I'd tell you 'bout dis heah."

Eddring turned at his desk for a moment. "Take this over to the telegraph office at once, Jack," said he. "It's a message to Colonel Blount. I want to see him; and I want you to stay around, so I can get you when he comes up."

CHAPTER II

THE OPINIONS OF CALVIN BLOUNT

It was nearly noon of the following day before Colonel Calvin Blount, in response to the summons of Eddring, presented himself at the office of the latter. He was Calvin Blount grown still more gaunt and gray and grizzled, though his eye lacked nothing of its accustomed fire. He seated himself, and cast one long leg across the other, as he threw his hat into a chair, in response to Eddring's invitation.

"First," said Eddring, "tell me about yourself. It has been quite a while since I've been down at your place, hasn't it?"

"Well, as to the place," replied Blount, "it's pretty much gone to pieces. You know my idea is that the chief end of man is to go b'ah hunting, and he oughtn't to be guilty of contributory negligence by staying at home too much. There's been no one to run the place, and I haven't cared. Least said about it, the best, I reckon."

"Who is your housekeeper now?" asked Eddring.

"No one, unless you call it that girl Delphine that used to work for Mrs. Ellison. She came back there a while ago, and said she hadn't any place to live, and wanted to go to work, so I told her to take hold. I don't care. I've been livin' out in the woods most of the time. There's more b'ahs now than you ever did see. You ought to come down and have a hunt. The high water has driven 'em all up to the ridges, and we can just get all of 'em we want."

"Well, I like to hunt once in a while," said Eddring, placing the tips of his fingers together judicially, "but, you see, I'm a poor man, and I have to do a little work once in a while, Now, you've got that big plantation of yours -"

"Plantation!" snorted Blount; "yes, about half my fields are grown up in sassafras brush. I rented out a thousand acres to the best niggers I had, and I give 'em mules and machinery and a stake at the store, and I told 'em to go ahead, and we'd split even at the end of the year. It's no use. I've got to begin all over again, the same as I did when I first started in there. It don't take long for that country to slide back into brush, if you don't keep after it. It would be cane and sassafras and cat briers all over to-day, so far as the niggers are concerned. Why, man, if you opened the gates of Heaven and showed them to Mr. Nigger, yon couldn't get him in, unless you kicked him in."

"You don't seem exactly in accord with the modern idea of uplifting the colored race, this morning, do you, Colonel?"

"No, I don't. Now, I wish our friends from the North would do one of two things, either leave Mr. Nigger alone, or else take him up North, and live with him themselves. You know what happened down at my place last month?"

"No, anything new?"

"No, nothing *new,* only another one of them investigatin' parties from up North. They had a good fat new educator, half-nigger, half-white, this time - educated a heap more'n I am. He was the king bee in that lot of evangelizers and elevators. Well, I took them out over my farms and showed them the sassafras shoots coming up where the cotton ought to be. 'Gentlemen,' said I, 'here's an instance of what an intelligent and industrious race can do. Here's the best plantation in the Delta turned over to these people to make or break. This is the richest soil in the world. They had half of all they could raise, and they had their living guaranteed them. Nobody guarantees *me* a living, not even God A'mighty. They didn't put up a dollar, nor an ounce of brains, nor a bit of worry. Now, did they work, or did they sit in the shade and loaf? You look around and tell me.'

"The big half-white man began to preach to me, and I says to him, 'Before you go on, I just want to ask you two questions. First, how much of you is nigger, and how much is white? Second, do you want to quit running a college up North, and come down here and take hold of this plantation, and so help out three hundred fellow-citizens of yours who are a heap more interested in the nigger question than you are yourself?' I asked that fellow that. That's when he shrunk some."

Eddring smiled, but it was a serious smile, for the South has small inclination to jest over questions such as these.

"Well, about all the fellow could do was to fall back on his old song about education uplifting the race. 'That's all right,' I said to him. 'I'll pay my share of that. But we've got to wait until your millennium comes. It's no use saying it has come, when it hasn't. It's going to take a long time before you get the real useful educating done.'

"I got riled, talking to him, and at last I called up one of my field hands - he had ruined twenty acres of the best cotton land I had - and I took him by the ear and pulled out a bunch of his hair. Said I to him, 'Sam, is your hair like mine! Would it ever get like mine?' 'No, boss,' said he, 'not in a hundred yeahs.' He laughed at me.

"Then I said to that white fellow from the North, 'How hard do you work? I want to know that.' He began to swell up a little at that. Well, I put it to him this way. Says I, 'There was a man came down through here a few years ago, and he got plumb rich. He told all these poor black people all around that for fifty cents he'd sell them a bottle of stuff that would make their hair straight like a white man's, in less'n a month. He always put it about a month ahead, so that he'd have time to get away. Now, that hair tonic man was what I call a professional benefactor of the nigger race,' said I. 'He got paid for it, just the same as you do. And,' says I, 'he'll straighten out their hair with his hair tonic just about as soon as you'll straighten out their problem with your particular kind of ointment - for which you are getting better paid than he did.'

"That riled the fellow plenty, but I went on talking to him. 'The only difference between you and him,' says I to him, 'is that he was whole white and was running a straight bluff, and you are part white, and are running a half-way sort of bluff. You pray to God A'mighty so much about this that you have just about got yourself half-persuaded that you're honest. Do you reckon that you have got God A'mighty persuaded that way, too?' said I to him. That made an awful disturbance in the evangelizing and elevating outfit, and finally I got out of patience. Says I to them, 'I don't want to forget that you are visitors at my place. You white folks can come to my table, if you want to, or you can eat with the oppressed and down-trodden out in my kitchen, if you like that better. Your fellow-citizen, with the specialty of elevating the downtrodden, can't eat at my table. After you get it fixed up the way that suits you best, and have had your dinner, I want you-all to go out and take one more look at the sassafras that's growing on as fine a cotton land as ever lay out of doors. If you can elevate my niggers so that they'll work, why go ahead and do it. God knows they need it. Learn 'em geometry, learn 'em to write poetry, send 'em to Europe to learn painting, but please put somewhere in your college a department showing how to dig up stumps and chop sassafras roots. 'You'll pardon *me*,' says I, 'for I'm a plain man; but I just want to say that that's the kind of elevating that the black race in America needs most. But whatever you do, don't be foolish. Don't say to me that that's done which you and I both know *ain't* done.'"

Both Eddring and Blount were silent for a time. "Those folks stayed in around our country for quite a while," resumed Blount, "and they succeeded in stirring up the niggers to thinking that they were not getting a square deal, but ought to break into politics once more. A few of us planters got together, and *we* were so stirred up about it that we thought we would do something right funny. Our county election was coming on, and you know we have got about ten black voters to one white down there. Under the Constitution we couldn't elect a white man down there in a hundred years - not if we followed the Constitution. This time, just for a joke - but listen - do you know what we did?"

"Well, it's pretty hard to tell just what Cal Blount would do, sometimes," said Eddring, "but I don't doubt you did something foolish."

"No, we didn't. We just had a joke. We let them elect a nigger sheriff for Tullahoma County! We just 'lowed we'd give 'em a touch of law as a sort of object lesson to the Northern elevators. Thought we'd take a shot at the educating business ourselves. The fellow's name is Mose Taylor, and say! he's the tickledest nigger you ever did see! He's about half-white, too, and he always did want to break into politics one way or another. Now, he's done broke in. We let him, just for a joke. Of course, when there's any need for a *real* sheriff, we white people allow that we'll have to use the old one - Jim Peters."

"Well, these things aren't always just exactly the best kind of jokes," said Eddring. "You have been having nothing but trouble down there for a long time."

"Trouble!" said Blount, "I should say we have. We've tried to keep it a white man's country, but it's been a fight every day of the year. Niggers stole and killed all the cattle of my neighbors down in there, and we hung two or three niggers last month for stealing cows. We put a sign on them, 'You stole a cow, cow killed you.' You've got to make things sort of plain, you know, to these people, so's they can understand 'em. Now, you know the trouble we had down there about that train wreck. It's morally sure the niggers were at the bottom of that, one way or another. That ain't all. I told you we were having a big overflow now. Well, the fact is, we found out a day or so ago that this overflow is mostly hand-made. They've been cutting the levees -"

"Blount," said Eddring, quietly, "that's just why I telegraphed you to come up here. I've got a boy here who knows about the whole proposition. They're organizing, as sure as you're born, and they've got a leader. They've got a Queen, they say."

"A Queen!" snorted Blount, jumping to his feet. "Queen, eh? Well, now! you look here, if we ever do get hold of that Queen, I want to tell you, she'll have the uneasiest head that ever did wear any kind of crown. *Queen*, eh!"

"And you've got a nigger sheriff now! Fine machinery for the law to have in that part of the Delta just at this time, isn't it?"

"Sheriff! What do we need of a *sheriff*, if we get down to the bottom of this devilment? We have got to put it *down*, and that's all there is to it, as you know very well. There's no two ways about it. These disturbances, most of them due to politics, have upset our whole country. Now, it is for us to set it right again. We've got to cut politics out, and get down to common sense, down to business. The South can't wait for ever on politics, Northern or Southern. This country's *bigger* than politics, and bigger than politicians. You know we can count on every white man in my part of the Delta. Can we count on you?"

Eddring hesitated, but finally looked his friend in the face. "I'm a white man," said he. Blount went on.

"What you tell me is not altogether news. We're going after these people, and we're going to put an end to this thing once for all. We're going to have a *country*. Now, we want as large a number of white gentlemen as possible. We will want you.

"Now, no matter what you are doing, or where you are, will you come when I send for you!"

Eddring repeated simply, "I am a white man, too."

"It's for the law, Eddring - for the country."

"Yes. I think it's for the law."

CHAPTER III

REGARDING LOUISE LOISSON

"Come out and eat with me, Cal," said Eddring. "I've some other matters to put before you. A great many things have been so confused in my mind that I have hardly known where to begin to straighten them out."

"I reckon you've got some new lawsuit or other on your hands," said Blount.

"You're right. At least it may be a lawsuit, and it certainly bids fair to be a puzzling study, lawsuit or not."

After they were seated at table in an adjoining cafe, Eddring tossed over to his friend a late copy of a New Orleans newspaper. "You see that headline?" said he. "It's all about a dancer, Miss Louise Loisson. You ever hear that name before?"

"Why, no, I don't seem to remember it, if I ever did."

"Well, that name is bothering me mightily just now. You know something of the history of those old Y. V. damage judgments, after I left the road?"

"Yes, I reckon I heard something about it. Some one seems to have got hold of the list of claims, and pushed them for all they were worth. Of course, I know you hadn't anything to do with that."

"It was an odd sort of thing," said Eddring, "and it has led up

EMERSON HOUGH

to a number of other things still more strange. Now, no one knows how that information regarding the claims got out. I told you that I found that complete list of the claims in the valise of the mysterious man, Mr. Thompson, who was killed in the train wreck at your place. Of course I turned over all this material to the company at once. But there must have been a duplicate list out somewhere. I had my own suspicions. I knew, or thought I knew, why the dogs ran that trail right up to your house. Here's one reason I had for that." He threw on the table before Blount a soiled and wrinkled bit of linen, the same mysterious handkerchief which he had put in his pocket at the train wreck long ago.

"Did you ever see that before?" asked he. Blount sat up straighter and looked closely at the object, but shook his head.

"It might be Delphine's," said Eddring. At this the other man shut his mouth hard and his face grew suddenly serious.

"Now, I say I had suspicions," resumed Eddring. "That list of claims was never written out by that traveling man, Thompson. It might have been done by Henry Decherd, might it not?"

"What makes you think so?"

"Nothing, except that I believe those papers were in Henry Decherd's valise. In fact, I know it. He did not want to claim the valise when he saw that I had it. This letter might very possibly have been written by Delphine to Decherd. See here." He placed before Blount the unsigned letter which he had preserved ever since the time of its discovery. Blount read it through in silence, flushing a bit to see his own name mentioned by a servant in such connection; but without comment he looked quietly at Eddring, now eager in the instinct of the chase.

"I'll tell you frankly, Cal," said the latter, "I guessed all along that these two were concerned in all this business, but I couldn't speak. I didn't dare tell my suspicions when I had no better proof than was possible to get at that time. I didn't want to tell the sheriff. I didn't dare tell even you what I thought. Now there was something else in that valise which I did not turn over to the company, because I did not think it was their property."

He took from his pocket the mysterious little volume, the same which had so strangely appeared at different times and in the hands of different parties, not all of whom were at that time known to himself. Blount turned it over curiously in his hand.

"Funny sort of book for a traveling man to have in his valise," said he. "You reckon he was some sort of book collector?"

"Well, I don't reckon that Thompson was. Upon the other hand, Henry Decherd might have been, for certain reasons. Let's see.

"Now, here is this little French book. It tells about a certain journey made from America to France in the year 1825 by several Indian chieftains. They went with one Paul Loise, interpreter. With them was a young girl, Louise Loisson - don't you see the name? - and she is carefully described as a descendant, not of Paul Loise, but of the Comte de Loisson, a nobleman who came to St. Louis shortly before 1825."

Blount sat up still straighter in his chair. "This here is mighty strange," said he. "Names sound right near alike."

"Yes," said Eddring. "But that Louise Loisson must have been dead, buried and forgotten half a hundred years ago. If so, what is she doing dancing down at New Orleans to-day? As soon as I saw that name in the newspaper, I looked it up again in my little book. Then I put together my suspicions about the letter, and the list, and the valise. If I hadn't seen the name in the newspaper, I might never have been so much interested in it; and certainly I should never have put the matter before you."

"I am mighty glad you did. There may be a heap under all this that I want to know about."

"There is. And now I want you to follow me closely; because this very same thing has come to me from another direction.

"You know that in my work I have to examine papers in all sorts of claim cases. Now, within the year, I ran across a United States Supreme Court brief, a case which came up from the Indian Nations, and which was decided not long ago. It seems that the plaintiff used to be on the Omaha pay-rolls. Some one in the tribe, apparently as a test case, covering certain other claims, objected that the claimant was not all Indian, indeed not Indian at all, and hence not entitled to be on the rolls; although you know Uncle Sam recognizes Indian blood to the one-two-hundred-and-fiftieth part.

"I might never have taken much interest in that suit, which I happened to be going over for other reasons, if I hadn't caught sight, in the testimony, of the names of Loise and Loisson, and if I hadn't found the name of Henry Decherd among counsel for the plaintiff!"

"Well, by jinks, *that's* mighty curious!" said Blount. "I didn't know he was a lawyer."

"Yes. He was a lawyer; so much the more dangerous, as I'll show you. Now Paul Loise was official interpreter for the United States government at St. Louis in 1825. He was of absolutely no kinship to the Comte de Loisson, the similarity of names being a mere coincidence, though one which has made much trouble in the records since that time, as I have discovered. The confusion of these two names was one of the most singular legal blunders ever known in the South. It was this entanglement of the records that gave Henry Decherd his chance.

"The Comte de Loisson was a widower, and he brought with him from France a young daughter. He pushed on up the

Missouri River in search of adventures, but he left this daughter, as nearly as can now be learned, in charge of the half-breed interpreter, Paul Loise, perhaps with the understanding that the latter was to obtain suitable care for her from officials in the government employ. That was about the time the Redhead Chief - Clark, of Lewis and Clark, you know - was Indian commissioner at St. Louis.

"Now Paul Loise, at that time engaged in the government treaty work with the tribes, was moving about from tribe to tribe, and he seems to have had an Indian wife in pretty much every one of them. He also had a white wife, or one nearly white, whom he left at his headquarters in St. Louis; and it was with this woman, white or partly white, that the young daughter of the Comte de Loisson was left, at least for a time. Paul Loise himself on one journey went up the river to the place where the Omaha tribe then lived. Whether he took this white child with him, or whether he left her in charge of his white wife at St. Louis, is something now very difficult to prove. This United States Supreme Court case hinges very largely on that same question; and hence it is of great interest to us, as I will show you after a while."

"Well, now, couldn't this dancer down at New Orleans - some sort of Creole like enough - have been a descendant of this Loise family of St. Louis?" asked Blount.

"That we can't tell," replied Eddring. "As I said, the similarity of the names set me looking up the whole matter as soon as I could."

"Well, didn't the French girl's father ever come back after her?"

"Wait. We'll come to that. The one thing certain is that he never came back down the Missouri River. He disappeared absolutely, no doubt killed somewhere by the Indians. His daughter grew up as best she might. She went to France, as our book shows. After a time Paul Loise, her erstwhile protector, died also. Here Louise Loisson disappears from view. She left behind her a very pretty legal question for others to solve, and a mightily mixed set of records to aid in the solution.

"Out of the uncertainty regarding the descendants of Paul Loise there arose a great deal of litigation. This lawsuit, which I have mentioned, no doubt originated by reason of that very confusion. Now, the attorneys in that suit had a knowledge of the existence of this very book which you have in your hand. They stated in this brief that there was but one copy of this book existing in America, that in the Congressional Library at Washington. They won their case by means of this book as evidence; for here is full proof, printed in Paris in 1825, that these Indians went to Paris, accompanied by Paul Loise, and by one Louise Loisson, a white girl, noble, and *not* his daughter; which meant that he had a mixed-blood daughter elsewhere, from whom the claimant had descent.

"How this book got into the possession of Henry Decherd - of course it did not belong to the man Thompson-is something I can't tell. He no doubt intended to use it for his own purposes, as I will try to show you after a while. As to this Supreme Court case from the Indian Nations, it simply proves that the claimant did have a status on the pay-rolls; and it stops at that. The case is irrefutable evidence on the Paul Loise descent question. Perhaps Decherd, for reasons which we shall possibly find out, was not willing to let the matter rest quite there.

"As to our little book, it is a gay one enough. It says that the chieftains from America were received with distinguished honors in the city of Paris. They had so much champagne that three of them died. A titled woman of France fell in love with one of them, and there were all sorts of high jinks. As to the young girl - *La Belle Americaine* they called her - it seems that Paris could not have enough of her. She was all the rage. She taught them the dances of the 'sauvages.' 'Tres interessantes' the Frenchmen thought these dances, it seems. That's all we know of her - she danced. Well, if Mademoiselle Louise Loisson, down at New Orleans to-day, is as successful with her line of dancing as her possible mamma or grandmamma was in Paris years ago, it would certainly seem she has no reason for complaint."

Blount sank back in his chair with a deep sigh. "You were right," said he. "It is a little hard to understand all this at first, but I'm beginning to see. And unless I'm mistaken, this thing is going to come home mighty close to us. Decherd has surely been mixed up in this, if this was really his book, or in his valise, as you think. Delphine is in it, too, if that letter to him means anything. But now, what was Decherd after?"

"I'll tell you," said Eddring, "or at least, I'll show you what I have discovered so far, and you can guess at the rest.

"When I got thus far along I was pretty deeply interested, as you see, and I followed it on out, just for the love of the mystery. Now I have unearthed the fact that the Comte de Loisson did leave some property when he died. Soon after his arrival in the neighborhood of St. Louis, he bought a good-sized tract of land, down in what is now St. Francois County, below St. Louis. The lands at that time were thought valueless, but perhaps the Comte de Loisson had more scientific knowledge than most of the inhabitants of St. Louis at that time. Perhaps he intended to develop his lands after he returned from his adventures up the Missouri River. He never did return, and the lands seem to have lain untouched for a generation or more, still for the most part considered valueless.

"Now, when I had got *that* far along, I took the trouble to look up the numbers of the sections of this land. Cal, I want to tell you that that land to-day is in the middle of the St. Francois lead region, which is full of this new disseminated lead ore, which everybody for a time thought was only flint!"

"On Jordan's *strand* -" began Blount, suddenly bursting into song.

"I don't blame you for being disturbed," said Eddring, himself smiling. "As you see, there is something under all this. Maybe Mr. Decherd is a bigger man than we gave him credit for being. Maybe this little book is a bigger book than we thought it was.

"Now, you know, the entail has been abolished in the state of Missouri. So we come directly to the question of the descent of these lead lands under a certain name. Of course, a single heir in each of three generations would carry the title down clear till to-day; provided, of course, that there was no escheat to the government - that all the taxes had been kept up. Very well. That means that it is at least a legal *possibility* for a living heir to-day to have title to those Loisson lead mines, which are very valuable. Cal -" and here Eddring rose, tapping with his finger on the table in front of him, "the Louise Loisson who went to France in 1825 was the owner of those lead mines! Now I have looked up the tax record. The taxes on these lands for several years back have been paid by Henry Decherd!"

Blount himself rose and stood back, hands in pockets, looking at the speaker. "- I'll *take* my stand!" he continued with his hymn.

"For a long time," went on Eddring, "these lands, not supposed to be worth anything, were not listed by any assessor, and hence did not appear upon the tax-rolls. Thus they were not forfeited by the original purchaser, who must have had his title pretty nearly direct from Uncle Sam himself. Louise Loisson, the first, the French noblewoman dancer, owned those lead mines. If this dancer at New Orleans be a relative of hers, a daughter or granddaughter, she won't have to dance unless she feels like it. For I am here to tell you, as a lawyer, her claim to this tract can be proved, just as readily as the claim to a place on the Omaha pay-rolls for a descendant of Paul Loise was proved in the United States Court five years ago, by means of this same book on the table there before you!"

"Well now, my son, that's what an ignorant fellow like me would call a mighty pretty lawsuit," said Blount, turning over the curious little red-bound volume in his hand.

"It's more than pretty," said Eddring, "it's deep, and it's important - important to you and me, for more reasons than one. There has been a heap of trouble down in the Delta, and there has been a head to all this trouble-making. We are now entitled to our guess as to whether or not we have in this curious way located the head. If we are right, we have at least connected Henry Decherd with an attempt to secure, either for himself or some one else, the title to these lands.

"Now, whether the rightful heir, if there be any heir, knows of the existence of these lands, or ever heard of this book, or ever heard of that Indian lawsuit, is something which we don't know. There may not be any living descendant of the Loisson family. All we know is that there *is* some one using the Loisson name; and that there *is* some one else who is after the Loisson estates. Now, just why this latter has had certain associates, or just why he has done certain other acts, you and I can't say at this time. But we'll know some time."

"The first thing to do, of course, is to go to New Orleans to see that dancer woman."

"Of course," said Eddring. "I shall start tomorrow. As for you, Blount, you've got hint enough about what's going on in your own neighborhood. You'd better watch that girl Delphine. What are you letting her stay around there for, anyway?"

"Because I've got to eat," said Blount, "and because I've got to have some one to run that place. As I told you, I haven't been there much of the time till lately. I reckon she's been boss, about as much as anybody. You know there wasn't a white woman on the place, not since Miss Lady left. I couldn't ever bear to try to get anybody else in there. I just let things go."

"What became of Mrs. Ellison, after she left your place?"

"I don't know; don't ask me. I was an awful fool ever to get caught in any such a way. I heard Mrs. Ellison went to St. Louis, but I don't know. As I look at it now, I believe Decherd was more than half willing to make up to Miss Lady. I reckon maybe Mrs. Ellison didn't like that, though why she should care I don't know. Don't ask me about all these things - I've had too much trouble to want to think about it. All I know is that the girl was as fine a one as ever lived. *She* was good - now I know that, and that's all I do know. I always thought she was Mrs. Ellison's daughter; but when the break-up came, they allowed it wasn't that way. I never did try to figure it all out. When Miss Lady disappeared, and we-all couldn't find her nowhere, I just marked the whole thing off the slate, and went out hunting."

"Cal," said Eddring, quietly, "did you ever stop to think that there is quite a similar sound in those three names, Loise, and Loisson, and Ellison?"

Blount threw out his hands before him. "Oh, go on *away,* man," said he. "You've got me half-crazy now. I don't know where I'm standing, nor where I've been standing. I don't feel safe in my own home - I *haven't* been safe. My whole place has gone to ruin, and all on account of this business. It's nigh about done me up, that's what it has. And now here you come making it worse and worse all the time."

"But we've got to see it through together."

"Oh, I reckon so. Yes, of course we must."

"Well, now, let's just look over the matter once more," said Eddring. "Let us suppose that Decherd has stumbled on this knowledge of the unclaimed Loisson estate. He works every possible string to get hold of it. He tries to get tax title - and that is where he uncovers his own hand. Meanwhile, he tries the still safer plan of finding a legal heir. We will suppose he has two claimants. From this letter here we may suppose that Delphine was one of them, his first one. He seems to have learned from this Indian lawsuit, whether or not he was concerned other than as counsel in that lawsuit - and the record does not show whether or not he was - that Delphine, or his claimant, whoever that was - we'll say Delphine, for we don't know Delphine's real name, perhaps - could and did stick on the pay-rolls of an Indian tribe. That meant that she was Loise, and not Loisson. The United States Court records hold that absolute evidence, *res adjudicata - stare decisis;* which means, in plain English, that ends it. It also means that that Indian claimant could *not* inherit the Loisson estate!

"Now here is an unknown woman, whom we will call Delphine, begging Decherd not to forsake her. There would seem to have been a failure on this line of the Decherd investigation. Perhaps the result of the test case didn't please Decherd very much, although he was on the winning side. At least, it marked the Loise claimant off the Loisson slate. So much for claimant number one. So much for Delphine, we'll say.

"But now, at some time or other, Miss Lady and Mrs. Ellison appeared on the scene. I don't know, any more than you do, how these three happened to know each other, or why Decherd happened to appear so steadily at your place, after you had so eagerly taken his suggestion and employed Mrs. Ellison as your household supervisor. But now, we will say, Decherd takes a great notion to Miss Lady. All the time Delphine is there watching him. She puts on a heap more airs than a colored mistress. Along about the time of the train wreck, she begins to charge him with faithlessness. She refers vaguely, as you see in the letter, to his interest in this other woman. Now, can that be our Miss Lady?

"We don't know. None of us can tell, as yet, who that mysterious other person is. Mrs. Ellison might tell us, if we could find her, or if we cared to find her."

"No, you don't," said Blount. "That woman stays off the map. The only one of the three we want to find is Miss Lady."

"Yes," said Eddring, "if we had Miss Lady, and if we could get Mrs. Ellison and Henry Decherd to tell the truth as Miss Lady would, then we would learn easily a great many things which perhaps it will cost us a great deal of trouble to uncover."

"Well," said Blount, sighing, as he walked moodily across the room, "my own little world seems to be pretty much turned upside down. I can't say you make me any happier by all this. The only thing I can see clear is that you've got to get to New Orleans as soon as you can. There's reasons plenty for you to go."

The two men looked at each other for a moment, but said nothing. "Give me my little book," said Eddring, finally. "I fancy Mr. Henry Decherd would be glad enough to have that back in his own hands again. There's his evidence. This is the key to his plans, whatever they are."

Blount groaned as he swung about on his heel. "Good God! man," he said, "don't! To hell with your lawsuit! What do we care about mixed names, or all this underhanded work? Never *mind* about me and my affairs - I'll take care of that. Man, it's *Miss Lady* we want. We don't know what has happened to her. The rest don't make any difference."

"Yes," said John Eddring, "it's Miss Lady. The rest makes little difference."

"Go on, then," said Blount, fiercely, smiting on the table. "Now, find out about this Louise Loisson. Maybe then you'll hear something, somewhere, that'll give you track of our Miss Lady. Start to New Orleans at once - I'm going down home, to watch that end of the line. We're going after those levee-cutters. As I said, we may want you, and if I send for you, get to my place as fast as you can. Never mind how you get there, but come. And man! if we could only get Miss Lady back! If she -"

"If we could!" said John Eddring, reverently.

CHAPTER IV

THE RELIGION OF JULES

Eddring made his journey to New Orleans, as he had promised. On the morning following his arrival he took his breakfast at one of the quaint cafes of the city, a place with sanded floors and clustered tables, and a frank view of a kitchen in full though deliberate operation. One Jules, duck-footed, solemn and deliberate, served him, and was constituted general philosopher and friend, as had for some time been Eddring's custom in his frequent visits to this place.

"Jules," said he, tapping the newspaper in his hand, "how about this? It seems you have a new dancer at the Odeon, very beautiful, very mysterious, very interesting!"

"Ah, Monsieur, all the young gentlemen they grow crezzy, that is now four, five month, Monsieur."

"Who is she, then, Jules, and what? Is she indeed very beautiful?"

"It is establish', Monsieur. No one has ever seen her face. As to her grace and youth, it is not to doubt. She dance always in the domino, and no man may say in truth he has pass' word with Louise Loisson. She is the idol, the *nouvelle sensation* of the city."

"Goes masked, eh? Young, beautiful, eh? Well, I should say that's not bad advertising, at least."

"Monsieur," said Jules, earnestly, "do not say it at the club. It would provoke discussion, and the young gentlemen might have anger. Mademoiselle Louise is worship' in this town. At first, *non!* It was thought as you say. But soon this feeling of the young men it has shange'. It has go into devotion. Now it is religion!"

"Well, that is a pretty state of affairs, isn't it?"

"But I say to you that this Louise Loisson, she dance not like the othair *femmes du ballet - absolument non."* Jules became excited, spreading out his hands and letting fall his napkin.

"It is different, the quality of the dance of mademoiselle," said he. "It is *quelque chose,* I do not know what. It is not to describe. It make you *think,* thass all. As I say, she has come to be a religion."

"But where does this divine creature live, Jules? Who is she? Come, now? you ought to tell me that much,"

Jules went on polishing a glass. "Ah, Monsieur, why you h'ask?" said he. "I may say so much, like this; she live with a lady in the French town - very fine, very quiet, very secret. It is the house of old family which was bought by Madame Delchasse. Madame, you have know, perhaps? She was long time the bes' cook in New Orleans. She make plenty money. When Mademoiselle Louise she first come here, she is very poor, she have no friend. Somehow she is found by this Madame Delchasse. Monsieur and Madame Delchasse, they have once together the res'traw. Monsieur is very fond of the *escargot a la Bourgogne,* and one day he eat too many *escargot.* Madame, she run the res'traw, sell great many meal to the dam-yankees; sell the cook-*book* to the dam-yankees *aussi.* Thus she get rich - very rich, and buy the house on l'Esplanade. But madame is lonely. She is not receive' by the old French *familles.* Monsieur Delchasse is dead, her shildren are dead - she is alone. She take Louise Loisson home to live. My faith! she is watch her like the cat."

"But how about this dancing? Why does she need to dance?" queried Eddring.

"Ah, she has dance two, t'ree time in the house of Madame Delchasse. 'It is zhenius,' exclaim Madame Pelchasse at this dance; and always, and always, *tou-jours,* she tell of the zhenius of this *jeune fille* who has come live with her. Thass all. The *proprietaire* of the Odeon, he fin' it hout. He insist, this *jeune fille* shall dance. She riffuse. He insist, he offer much money. At las', she say she dance if she have always the masque. *'Bon!'* he cry, and so it is determine'. She dance always in the domino. It is most romantique, most a'mirab'. So this is now the religion of all the young men, *mais, oui,* this *jeune fille,* Mademoiselle Louise Loisson!"

"And how does Madame Delchasse regard this public dancing by her *jeune fille?"*

"Monsieur, she worship' Mademoiselle Louise. But she say, 'This is art, and of art the world it is not to be deprive!' It is well for both madame and for Mademoiselle Louise. The luxury of those room in those old house, they far surpass the best of what one find in the new hotel. Mademoiselle have the best cook in New Orleans. She come in her carriage, she go the same. She drive up to the gate on l'Esplanade, and the gate is close! Behold all! You know so much as any gentleman of *Nouvelle Orleans* - you have the tenderloin of trout?"

After breakfast Eddring strolled over to the box office of the Odeon; but though he made diligent inquiry of the young man who met him at the window, the latter could give him no satisfaction beyond the mention of the address on the Esplanade where dwelt Madame Delchasse. He was very lukewarm in regard to further inquiries from the stranger.

The flavor of this little adventure began now to appeal to Eddring, and thus left to his own resources, he determined to assume a bold front and call in person at the old house on the Esplanade. It being still early, he wandered for a time about the strange old city; but the crooked streets and their quaint shops had lost their charm. The ancient Place d'Armes, the old Cabildo, the French market, the tumble-down buildings which house the courts of justice ceased to interest him. He was relieved when finally he felt it proper to turn up the old Esplanade, which wandered away with its rows of whitened trees, out among the dignified and reticent residences of the *vieux carre.*

The flavor of another day came to him. This, indeed, was the same *Nouvelle Orleans,* he reflected, from which in an earlier day the first Louise Loisson had set sail for France! He, by virtue of this old volume now resting in his pocket, was concerned with the fortunes of that earlier Louise Loisson. And yet, he acknowledged the growing feeling that in this matter there was coming to be for him something more than a professional interest. This thought he put away as best he could, chiding himself as perpetually visionary, though old enough now to dream no more.

In time he arrived at the street number to which he had been directed, and paused at the iron street gate which shielded even the carriage drive from the public. Through the bars of the gate he could see a well-kept, formal lawn and the peaked roof of the close-shuttered, green-balconied dwelling beyond. There could not have been a better abode, he reflected, for this mysterious personage who had called him hither on this fantastic, will-o'-the-wisp journey. Yet he pulled himself up with disgust. He dared not hope! He reproved himself sharply. No doubt he was to see presently a gushing or garrulous or ignorant young woman, whose pretended modesty was but an artifice, whose real soul was set upon the adulation of the public and the pecuniary gain received thereby. He was almost of a mind to turn away, and end his quest then and there.

He was not prepared for what was soon to happen. There came a hum of wheels along the old roadway, and a carriage pulled up at the walk. There alighted quickly the figure of a young girl, tall, slender, round, full-chested, abounding in health and vigor. So much could be seen at a glance. As to the face of the new-comer, the eyes were shielded by a dark blue domino, or short mask. Eddring saw beneath, this concealment a strong, round, tender chin; above, a pile of red-brown hair. He caught the flash of a sweeping bunch of scarlet ribbons, heard a quick rustling of skirts, saw an inscrutable face turned toward him; and then, before he had time to think or speak, a servant had swept open the great iron gate and the young woman had stepped within. She did not look back, but passed on rapidly up the gravel walk toward the house. And John Eddring, foolish, stunned, abashed, knew that he had seen the mysterious Louise Loisson! Ah, he had seen more - he had seen another!

He turned as he heard a footstep and a soft voice at his elbow. The passerby accosted him smiling, and he recognized Jules, the duck-footed.

"Ah, Monsieur," said the latter, "I see you have also discover' the shrine. Is it not beautiful, Monsieur - this worship of a pure *jeune fille?*"

The words brought Eddring back to his own proper senses. Forgetting all else, he sprang through the big gate, past the servant, and hastened up the walk. "Miss Lady! Miss Lady!" he cried.

CHAPTER V

DISCOVERY

"Miss Lady!" cried Eddring, yet again; and even as the hurrying figure before him reached the gallery steps, she heard the entreaty of his voice and turned. As she did so she tore from her face the concealing mask and stood before him, Miss Lady indeed - tall, straight, young and beautiful. Eddring moved forward impetuously, feeling all the thrill of her presence; all the lambency of woman, planet-like, far-off, mysterious. Eagerly he looked, and questioningly, doubtingly, and then there came a quick content to his heart. In spite of all, in spite of what might have been, this was Miss Lady herself and none other! Sweet as of old, and ah, fit indeed for worship! Ah, here, he cried out to himself, was that friend of his soul, lost now for a time, but found, now found again!

But even as he pressed forward, holding out his hands, his emotion shining in his eyes, there came a change upon Miss Lady's face.

"Ah, Mr. Eddring, it is you?" she said, and her voice had the upward inflection, as though she carelessly addressed an inferior. "I remember you very well, but I hardly thought to see you. Indeed, I should hardly have expected to see any one in just this way."

All that Eddring could do was to falter and cry out, "Yes, I have come! I have found you!"

"Indeed? But we do not receive callers. Our plan of life has been arranged otherwise. You might be observed even now. It would cause talk."

"Talk!" cried Eddring, now suddenly breaking into flame. "Why, let them talk! It is time there was talk - time you talked to some of your old friends - you, Miss Lady, who had so many friends."

"Friends!" said the girl, bitterly. "Friends!"

"Yes, friends!" cried Eddring. "Surely you know that Blount and I have moved heaven and earth trying to find you. Why you should go, why you should leave every one in ignorance and take up with mummery like *this* - it is something no sane person can tell. You have not done right, Miss Lady. You have not done right!"

The girl raised her head, a flame of anger upon her own cheek at this presumption. Yet she reserved her speech, and by gesture led Eddring to a spot concealed by the ivy-covered lattice. Her cheeks burned all the more hotly as Eddring went on.

"What mockery!" he cried.

"Yes, what mockery!" repeated Miss Lady. "What mockery that you should say these things to me! What had I up there? What was I? I was a servant, a dependent. Besides all that, things came up which would have driven any decent girl away. I could do nothing else but go. Oh, you don't know all. You can't be just, for you don't know."

"But your mother?"

"You mean Mrs. Ellison? She was not my mother, Mr. Eddring. I thought you knew that. That is one reason why I am here."

"She was not your mother? Then that was true?"

"She never was. She disappeared out of my life, and I know little about her now, excepting that she was the only mother I ever knew. There has been deception of some sort. There were so many sad and troublesome things that I could no longer endure my life as it was. I went away. I came here, I found a home."

"But Colonel Blount?"

"Sir, he was my friend. I can only say that in justice it was better for me to go. He is a noble man. If ever I pained him I am sorry. But as to friends -" she dangled the little domino on her finger, "this has been my only friend. It has kept me from seeing even myself. Without it I should have died." There were no tears in her eyes as she spoke. Eddring felt that he had now to do with a woman grown, sad, not light and unstable. There crowded to his tongue a thousand things.

"*That!*" said he. "You, Louise Loisson - you have indeed been masquerading. Tell me, how did you get that name?"

"It was an accident purely," said Miss Lady. "I found it in a book, years ago. It was unusual, and I took it for that reason. I wanted to get as far away from any possibility of detection by my friends as I possibly could. See," she smiled bitterly, "I am Louise Loisson now, the common dancer! I make my living in that way. But for that, and for the kindness of Madame Delchasse here, I might have starved. I am no longer any one you ever knew. Behind this mask sometimes I forget."

Eddring looked at her with strange earnestness. "You don't know how true is every word you speak," said he. "There is absolute fatality under all this. On my honor, I believe you *are* Louise Loisson, born over again! But look how fate brings you and me together: I did not know where Miss Lady Ellison had gone; I did not know who Louise Loisson might be; by chance, by the merest chance, I wished to learn - for other reasons only. Now, see! Why, it is fate, Miss Lady! I have found you both. Miss Lady, my dear girl, see! I have found everything else in the world at the same time." The pent-up yearning of his soul was in his voice, his eyes. The girl caught swift warning.

"I shall go in," said she; but he stopped her. She tore loose the hand which he would have taken. "Go!" said she, "and never must you come through that gate again. You were unasked, and never will be asked. You, to talk of friends! Why, you were the very last of any I ever knew whom I should have cared to see again."

"What - what is that?" He stumbled under this sudden blow.

"Oh, I have enough of men," said the girl, bitterly, "enough of humanity. But I will tell you this much, a friend of mine must first of all be an honest man. You talk to me of masquerading; take off your own mask, and let me set my foot upon it, as I have set foot upon all my past! Sincerity, truth - I wonder if there is such a thing left in all of God's world. I did not ask you here, I do not welcome you here. Good-by. You must go."

He stood dumb, simply gazing at her, not understanding; and his absolute horror she took to be his mere confusion. Yet her eyes were more sad than angry as she went on.

"You've prospered, Mr. Eddring, I know," said she. "What a difference for you and me! A girl must walk so carefully, but a man may do as he pleases. You talk about fate, and that sort of thing, but no man with a life like yours can come into my life, mere dancer though I be. Before you go I want to say to you that I know the story of your discharge from the railroad. I know how you profited by your knowledge of the company's affairs - know other things not public regarding you. Since I do know these things, for you to dare to come to me in this way seems to me the worst of effrontery."

Still Eddring stood uncomprehending, stunned. "I - I do that?" he whispered, half to himself. "Did you think - could you believe -"

"I could believe nothing else."

"Who told you these things?" blazed he at length, as at last his heart once more sent the blood back through his veins.

"If you wish to know, I will tell you. It was Henry Decherd. I imagine he could furnish proof enough." She spoke defiantly, if perhaps wearily.

"Henry Decherd!" exclaimed Eddring. "Henry Decherd! Miss Lady, is it possible that you can stand alive under the sun of heaven and say these things to me? Is he here? Tell me, what right -"

But now the anger of Miss Lady herself was blazing, and all the cruelty of her sex was in her tone as she answered. "I need not tell you," said she, "but I will. Mr. Decherd is the only friend of my former life who cared enough for me to follow and find me. And so he has the right -"

"For what? Tell me, is there any truth in this newspaper paragraph - 'There is talk about the marriage of the mysterious Louise Loisson'? Don't tell me that he - that Decherd - " He gazed steadily into her eyes, but saw there that which made him forget all his purposes, forced him to remember nothing in the world but his sudden personal misery. And so for an instant he stood and suffered - until the sheer bigness of his soul began to reassert itself. All his love for her came back, and he forgot even his deadly hurt in the great wave of pity and tenderness which swept over him.

"Miss Lady," said he simply, after a time, "for myself it doesn't make so much difference, after all, I am one of the unlucky. But for you, as you say, it is at least your due that you should have honest men for your friends, and an honest man for your husband. I wanted you to trust me. I loved you. I wanted you to believe in me. I wanted you to *marry* me, Miss Lady - I *will* say it - and I wanted to tell you that long ago, before you left us. That is over now. You are unjust and cruel beyond all toleration - beyond all belief. You could by no possibility ever love me. But listen. You shall never marry Henry Decherd."

EMERSON HOUGH

CHAPTER VI

THE DANCER

Ah, but it was a sweet and wonderful thing to see La Belle Louise dance; a strange and wonderful thing. She was so light, so strong, so full of grace, so like a bird in all her motions. She swam through the air as though her feet scarce touched the floor, her loose silken skirts resembling wings. Now on one side of the lighted stage, now back again, nodding, beckoning, courtesying to something which she saw - this spectacle must have moved any one of us to applause, as it did these thousands who came to witness it. The stage has no traditions of any dance like this of La Belle Louise. It is now danced no more, this dance which a maid or a lily or a tall white stork might understand, each after its own fashion.

Scores of times had La Belle Louise given this dance, each time with but trifling variations, each time to thunders of applause, with an art so free of effort that it was above all art. But what had now, for the first time, come to La Belle Louise? Did her bosom labor in the physical exertion of these measured steps? Was the quality of lightness and freedom lacking? Was the self-absorption, the abandonment, the impersonal, bird-like quality less to-night than before? And was the subtile, cruelly just sense of the public right in its hesitation, in its half-applause? Had there been actual change in the dancing of La Belle Louise?

The dancer looked from side to side, as though in search of some face or figure; as though in fear, in distress. Was she actually panting when she left the stage - she, La Belle Louise, the ethereal, the spirituelle, the very imponderable dream of the dance itself? This might have been; for presently she cast herself into the arms of Madame Delchasse in a state bordering upon actual panic.

"Auntie!" she cried, "I can not dance! I am done with it! I shall never dance again. I can not! I can not!" She trembled as though in actual fear or suffering as she spoke.

"Now, now, my cherished!" said the old French lady, gathering her to her ample bosom, "what is it that has come to you? You have illness? Come, we'll go at 'ome."

The dancer was slow in laying aside her silken skirts and putting on her street attire. Madame waited some time before thrusting her head through the half-open door, "See! my dearie," she cried, "I have the surprise for you. Monsieur shall ride home with you. He has ordered for to-night the second carriage, which I shall myself take - since you are so soon to ride with monsieur all the time, is it not?"

The head of madame disappeared. The girl, when at last ready to depart, sat with her gaze fixed on the door; yet she started when presently there came a knock. Henry Decherd entered.

"Louise!" he cried, "Louise!" and would have caught her in his arms. She repulsed him and stood back, pale and trembling.

"Oh, I say," protested Decherd, "one would think I had no right."

"You have no right to touch me," she replied. "You shall not. Go on away with auntie in the other carriage. I will follow you home."

"Come, now," said Decherd, approaching; "this sort of thing won't do. I don't understand what you mean."

"No, you don't understand a girl," she said.

"At least I understand how a girl ought to treat the man she is to marry."

"Marry!" said Miss Lady, whispering to herself. "Marry!" There was silence between them for a time, but she turned to him at length.

"I shall never dance again," said she. "Neither to-morrow, nor at any other time, shall I set foot upon the stage again."

"You will not need to do so, when once we are married," said he. "I shall be willing - but tell me, what's the matter to-night? You are only tired. You will wake up again."

"Wake up!" cried she, "that is the very word. I feel as though I had suddenly awakened, this very night." She pressed her hands to her reddening cheeks. "Can't you see?" she cried. "To-night for the first time I felt them! I felt their eyes. I *felt* them, out there in front, as though there were many; as though there were more than one. I felt that they were women-that they were *men!*"

"Well, they have been there all the time," said Decherd. "It's odd you should just realize that."

"I never did before," said she. "It kills me. Why, can't you see? I have been selling myself - my body, my face, my eyes, *myself,* a little at a time, a little to each of them. I've been selling myself. They paid to see *me.* Now I can dance no more. Yes, you are right, I am awake at last; and I tell you I am some one else. I have been in a dream, it seems to me, for years. But now I can see."

"Well, let the dancing go," said Decherd, rising and coming toward her. "Never mind about that."

"Let everything go!" cried Miss Lady, fiercely. "Let everything go! Marry you? Why, sir, if indeed you understood a girl, you would not want me to come to you feeling as I do now. Can't you see that a girl must *depend* on the man she loves? I have tried to feel sure. I have tried to see you clearly. Now, to-night, it is just as it was that time years ago when you spoke to me; something comes between us. I can not see you clearly. I can not understand. And so long as that is true, I can never, never marry you. I can not talk about it. Go! I do not want to see you!"

A sudden alarm seized upon Henry Decherd. "Listen," he said; "listen to me. I can not have you talk this way. Why, you know this sort of thing is absolutely wrong."

"Everything's wrong!" cried Miss Lady, burying her face in her hands as she sank on a couch. "Everything is wrong! I am ashamed, I can not tell you why. I don't know why, but I have changed, all at once. I'm not myself any more. I'm some one else. I don't know *who* I am! I never knew. Oh, shall I never know - shall I never understand why I am not myself!"

Decherd caught her hands. "We shall not wait," said he, "we'll be married to-morrow." His voice trembled in a real emotion, although on his face there sat an uneasiness not easily read. "Dearest, forget all this," he repeated. "Go home and sleep, and to-morrow -"

Her eyes flashed in the swift, imperious anger wherewith upon the instant sex may dominate sex, leaving no argument or answer. Yet in the next breath the girl turned away, her anger faded into anxiety. She wavered, softened in her attitude.

"Oh, he told me, he told me!" murmured she to herself. "I can not - I can not!" She seemed unconscious of Decherd's presence. But soon she forgot her own soliloquy. Once more she looked Decherd squarely in the face.

"I can not marry you," she said. "I *will* not!"

"I'll not allow you to make a fool of yourself, or of me," said Decherd. "What do you mean - who is 'he'?"

He had his answer on the moment, not from her lips, but by one of those strange freaks of fate which often set us wondering in our commonplace lives.

There came a tap at the door, and a call boy offered a card. "It's against orders, I know, ma'am," he began, "but then -"

Decherd, full of suspicion, sprang at the messenger and caught the card before Miss Lady saw it. His swift glance gave him small comfort.

"Eddring!" he cried. "By God! John Eddring! So -"

"Yes," she flashed again at him. "You are rude; and there is your answer; and here is mine to you, and him." She turned to the call boy.

"Tell the gentleman that Miss Loisson can not be seen," said she.

A ghastly look had come upon Henry Decherd's face at these words. His features were livid in his rage. "So Eddring is here, is he!" said he, "and he has been talking to you! By God, I'd kill him if I thought -"

"Carry my wrap, sir!" said Miss Lady, rising like a queen. "You may do so much for the last time. At the gate I shall bid you good-by. Open the door!"

CHAPTER VII

THE SUMMONS

As though in a dream, Miss Lady followed Decherd to the entrance, near which stood a carriage in the narrow little street. She scarcely looked at his face, and did not note his hurried words to the driver. Silent and distraught, she took no note of their direction as the wheels rattled over the rude flags of the medieval passageway. The carriage turned corner after corner in its jolting progress, and finally trundled smoothly for a time, but Miss Lady, hoping only that this journey might soon end, scarce noticed where it had ended. She saw only that it was not at the gate of Madame Delchasse's house, and, startled at this, expostulated with Decherd, who reasoned, argued, pleaded.

Meantime, at the gate of the old house on the Esplanade, Madame Delchasse waited uneasily alone. Perhaps half an hour had passed, and madame could scarce contain herself longer, when finally she heard the rattle of wheels and saw descending at the curb a stranger, who hurriedly approached her carriage window.

"Pardon, Madame," said he, as he removed his hat, "this carriage is, perhaps, for the house of Madame Delchasse?"

"It is, Monsieur," said madame, frigidly. "I am Madame Delchasse."

"Pardon me, Madame," said the new-comer, "my name is Eddring, John Eddring. I would not presume to come at such an hour were it not that I have a message, a very urgent one, for Miss Loisson. She refused to see me at the theater, and I came here; she *must* have this message. It is not for myself that -"

Madame drew back into her carriage. "Monsieur," said she, "I say to you, bah! and again, bah!"

"You mistake," said Eddring, hurriedly. "It is only the message which I would have delivered. It is only on her account." Something in his voice caught the attention of madame, and she hesitated. "It is strange mademoiselle do not arrive," she said. "Monsieur Decherd should have brought her 'ome before this."

"Decherd!" cried Eddring.

"*Mais oui.* He is her *fiance.* What is it that it is to you, Monsieur?"

"Listen, listen, Madame!" cried Eddring, "We must find them. This message is one of life and death. Come, your carriage -" and before madame could expostulate the two were seated together in madame's carriage, and it was whirling back on the return journey to the Odeon.

Eddring fell on the doorkeeper. "Miss Loisson! Where is she? When did she leave?" he demanded; and madame added much voluble French.

"Mademoiselle left with a young gentleman a half-hour ago," said the doorkeeper. "I heard him say, 'Drive to the levee.' Perhaps they would see the high water, yes?"

"That's likely!" cried Eddring, springing back into the carriage, "but we will go there, too." Hence their carriage also whirled around corner after corner, and presently trundled along the smoother way of the levee. Passing between the interminably long rows of cotton-bales they met a carriage coming away as they approached, and Eddring, upon the mere chance of it, accosted the driver.

"Did you bring two persons, a young lady and a young man, here a moment ago?" said he.

"Not here," said the driver, pulling up. "But I took them lower down on the levee. They went on board the *Opelousas Queen*. You'll have to hurry if you want to catch, them. She's done whistled, an' 'll be backin' out mighty quick."

Eddring hardly waited for the end of his speech. "We must find them," said he to madame at his side, who now was becoming thoroughly frightened. "There is something wrong in this. I must get this message to Miss Loisson, and I must find out what all this means."

A few moments later their own carriage brought up with a jerk, and Eddring, dragging madame by the arm, hurried across the stage plank almost as it was on the point of being raised.

"What do you mean?" growled the clerk to the hurried arrivals, as the *Queen* slowly turned out into the stream.

"Did a couple come aboard just now, a few minutes ahead of us?" cried Eddring, taking him by the shoulder in his excitement.

"Why, yes. But they didn't come in such a hurry as you do. Where are you going?"

"Wait," said Eddring. "What was the girl like? Tall, dark hair, wore a cloak, perhaps? And the man - was he rather thin, dark - had oddish eyes?"

"Why, yes; I reckon that's who they were," grumbled the clerk.

Eddring paid no attention to him. "Madame," said he, "they must be on the boat.

"Now look; here is my message, Madame," he resumed, as he led her apart to avoid the clerk. "You will see why I have brought you here, and why I had to find Miss Loisson and this Mr. Decherd." He handed to her two pieces of paper - messages from Colonel Calvin Blount addressed to him at New Orleans. The first one read: "We are organized; come quick. More levee-cutting."

"That is three days old," said Eddring. "Here is one sent yesterday. It must have gone out by boat to some railway station, for the roads are washed out for miles in all the upper Delta. 'Shot bad in levee fight. Come quick. We have caught Delphine, ring-leader. More proof implicating Decherd. Louise Loisson our Miss Lady. Find her; bring her. Watch Decherd. Come quick. - Calvin Blount.'

"Madame," said Eddring, "Miss Louise Loisson was once Miss Lady Ellison, at the Big House plantation of Calvin Blount, in the northern part of Mississippi. Her friends have been looking for her for years, but in some way have missed her. I will say to you that she is a young woman lawfully entitled to property in her own name. This Henry Decherd is unfit company for her, if not dangerous company. As to this marriage, it must not be. Madame, take this message to Miss Loisson; if you can, induce her to go to her old and true friend, Colonel Blount, - if it be not too late now for that. I am sure you will be thankful all your life; and so will she. Find her; I will find Decherd. We must get up to Blount's place then. He's hurt. He may be killed."

Madame stood troubled, fumbling the papers in her hand. She scarce had time to speak ere there came from the ladies' cabin a sudden rush of footsteps, and in an instant Miss Lady and she were in each other's arms.

CHAPTER VIII

THE STOLEN STEAMBOAT

"My shild! My soul!" cried madame. "What is it? Where have you been? What is this!" She patted Miss Lady with one plump hand, even as she wept; and all Miss Lady could do in turn was to put her face on the older woman's shoulder and sob in sheer relief.

"Why you don' come at 'ome?" cried madame, severely. "We have wait' so long. See, this boat, she don' stop. Why do you come to the boat, when you say you come at 'ome to me? Ah, Mademoiselle, you have never deceive' me before."

"I have not deceived you," said Miss Lady. "I did not know that we were coming to the river-front in the carriage - I thought we were going home. When we got here he pleaded, he begged - it was just to ride across to Algiers, and come back, he said. He said it was the last time, the last hour that we would ever spend together. He threatened - what could I do, Madame? You would not have me make a scene; it was dark out there, I thought it safer to come aboard the boat - where there were lights - and other ladies. I went back to the ladies' cabin. O Madame, Madame -"

Madame Delehasse threw her arms about the girl and they passed down the long cabin of the boat. Eddring turned to the clerk, grieved and wondering.

"Can you put these ladies ashore at Algiers across the river?" asked he. "There has been a mistake. They don't want to go up river."

"They'll have to go, now," said the clerk. "We'll put them out at the ferry, up above a few miles. Best we can do. Algiers! Do you think we are running a street-car?"

"Very well," said Eddring. "Get two state-rooms, then. We'll go on up the river. You can put us ashore sometime after daylight. We wanted to catch a train up country, but if we can't do that to-night, we'll try it from some stopping-place up river."

There had come to Eddring the lightning-like conviction that he was now suddenly flung into the chief crisis of his life. He looked hard at the widening gap of black water between him and the shore, and at the hurrying floods into which the boat was now beginning steadily to plow; but the night and the floods gave him no answer. He knew that he had taken upon himself responsibility for two women, one of whom he believed to have been practically a victim of abduction - this woman whom he had loved for years, had lost, and lost again, but who was now here, under his care, dependent on his own courage, his own resolution and decision. It was but for a moment that Eddring hesitated. The heart of the great boat throbbed on beneath him, but even with her strong pulse there rose his own resolve. He left the forward deck and passed back to seek out the clerk.

"Go tell the captain of this boat to come to me," said he.

"What do you mean? Who are you?" the clerk asked.

"I must see the captain," Eddring answered with a wave of the hand, and again turned away. Perhaps it was the very stress of that moment which finally indeed brought Captain Wilson of the *Opelousas Queen* into the presence of his enigmatical passenger.

"Well, sir?" cried Wilson, as he approached, "what can I do

for *you?*"

"Captain Wilson," said Eddring, quietly, "I want to take your boat off her regular run. I have got to get up the river, and I am afraid the roads are wiped out."

The river-man's astonishment at this bade fair to end in explosion. "My boat!" he ejaculated. "Quit my run?"

"Yes," said Eddring. "I'll explain to you later the necessity I have for getting up the river quickly - and why it means that I have got to have your boat."

"Have my boat!" said Wilson, his voice sinking into an inarticulate whisper. "And me with mail, and passengers, and freight to leave from Plaquemine to St. Louis! Have my boat! Have my -"

"Put your passengers off at Baton Rouge in the morning. Transfer your mails there. Let everything get through the best it can. It can wait. As for me, I can't wait; I must go through direct."

Wilson endeavored to look at him calmly. "If you talk that way to me much longer," said he, "I'll say you're surely crazy."

"I'll see you about it in the morning," said Eddring, quietly. His singleness of purpose had its effect. Captain Wilson abruptly turned on his heel.

Meantime Miss Lady and Madame Delchasse had drawn apart in their own excitement, exclaiming only against the fact that this boat, so far from crossing the river, was now forging steadily upstream. Along the distant bends there could be seen the black masses of shadow, picked out here and there by the star-like points of the channel lights; while the low banks of the western shore, dimly indicated by the ferry lights, slowly slipped away.

"We are h'run away," cried Madame Delchasse. "It is not to Algiers. Ah, my angel, what fortune I am here!" Miss Lady silently pressed her hand, and they moved farther forward on the guards.

Eddring heard them talking, and knew the cause of their uneasiness. He sat apart on the forward guards planning for a further attempt with Captain Wilson, and planning also for another meeting which he knew he might presently expect. He needed all his faculties at that moment, as he sat with his back to the rail, and his eyes commanding the approaches to the deck. He was waiting for what he knew would be the most exacting situation he had known in all his life - the encounter with Henry Decherd.

As for the latter, it had been his plan to absent himself from Miss Lady until after the boat should have swung well into the up-stream journey; then, he meant to do whatever might be necessary to carry out his main purpose. Abduction, compulsion, force - none of these things would have caused Henry Decherd to hesitate at this time of desperation. Miss Lady's sudden desertion and flight to the ladies' cabin disconcerted him. The sound of Eddring's voice and that of madame filled him with dismay. He tried to compose himself, but found his nerves trembling. Hurrying to the bar, he sought aid in a glass of liquor. He knew there must be a reckoning. As he returned from the bar he met Madame Delchasse with Miss Lady, and was obliged to speak.

"Madame, how did you come here?" he stammered. "Why, where is this boat going?"

"It is not go to Algiers, no?" said madame, freezingly. "By this time, Monsieur Decherd, I have expect mademoiselle to be at my 'ome."

"Why, we only wanted to run across the river together. We were coming home," protested Decherd. "We did not know this was an up-river boat."

Madame Delchasse drew herself up magnificently. "I, Clarisse Delchasse," said she, "have arrive'. I shall take care of mademoiselle." Decherd again began, but she interrupted him. "If it is not for this stranger, this Mr. Eddrang," said madame, "I am not here this moment to care for mademoiselle. What care have you take? People would not talk, no? You to protect! Bah!" She slammed the glass door of the cabin in his face.

Decherd stood irresolute, ill-armed in the injustice of his quarrel. He had not a moment to wait.

"Decherd!" The voice was John Eddring's.

Decherd turned. The silent watcher beside the rail had risen and was coming straight toward him.

CHAPTER IX

THE ACCUSER

Henry Decherd paused under the steadfast gaze which met him.

"Decherd," said Eddring, simply, "I want to talk to you. Come and sit down." They moved a pace or two forward, Eddring taking care that the other should sit facing the light which streamed through the glass doors of the cabin.

"Stop! Decherd, I wouldn't do that." Eddring glanced at the hand which Decherd would have moved toward a weapon. Eddring's own hands hung idly between his knees as he leaned forward in his chair.

"I would like to know what you mean by meddling in my affairs," began Decherd. "You are interfering -"

"Yes," said a voice, soft but very cold, "I'm interfering. I am going to spoil your chances, Decherd. Sit down." The man thus accosted involuntarily sank back into a seat. Then a sudden rage caught him, and he half-started up again. This time he saw something blue gleaming dully in the idle hand which hung between Eddring's knees.

"Be careful," said the latter. "I told you not to do that. Sit down, now, and listen." An unreasoning, blind terror seized Henry Decherd, and in spite of himself, he obeyed.

"In the first place, Decherd," said Eddring, "I want to say that it was not lucky for you when I got hold of your valise by mistake at the Big House wreck - the time I found that list of claims, and the little old book in French. I have studied all those things over carefully, together with other things. I've been thinking a great deal. That's why I am going to spoil your chances."

"Does she know?" whispered Decherd, hoarsely.

"No, she knows nothing about it at all. She doesn't know who she is - not even why she happened to take the name of Louise Loisson." Decherd gasped, but the cold voice went on. "You might have told her some of these things. You might have told her who her real mother was, and who her false mother. You might have given her a chance to know herself. I don't fancy that you did. I don't think you told her anything which did not serve your own purposes."

"We were going to be married," began Decherd.

"We are going to be married -"

"You *were,* perhaps," said Eddring, "but not now. Oh, I don't doubt that you are willing enough to marry Louise Loisson, and to deceive her after your marriage as you did before. I don't doubt that in the least."

"What business is it of yours?" said Decherd, now becoming more sullen than blustering.

"I can't say that it was my business at all," said Eddring. "It's accident, largely; and surely it was not your fault that I blundered on these matters. It was rather fate, or the occasional good fortune of the innocent. You covered up your trail fairly well; but a criminal will always leave behind him some egotistical mark of his crime, either by accident or by intent. You left marks all along your trail, Decherd - there, there, keep quiet. I don't want to use force with you. I'm not going to be the agent of justice. But it won't be altogether healthy for the man on whose shoulders a great many of these things are finally loaded. You were enterprising, Decherd, and you were an abler man than I thought, far abler; but you undertook too much.

"Now, here's a message from Colonel Blount," Eddring resumed. "It looks as though things were coming pretty nearly to a show-down up there. We are going to find out all about that. Incidentally, we are going to find out everything about this poor girl here, whose name and reputation only the mercy of God kept you from ruining this very night." The two now sat looking each other fairly and fully in the eye. For the first time in many years Henry Decherd recognized the whip hand.

"I might as well tell you," said Eddring, "that I know about the old Loisson estate - a great deal more than its lawful heiress does. I know who paid the taxes on the lands. I know as well as you do about the suit in the United States Supreme Court, where you won and lost at the same time. In that case you proved your client, Delphine, to be Indian, and therefore not French - in plain language, you proved that she was the heiress of the Indian, Paul Loise, and therefore could *not* inherit certain valuable lands of which we both know. Before you found yourself on that account forced to pin your faith to the descendants of the French Comte de Loisson, you were willing to use either line of descent, provided it made it possible for you to get possession of these lands. You were willing to deal with a woman of mixed blood, or with one of pure blood, of noble descent. Let me be frank with you, Decherd. You were playing these girls one against the other. It was Delphine against the descendants of the Comte de Loisson - a delicate game; and you came near winning."

Decherd passed a hand across his forehead, now grown clammy, but he could see no method either of attack or of escape, for the cold gray eye still held him, and the blue barrel hung steady beneath the idle hand, as the same steel-like voice went on:

"I will just go over the proof once more, Decherd," said Eddring, "and see if we don't look at it about alike. For instance, if Delphine is Indian, she isn't white. Uncle Sam's Supreme Court says she's Indian. That's record, that's evidence. Take the two girls, one of noble blood, the other of questionable descent, and they are together equal, *in posse*, as we will say, to these valuable lands. Do you follow me? Oh, give up thinking of your gun. I'll kill you if you move your hand.

"Very well, then, my friend, it comes simply to a case of cancelation. No matter what you have told or promised either, there can be but one heiress. Mark out one girl, and the other is equal to that estate, we'll say. You yourself marked out Delphine when you proved her to be of Indian descent. That leaves Miss Lady as the heiress of the estate of the Comte de Loisson, doesn't it, Decherd?

"It leaves, also, two ways of getting the estate. You could marry the girl, or kill her. You might possibly get a tax-title in the latter case; if you killed the girl the tax-title would mature in your name. You may count that string as broken. Mrs. Ellison, we will say, wanted your paramour, Delphine, canceled, and wanted also to put the remaining claimant out of sight. Then, as mother of this heiress - the false mother, as you and I know - she thought that she would inherit the lands - and you.

"That was Mrs. Ellison's plan - a very ignorant plan. Then the simple matter of a marriage - or of no marriage - between Mr. Henry Decherd and this Mrs. Alice Ellison, would enable them comfortably to share this estate. That was the way Mrs. Ellison wanted it, perhaps. But you preferred to marry the true claimant, and get rid of Mrs. Ellison. That was your plan. You wanted to cancel every possible claimant except Miss Lady, and then you wanted to force Miss Lady into a marriage with you. Do I make myself clear to you, Mr. Decherd? And do I make myself clear that this country isn't big enough for both of us? Keep quiet now. You've come to your show-down right here.

"Meantime, it was part of your scheme, as I now see, to keep Miss Lady away from her friends, to poison her against those friends. You had to live, and you were a lawyer, or a sort of a lawyer. You got hold of these judgment claims against the railroad which discharged me. You told this girl that I stole those claims. You know you lied. For a time you deluded this poor girl, poisoning her mind, killing her nature with your deceit. None the less, you left behind you open proofs, ready-made for your own undoing. Why, this very name, this stage name of Louise Loisson, was banner enough to bring her real friends to her side. But you didn't know, did you, Mr. Decherd, that I had read the little book, and that I knew the Loisson history? I said it was by chance I found the book. I am ready now to say it was by fate - by justice. It's like the fetish mark on the church-door - that negro church in the woods - like the sign on Delphine's handkerchief. Guilt always leaves a sign. Justice always finds some proof.

"Now, I have a message from Colonel Blount. Here it is. He says, 'Louise Loisson our Miss Lady.' He has found out some-thing, too, at the other end of the line, hasn't he, Decherd? Notice, he says, 'our Miss Lady.' She is ours, not yours. I am going to take her along with me, back to the Big House, and to her friend, Colonel Blount. He says, 'Watch out for Decherd.' I am watching out for him. He also says that they have caught the leader who has been making all the trouble up there in the Delta, near the Big House plantation."

"Delphine!" gasped Decherd, from tightened lips, a pale horror now written on every feature. "Has she talked?"

"Yes, Delphine! You were able to guess that, were you, Decherd? Thank you. You were right. I do not know whether or not Delphine has talked. But whether she has or not, there will presently be no chance for you. You are at the end of your string, Decherd.

"And now, get up," said Eddring to him sharply, rising. "Get up, you damned hound, you liar, you thief, you cur. This boat's not big enough for you and me. The world will be barely big enough for a little while, if you're careful. We are not afraid of you, now that we know you. Go back to Mrs. Ellison, if you like. You can't go back to Delphine now, and you can't speak to Miss Lady again. She is *our* Miss Lady. You can't stay on this boat tonight, where that girl is."

"So you - you're trying to cut in?" began Decherd.

Eddring did not answer.

He caught Decherd by the collar, wrenched the revolver from his pocket and pushed him down the stair, then dragged him along the lower deck. They passed a line of sleeping deck-hands too stupid to observe them. Dragging astern of the boat, high between the two long diverging lines of the rolling wake, there rode a river skiff at the end of its taut line.

"Those lights below are at the ferry, eight miles from town," said Eddring. "Get into the boat."

"For God's sake, can't you get them to slow down?" whined Decherd; but Eddring shook his head. Decherd let himself over the rail of the lower deck, and for an instant the strained line bade fair to hold his weight. Then his feet and legs dropped into the water as he and the boat approached. Desperately he clambered on, and so fell panting and dripping into the bow of the skiff. A moment later the boat and its huddled occupant dropped back into the night, tossing in the wake of the churning wheels.

From above there came pouring down the somber flood of Messasebe, bearing tribute of his wilderness, in part made up of broken, worthless and discarded things.

Eddring gazed after the disappearing boat. He was relaxed, silent, worn. The grip of a great loneliness seized upon him. What had he gained? Why had he interfered? The world about him seemed void and vacant. He felt himself, no less than the other man, a worthless and discarded thing - a bit of flotsam on the flood of fate.

CHAPTER X

THE VOYAGE

"As to the law, Captain Wilson," said Eddring, to the master of the *Opelousas Queen* the following morning, as he sat in the cabin; "I'm a lawyer myself, and I want to tell you, the law is a strange thing. It will, and it won't. It can, and it can't. It does, and it doesn't. It's blind, crosseyed and clear-sighted all at the same time. It offers a precedent for everything, right or wrong. Now, as you say, it is unlawful for us to stop the delivery of these mails. I know it - big penalty for non-delivery. But let's talk it over a little."

The *Opelousas Queen* was now plowing steadily up-stream, far above Baton Rouge, meeting the crest of the greatest flood she had ever known in all her days upon the turbid waterway. Her master now, surly but none the less interested, out of sheer curiosity in this strange visitor, sat looking at him without present speech.

"Are you a married man, Captain Wilson?" said Eddring. "Have a cigar with me, won't you?"

"What difference is it to you?" said Wilson, waving aside the courtesy.

"Yes; but *are* you?"

"Wife died six years ago," said Wilson, gruffly. The muscles ridged up along his jaw as he closed his lips tightly.

"Any children?" said Eddring.

"Daughter, eighteen years old; and a beauty, if I do say it."

"I reckon you love her some, don't you, Captain? Thought a heap of your wife, too, maybe, didn't you?"

Wilson half-rose, one hand upon his chair back, as he pounded on the table in front of him with the other. "Now look here, Mister Who-ever-you-are, I've stood a lot of foolishness from you already," said he, "but those are my matters, and not yours. Get on out of here." Yet Eddring only looked at him smiling, and into his eyes there came a flash of pleasure.

"I'm mighty glad to hear you say those very words, Captain," said he; "because now I know you'd do anything in the world to help a good girl out of trouble, or to keep her out of it. Now, about the law. I'm sure, Captain, you believe in the higher law - the supreme law - the chivalry of the southern man, don't you?" Wilson waved him away again, but still gazed at him curiously. "Now listen, Captain," Eddring persisted.

"I am listening," blurted out Wilson. "Say, man, if I had your nerve, and what I know about poker on this river, I'd own the country."

"But listen -"

"No. I just want to set here and admire you a few minutes before I tell the deck-hands to throw you into the river."

"Captain," said Eddring, pulling up his chair, "after I'm done with what I have on hand, you may throw me into the river, if you like. I don't think it will make much difference. But now, don't you think you're running this boat. The real commander of this boat, Captain Wilson, is the supreme law of this land - that law under which the gentlemen of the South are bound at any time and all times to give courtesy and comfort to a woman when she needs them." Wilson looked at him mutely, the muscles on his jaw straining up again. He jerked his head toward the aft state-rooms with a gesture of query. Eddring nodded.

"She's a beauty, too," said Wilson, sighing. "Reminds me of my own wife, the way she used to look - the way my own girl looks now. You're a lucky man."

"Captain Wilson, I don't figure in this thing personally at all. But now I'll tell you the whole story, and let you decide for yourself."

He went on speaking slowly, evenly, gently, impersonally, telling what had been the case of Miss Lady upon the very night preceding; telling how great was the stress of events at the head of the Delta, very far away, and impossible now of access. He made no offer of pecuniary reward, but stated his case simply and asked his auditor to put himself in his own position.

As he spoke, the chair of Captain Wilson began to edge toward his own. In the eyes of the old steamboat man there came a glisten strange to them. His hand unconsciously reached out. "Stop!" he roared. "Give me your hand. The boat is yours! Of *course* she is."

Eddring was silent, for there came a lump in his own throat, as he felt Wilson's assuring hand clap him on the shoulder.

"You're what *I* call a thoroughbred," said the latter. "Man, can you play poker? You certainly can make a pair of deuces look like a full house. Get up an' shake hands. You're right. The boat's yours. Uncle Sam can wait - the whole damned North American continent can wait -"

Eddring rose and took him by the hand.

"Well, that's my case, Captain," said he. "We've both one

errand, and that's to protect the white people of the Delta; and to get hold of the truth which will put this girl where she belongs. Public necessity is the greatest of all laws; unless it be the unwritten and general law which I know you've respected all your life."

"Well, man -" Wilson broke into an uproarious laugh, "you certainly are the yellow flower of the forest. It's mighty seldom I've laid down to a line of talk, but I ain't ashamed to do it now. Here's the boat, and we'll run her express, as soon as we can get rid of the mail and passengers up above. Any river-man knows what levee-cutting means, and what it means if the niggers get out of hand. I'll take you in - why, I know Cal Blount myself - and I couldn't look my own daughter in the face again if I didn't do just what you say."

CHAPTER XI

THE WILDERNESS

Between the cities of Memphis and Vicksburg there lies a great battle-ground. It has known encounters between red men and red, between red men and white, and has known the shock of arms when white has been arrayed against white. Most of all, it is a battle-ground yet to be, whereon perhaps there shall be waged a conflict between white and black. Always, too, it will be the battle-ground between civilized man and the relapsing savagery of nature; between man and the wilderness; between the white race and great Messasebe, Father of the Waters.

Father Messasebe is, after all, but weakly bound to the ways of commerce. His voice is always for the wild; his wish is for the ancient ways. Here in the far wild country - a part of which even to-day is a more trackless and a less known wilderness than any in the heart of our remotest mountain ranges - the great river reaches out a thousand clutching fingers for his own, claiming it as a home even now for his savagery; asking it, if not for a wild red race, then for the black one which may one day prove its savage successor.

Here is the reekingly rich soil of the great Delta - that name not meaning the wide marshes of the actual mouth of the Mississippi, but the fat accumulated soil of centuries caged in by that long, incurving dam of the hills which, far inland from the current of the swift water-way, begins at the head of the vast body of tangled Yazoo lands, and drops down, pinching in at the base of a great "V," where the bluffs converge near Vicksburg. These hills spreading out on either side hold in their wide arms an empire, the richest and most fertile land, though perhaps still the least known, of any to be found in this America. They hold also a population little understood; a people bold, undaunted, American. These arms of the hills hold also a vast problem; the problem of black and white, less settled to-day than it has been at any time these one hundred years.

Here in this land, more than two hundred miles in length and half as much in width, Father Messasebe extends his fingers. Sluggish bayous run across the waste as their fancy leads them, their current depending upon the whim of the river, or perhaps on that of the streams from the hill country which constitutes the great dam of the Delta. The crooked Yazoo is marked on the maps as crossing almost from the north to the south of this wilderness; yet the Yazoo can scarce claim a bed all its own, for it passes through many ancient bayous, and is fed by many of the old "hatchees" which the canoes of the red man explored long ago. Upon one side of the Yazoo comes the Sunflower, deep cut into the fathomless loam; yet sometimes the Sunflower is reversed in current; and the Sunflower and the Hushpuckenay may be one stream or two; and the latter may run as the levees say, or as the floods dictate; while above them both, at the head of the Yazoo, are bayous and "passes" which make a water-way once continuous from the great river into its lesser parallel.

Messasebe sometimes flows peacefully through channels marked out for him by man, yet this is but his whim; for a thousand years are as naught to the Maker of Messasebe, and Messasebe therefore may bide his time. But when the sport of the floods begins, and the currents are reversed, and the streams hurry down with cross tributes from the hills, and the wild waters have forgotten all control - then is when Messasebe the Mighty grasps and clutches with his wide fingers, and exults as of old in his wilderness!

Here in the heart of the Delta lay the Big House, a dot on the face of things; having, however, its problems, personal or impersonal, small and great. As John Eddring knew, there was trouble at the Big House now. The hours passed slowly enough on the journey up the turbulent flood of the great river. The railways were in places gone for miles. All that Eddring could do was to get by steamer as nearly as possible opposite the Big House plantation, and then win through by small boat as best he might, across the overflow.

Even the most diligent makers of maps can not keep pace with Father Messasebe. Along its southernmost course there are thousands of arms and lakes and bayous where for a time the river ran until it tired, and sought new scenes, new ways across the forests and cane-brakes. The charts may show you that this river is the boundary of a certain state; but who shall tell where or what that boundary may be? Who can trace the *filum aquae* of the most erratic and arrogant river in all the world? The river is not now as it was ten years ago, nor the same to-day as it will be ten years hence. Channel and cut-off and island and main current go on in their juggling, and will do so when generations shall have been forgotten. When the floods are out, and when Messasebe is at his ancient game, there is no channel; there is no map, no chart; there is a wilderness.

It was across this watery wilderness that John Eddring and his ally, Captain Wilson, urged their way on the wildest journey ever known even in the mad times of this great river. In a half-delirium which set aside all reason and all reckoning, the bow of the sturdy boat was driven against the down-coming seas, opening up one after another of the channel marks; parting one after another of the massed groups of shadows; churning round bend after bend, faster and faster, day and night, until, far up in the welter of the new waters, she forsook all charts and guides in the fury of her quest, and steamed forward in her own fashion, black smoke belching continually from her flues, and the pant of her fuming engine bidding fair to tear out the inadequate covering of her sides. Pilot and captain let go all track of the miles behind, looking only at those ahead. They got contempt for ordinary dangers. So, pushing her way on, against and across currents, shaving the bends, essaying every cut-off, the boat in her strange race hurried on, running express for the purposes of justice, and in the cause of the permanency of society.

At last they were far up the river, above the mouth of the Arkansas, and opposite the great swamps which lie between the Arkansas and the White upon the western side; so that now the greater portion of the journey was well-nigh done. Eddring and Wilson, both haggard with fatigue, stood on the bridge together and gazed out over the watery prospect.

"This overflow means millions in losses to the planters in the Delta," said Wilson. Eddring nodded.

"If levee-cutters started this flood up in Tullahoma, and the planters ever get hold of them, I shouldn't think it would be exactly healthy," added Wilson. "This means everything under water, clean to the Yazoo. Looks like those fellows in there had had their share of trouble lately."

"Nothing but trouble for four or five years," said Eddring. "Black politics."

"Yes," said Wilson, sighing, "when Mr. Nigger gets the notion that he'd like to be school superintendent or county treasurer, or something of the kind, he's goin' to be mighty willin' to lay down the hoe. I even think he would be willin', if he was asked, to let the white man do the hoein', and him do the governin'." Eddring made no answer, but gazed steadily out over the racing seas of tawny water.

"At any rate, we'll soon be there now," said he at length. "How can I pay you, Captain Wilson? How can I thank you?"

"Well," said Wilson, thoughtfully, "you might give me your note, the way a friend of mine, Judge Osborn, down at New Orleans, did once. That was in the war, you know, and Judge Osborn was a Confederate colonel. He had to take passage on a river boat, and they got hung up somewhere, and he and the

Cap'n played a little poker for several days. Colonel couldn't win nohow. At the end of the week he owed the Cap'n four hundred thousand dollars - Confederate money, of course. At last says he, 'See here, Cap'n, now I owe you this four hundred thousand dollars, and I can't pay you by about one hundred and fifty thousand dollars. Now, what am I going to go? Shall I give you my note?' The Cap'n he looks at the Colonel, and says he, 'Ain't I treated you all right, Colonel? Ain't I fed you good enough? Did I ever do you any harm?' The Colonel 'lowed he had been treated all right. 'Well, then,' says the Cap'n, 'what have you got against me? What do you want to give me your note for? Take everything I've got; take my boat, but please, sir, don't give me your note.' Now that's the way I feel. I don't want your thanks, and I don't want your note."

Eddring laughed frankly. "Well, Captain," said he, "let it go that way. I won't give you my note, nor my thanks; but when you are in my part of the world, come and live with me. After I get through with these things in there, I shall see you again sometime. There are some gentlemen of the Delta who will never forget Captain Wilson."

"Well," the gruff old Captain answered him, "I'll tell my little girl about it, and I reckon I'll get my pay from her. But now I shall have to be leavin' you before long," he resumed, as he studied again the appearance of the country into which they had now come. "We're raisin' the Old Bend landin', or the place where it ought to be."

"Wait a minute, Captain," said Eddring, "we'll need a skiff. Put in two or three blankets and something for coffee, if you will. It looks pretty rough in there, and we might not get through before dark." Eddring swept a hand toward the submerged forest, which, shoreless and all afloat, appeared upon their right, stretching away in every direction as far as the eye could reach through the evening haze.

"I will fix you up the best I can," said Wilson. "But now, do you know that country in yonder? Are you safe in going in?"

"I have hunted bear and deer all over there," said Eddring. "The main current across this big bend ought to carry us inland into a bayou that runs not far from the Big House. It is not more than twenty miles or so to the plantation. If I can strike the course of the Tippohatchee bayou, a few hours ought to take us through. If it comes dark before we get there, we shall have to camp, that is all about it. If a fellow tried to travel through in the night-time, he might land at Greeneville, or Vicksburg, or anywhere else."

"Well," said Wilson, "if you must go, I won't try to stop you. I'll have the skiff fixed up."

So, finally, after her journey up the river, the *Opelousas Queen* rounded the thin neck of the long river bend, and with a hoarse growl of relief, rather than of signal, slowed down and reversed, plowed up the yellow waters into billows half-white, and so lay breathing heavily, with just enough way to hold her against the current.

During the entire course of the journey, Eddring had not approached either Madame Delchasse or Miss Lady in personal conversation, and the latter had proved quite as willing to avoid him. Madame Delchasse had taken great and voluble interest in matters about the boat, and was often seen on deck. To her Eddring now sent his message, which brought both the ladies to the lower deck, for the first time in two days.

"What," cried madame, "we go in that leedle boat! *Ah, non!* I stay by the ship; also mademoiselle."

Miss Lady said nothing; she looked at the frail skiff, the turbulent river, and the great woods beyond, already growing mysterious beneath the veil of coming evening.

"Madame," said Eddring, "I can't argue about it. You must go." He turned upon her the stern face of one who, having assumed all responsibility, exacts in return implicit obedience.

"We shall drown," said madame.

Eddring turned gravely to the girl. "There is no danger. I can assure you of that. I shall do my best. I am sorry that it is so. But we must go. It is the only way to reach Colonel Blount's."

Upon Miss Lady's pale face there sat the look of one resigned with fatalism to whatever issue might appear. She made no further speech, but was the first to step into the boat. Madame Delchasse, still grumbling, followed clumsily. Eddring helped them in, took up the oars, and the two deck-hands, who had been holding the skiff, clambered back aboard the *Queen*. Eddring settled himself to the oars, and they cast off. The little skiff rocked, tossed, turned, and headed toward the shore under the strong stroke of the oars. Presently the set of the inbound current aided the oars, so that soon they were at the fringe of the forest. Eddring rose and waved a hand back to the watchers who were looking after them from the guards of the steamer. The *Queen* roared out a deep salute, and then the little skiff passed out of sight into the wilderness.

CHAPTER XII

THE HOUSE OF HORROR

"Me, I have thought never to cook again," said Madame Delchasse, "but now I shall have the honger. See! if I had the coffee-pot and the what-you-call the soss-*pan,* I should make of this the grand peok-*neek.* This journey through the h'wood, it is fine."

As madame spoke, the little boat was hurrying forward through the half-submerged forest, and the party had by this time reached a point some miles distant from their embarkation at what had formerly been the river-bank. Of shores along the river proper it could hardly be said that any remained, and at this point of pause, near to one of the long ridges which still here and there remained above the water, there appeared small trace of the accustomed landmarks. Here, deep in the forest, the inset of the main current through the broken levee was arrested by the forest itself, and by the channels of many intersecting bayous. It was not a river, but a vast, shallow lake that lay about them. Water was everywhere, and in this wide expanse Eddring confessed to himself that he had lost his course and had no definite knowledge of the way to find it. It gave him pleasure to see that the spirits of madame were buoyant, and that even Miss Lady, silent as she was for the most part, seemed to lose a portion of the apathy which had at first oppressed her.

Hoping that he might at any time reach country familiar to himself, Eddring sought to maintain the spirits of his companions by pointing out to them the unfamiliar objects of the world in which they now found themselves. Explaining that they were quite safe in their little craft, he showed to them the repulsive moccasin snakes, whose rusty forms lay wreathed on the logs or on such dry ground as here and there appeared. Again he showed them the log-like bulk of the alligator, lying motionless and invisible to the unpractised eye; or called their gaze to a group of noble wild turkeys, which craned out their necks from their perch on a tall dead tree.

"The game is all driven to the dry ridges," said he. "You will see that the birds and beasts are afraid to move. Their fright makes them almost tame. Do you see that little fellow there?"

He pointed out a wild deer, cowering beside a log on the little island near which they were passing. Here he stopped, and disembarking, soon called out to them that he had seen the track of a bear, fresh in the loam near-by. They being terrified at this, he returned to the boat, and skirted the muddy edge of the ridge, showing them the footprints of the raccoon, small and baby-like, the round tread of the timber wolf, the pointed footmark of the wild hog.

"Look," said he, "here is where an otter has been playing," - and he showed them a little huddle of twigs and dirt scraped together at the end of a log which projected over the water. "Why does he do it?" he said. "I don't know. It's his way of playing. There are a great many strange ways in the world of wild things. By to-morrow I shall have made good hunters of you both."

"To-morrow?" cried Madame Delchasse; and Miss Lady also turned upon him a startled and supplicating look.

"Yes," said he, "it's no use to promise what one can't be sure of doing. I know that we are not very far from the Big House station. We can't miss it, because we can't cross the railroad without knowing it, and you know the railroad would lead us directly to the place. At the same time, for us to attempt traveling in the night might mean that we should get hopelessly lost. I assure you, you have no need to be alarmed. There is plenty in the boat to keep you comfortable, and, as madame says, we will just make a picnic of it. I am sure none of us will be the worse for a night out in the woods."

Eddring bent steadily to his oars. He was forced to admit that their case showed small improvement as the shadows began to thicken. He stood up in the boat at length and gazed steadily at a little ridge of dry land which appeared before him. "I think we'll land here," said he, "and make our camp for the night." Miss Lady edged toward madame and laid a hand upon her arm.

"My shild," murmured madame, "yes, yes, it is the grand peek-*neek;* I, Clarisse Delchasse, will protect you." Rejoiced that matters were at least no worse with his passengers, John Eddring helped them from the boat, and as he did so caught sight of the tears which stood in Miss Lady's eyes. The strain of the last few days had begun to tell, and as she looked into the dense shadows of the forest in this precarious spot of refuge, it seemed to her that all the world had suddenly gone dark, and must so remain for ever. Eddring was wretched enough without this sight, but he went methodically about the work of making them both comfortable.

"First, the fire," he cried gaily; and presently under his skilled hands a tiny flame began to light up the gloom. He worked rapidly, for now night was coming on. "Watch me build the house," he cried; and soon he was absorbed in his own work of making an out-door structure, hunter fashion, as he had done many times in his expeditions in this very region. He cut some long poles and thrust their sharpened ends into the ground, and bending over the tops, wove them together. Then he thatched this framework with bundles of fresh green cane cut near at hand, and in a few moments had a sort of *wickiup.* On the bottom of this he threw brush and yet more cane, and then spread down the blankets. The opening of the little house was toward the fire, and presently both the women were sitting within, their fears allayed by the sparkle of the cheering flame.

"But, Monsieur, where you yourself sleep?" asked madame.

"Oh, my house is already built," replied Eddring, and pointed to a giant oak-tree some fifty yards away in the little glade. "You see how the knees of the big tree stand out. Well, I just get some pieces of bark, and put them down on the ground, and then I lean back against the tree-trunk, and the dew doesn't bother me at all. Of course, the main thing is to keep dry."

"Sir," said Miss Lady, almost for the first time accosting him, "do you mean to say that you sit up and do not lie down to sleep at all during the whole night? Why, you would be wretched. You must take one of the blankets, at least."

"Not at all," said Eddring. "I have sat up that way many a night on the hunt, and been glad enough of so good a chance. Now, you ladies begin to get ready for supper, if you please. Madame, I am sure that to-night you will prepare the best meal of your career. I think we can promise you that it will be enjoyed. Excuse me now for a while, and I will go and see about some more wood. An open fire eats up a lot of wood during a night."

He disappeared down a faint path which he had detected opening into the cane at the end of their little glade. His real purpose was to explore this path; for there now came upon him the growing conviction that he had seen this place before. He found the path to be plainer than the usual "hack" of the mounted cane-brake hunter, and here and there he caught sight of a faint blaze upon a tree. Hurrying along through the enveloping foliage of the cane, he had traversed some three or four hundred yards of this tangle before he saw a thinning of the shadows ahead of him, and came out, as he had more than half expected to do, at the edge of a little opening in the forest.

There, near the edge of the cleared space whose surface showed even now the prints of many feet, he saw a long, low house of logs. It was as he had seen it years ago! It was now, as then, the temple of the tribesmen. Around it now swept, open and uncontrollable, Father Messasebe, building anew his wilderness.

The white men had spared this temple. Perhaps they knew that sometime it would serve as a trap. And so it had served.

That there had been fateful happenings at this spot Eddring felt even before he had stepped out into the opening before him. He was oppressed by a heavy feeling of dread. Yet he went on, looking down closely in the failing light at the footprints which marked the ground.

These footprints blended confusedly, leading up to the door of the house, disappearing in the rank growth all about. And crossing these human trails from one side to the other of the narrow island left by the rising waters, there ran a strange and distinct mark, as though one had swept here with a mighty broom, or had dragged across the ground repeatedly some soft and heavy body! In this path there were marks of feet deeply indented, with pointed toes. This trail, these foot-marks, horrid, suggestive, led up to the open door. Eddring hesitated to look in. He knew the tracks of the alligators, but guessed not why these creatures should enter a building, as was never their wont to do. It required determination to look into the door of what he knew was a house of mystery, perhaps of horror.

Within the long room, now lighted faintly by the late twilight which filtered through the heavy growth about, he saw dimly the long benches fastened to the walls, as they had been when he first saw this place years before. In spite of himself, he started back in affright. The benches were tenanted! He could see figures here and there, a row of them.

Some of them were bending forward, some sitting erect. But all of them were motionless, the postures of all were strained, as though they were bound! The house had its tenantry. But there was no central figure here now, no leader, no exhorter, no priest nor priestess. There was no shouting, nor any note of the savage drum. The drum itself, its head broken in, the drum of the savage tribes, lay near the door, its mission ended. This audience, whoever or whatever it might be, was silent, as though sleep had made fast the eyes of all!

Eddring sprang back as he heard the scuffling of feet at the farther end of the hall. His teeth chattered in spite of himself, as this Thing, this creature of terror, came shuffling forward in the darkness, and with clanking jaws pushed past him, to disappear with a heavy splash in the water which now stood close at hand.

It was a house of horror. It was the place of the black man's savage religion and of the white man's savage justice. Here the white man had wrought sternly in the name of his civilization, and his keel, departing like that of the fierce Norseman in the ancient past, had left no trail on the waters lapping the shore which had known his visitation.

CHAPTER XIII

THE NIGHT IN THE FOREST

It was some time before Eddring could trust himself to appear before the companions whom he had left at the little bivouac. Night had practically fallen when he finally emerged into the little glade, now well-lighted by the fire. He paused at the edge of the cover and looked at the picture before him. Sick at heart and full of horror as he was from that which he had seen, none the less he felt a swift burst of savagery come upon his own soul. What was the world to him, its strivings, its disappointments, its paltry successes? Almost he wished, for one fierce instant, that he might exchange the world beyond for this world near at hand. A little fire, a little shelter, and the presence of the woman whom he loved - what more could the world give? He gazed hungrily at the figure of the tall young woman, defined well in the bright firelight. Yearning, he coveted the endurance of the picture, saying again and again to himself, "Would this might last for ever, even as it is!"

Madame Delchasse meantime was adding support to her well-founded reputation as artist in matters culinary. When presently Eddring joined them at the fire, he was invited to a repast in which madame had done wonders. It seemed to him that even Miss Lady began to revive under the summons of these unusual surroundings. Once, he noted, she actually laughed.

As they sat on the rude floor of cane-stalks, engaged with their evening meal, there came suddenly from across the forest the sound of a long, hoarse wail, ending in a tremulous crescendo;

the cry of the panther, rarely heard in that or any other region. In terror the women sprang to each other, and Eddring felt Miss Lady's hand close tight upon his arm in her unconscious recognition of the need of a protector.

"What - what was it?" she cried.

"Nothing," said Eddring; "nothing but a cat."

"A cat?" cried madame. "Never did I hear the cat with voice so big like that."

"Wasn't it a panther?" asked Miss Lady. "Will it get us?"

"Yes, Madame Delchasse," said Eddring, "it's a cat about eight feet long - a panther, as Miss Lady says. But it's a mile away, and it doesn't want to get any wetter than it is; and it wouldn't hurt us anyhow. I assure you, you need have not the slightest fear. Water and fire are not exactly in the panther's line, so you can rest assured that he will not trouble you. He wouldn't even have screamed that way if his disposition hadn't been spoiled by all this water."

Inwardly he noted the fact that Miss Lady did not again remove to a greater distance from him. His heart leaped at her near presence, and again there came the fierce demand of his soul, the wish that this night might last for ever.

Finally, building anew the fire, and showing the two how they might best use their blankets to make themselves comfortable, Eddring withdrew for his vigil at the tree-trunk. Now and again he dozed, wearied by the strain and the physical exertion lately undergone. Madame Delchasse slept heavily.

Upon her couch Miss Lady lay, and watched the flickering of the fire and the heavy masses of the shadows. She could not sleep. There came upon her the feeling of unreality in her surroundings which is experienced by nearly all civilized human beings when thrown into the uncivilized surroundings of nature. It all seemed to her like some rapid and fevered dream. She wondered what had become of Henry Decherd, what had been the cause of his sudden departure from the steamer. She resolved to summon courage on the morrow and to accost this uninvited new-comer upon the scenes of her life. She pondered again upon this strange man; asked herself why he had sought her out, why he had left her so soon and had since then been so frigidly aloof, even though he still carried her with him forward, virtually a prisoner. By all rights a thief, a dishonest man, ought not to be a gentleman; yet strive as she might, she could recall no single instance where the conduct of this man had been anything but that of a gentleman, delicate, kindly, brave, unselfish. Miss Lady could not understand. The shadows hung too black over all - the shadows of the past, of the future. About her there were vague, mysterious sounds, rustlings, coughings, barkings, sometimes sullen splashes in the water not far away. Terrors on all sides oppressed Miss Lady's soul. She had no hope; she could not understand. Her thoughts were in part upon that silent figure sitting in the darkness beside the tree. And then there came again the voice of the great panther, wailing across the woods. Miss Lady could endure it no longer. She sprang up.

"Sir!" she cried, "Mr. Eddring, come!" And so he came and comforted her once more, his voice grave and quiet, fearless, strong.

"I will build up the fire," said he, "and then I will sit by another tree, closer to the camp and just back of your house. I shall be between you and the water, and you need not be afraid."

And then there came about a wonderful thing, which not even Miss Lady herself could understand. She ceased to fear! She found herself wondering at the meaning of the word "depend." In spite of herself, in spite of all the evidence in her hands to the contrary, she felt herself growing vaguely sure that she could depend upon this man. Gradually the night lost its terrors. The whispers of the leaves grew kindly and not ominous. The fire seemed to her a reviving flame of hope. Presently she slept.

In the night the wild life of the forest went on. The barkings and rustlings and splashings still were heard, and the great cat called again. But all these savage things went by, passing apart, avoiding this spot where the White Man, most savage and most potent of all animals, had made his lair and now guarded his own.

In the night the voice of the wilderness spoke to John Eddring: "Old, old are we!" the trees seemed to whisper: "Only the strong! Only the strong!" This seemed the whisper of the wind in its monotone. He sat upright, rigid, wide-awake, his eyes looking straight before him in his vigil, his heart throbbing boldly, strangely. All the fierceness, all the desire, all the sternness of the wilderness in its aeons ran in his blood. His heart throbbed steadily. Peace came to his soul now as never before; since now he knew that he was of the strong, that he was ready for life and what combat it might bring.

CHAPTER XIV

AT THE BIG HOUSE

The fire lay gray in ashes at the dawn, when Eddring awoke, and the gray reek of the cane-brake mist was over everything. The leaves of the trees and of the cane dripped moisture, and the dew stood also in heavy beads upon the roof of the little green-thatched house. A short distance apart Eddring built another fire. Presently the sleepers in the little house awoke, and he saw emerge madame, tucking at her hair, and Miss Lady, in spite of all fresh and rosy in the wondrous possession of youth, as though she were a Dryad born of these surrounding trees. There seemed to sit upon her the primeval vigor of the wilderness. She came to him gaily enough and said good morning as though there had been but recent friendship and not aloofness. She pushed back her hair, and smoothed down her skirt and combed out with her fingers the bunch of bright ribbons at her waist. She and madame, having made ablutions at the island brink, returned, all the fresher and more laughing. Eddring's heart quickened in his bosom as he saw Miss Lady smile once more.

"Come," said she, "let's explore our desert island; yonder's such a pretty little path," - and she pointed down the path which Eddring had already investigated.

"No," he said, "the cane is very wet; you'd better sit close by the fire, so that you will not feel the damp. Now, I will get the breakfast; and I promise you, this is to be our last meal in the forest."

"Our last?" said madame. "What you mean?"

"In a couple of hours we shall be at the Big House," said Eddring. "I have looked about, and I know this place perfectly. We are only four or five miles from the station, and the way will be plain."

"Monsieur," said madame, "I shall be almost sorry. It is the fine peek-*neek*. Never have I slept so before."

"I, too, have slept nicely," said Miss Lady, "and I want to thank you. Shall we be out of the wood so soon?" There was small elation in her own voice, after all. In her soul there was a wild, inexplicable longing that this present hour might endure. Fear was gone, in some way, she knew not how. What there might be ahead, Miss Lady did not know. Here in the forest she felt safe.

The hurried breakfast was soon despatched and Eddring, taking aboard his passengers once more, pushed out into the broad sea which lay through all the heavy forest. The nearest road to the station was under water, and, as it offered few obstructions, Eddring for the most part followed its curves for the remainder of his boat journey. At length, as he had said, he brought up within sight of the telegraph poles along the railway. He passed by boat even beyond the little station-house, and landed at the edge of what had been the Big House lawn.

On every side there was ruin and desolation. The rude fence of the railway track had caught and held a certain amount of wreckage. Most of the field cabins were above the water, but others were half out of sight, deep in the flood. Fences were well-nigh obliterated. Half of the Big House plantation was under water. Above all this scene of ruin, high, strong and grim, the Big House itself stood, now silent and apparently deserted. Toward it the voyagers hurried. It was not until they knocked at the door that they met signs of life.

In response to repeated summons there appeared at the door the gaunt figure of Colonel Calvin Blount himself, shirt-sleeved, unshaven, pale, his left arm tightly bandaged to his side, his hawk-like eye alone showing the wonted fire of his disposition. Each man threw an arm over the other's shoulder after their hands had met in silent grasp.

"I am not too late," said Eddring. "Thank God!"

"No, not quite too late," said Blount. "There is a little left - not much. Who's with you?"

"The one you sent for," said Eddring, stepping aside, "and this is Madame Delchasse, the one woman, Colonel, whom you and I ought to thank with all our hearts. She has been the friend of Miss Lady when certainly she needed one."

Blount stepped forward, a smile softening his grim face. "Oh, Miss Lady, Miss Lady," he cried, extending his unhampered hand. "You ran away from us! You didn't do right! What made you? Where have you been? What have you been doing?" Miss Lady's eyes only filled, and she found no speech.

"But now you're back," Blount went on. "You need friends, and you've come back to the right place. Here are three friends of yours. Madame Delchasse - " this as Miss Lady drew her companion toward him with one hand, "I am glad to see you. It you ever befriended this girl, you are our friend here. Come in, and we will take care of you the best we can, though we've not much left - not much left.

"You see," said he, turning toward Eddring, "that boy Jack of yours came down with the news of this uprising that I mentioned in my message. He brought along his woman; and I must say that though I don't much mind this -" - he pointed to his injured arm - "if I have to eat that woman's cooking much longer, I'm going to die."

Then it was that Clarisse Delchasse arose grandly to the

occasion. "Monsieur Colonel," she said, as she divested herself of her bonnet, "I have swear I would cook no more; but me? I am once the best cook in New Orleans. I cook not for money, ah, *non!* but from pity! Sir, humanity it is so outrage' by the poor cook that I have pity! So, Monsieur, I have pity also of you. Show me this girl that can not cook, and show me also the kitshen. Ah, we shall see whether Clarisse Delchasse have forget!"

"Show her, Miss Lady," said Blount. "Show her. The place is yours. Oh, girl, we're glad enough to have you back. Go get that gold-toothed woman of Jack's, go get 'em all, if you can find any of 'em around. Get Bill, he's around somewhere - get any of 'em you can find, and tell 'em to take care of you. Child, child, it's glad enough we all are to have you back again. Ah, Miss Lady, what made you go away?"

Even as he spoke, Madame Delchasse, rolling up her cuffs, was marching down the hall. "By jinks!" said Blount, looking after her admiringly. "By jinks! It looks like things were going to happen, don't it?" His strained features relaxed into a smile.

"But now come on, son," he said, turning to Eddring, "you and I have got to have a talk. I'll tell you about some of the things that *have* happened. We've been busy here in Tullahoma."

Drawing apart into another room, Blount met Eddring's hurried queries as to his own safety, and heard in turn the strange story of the late voyage and the incidents immediately preceding it. He told Blount of the discovery of Miss Lady living in the care of the old Frenchwoman, Madame Delchasse - Miss Lady, as they had both more than suspected, none other than Louise Loisson, the mysterious dancer in the city of New Orleans; told of the plot which he was satisfied had been the motive of Henry Decherd in inducing Miss Lady to accompany him upon the steamer. Blount added rapid confirmation here and there, and presently they came to a topic which could no longer be avoided.

"I know what was done," said Eddring at length, after a slight pause in the conversation. "I found the place where it all happened. That's where we spent the night, on the ridge, near the house."

"Did they see? Did they know?" asked Blount, nodding toward the place where the two women had disappeared.

"No," said Eddring. "I did not tell them. Blount, it's awful. Where's the law gone in this country?"

"Law?" cried Blount, fiercely, "*we* were the law! We sent for that nigger sheriff - the one they elected for a joke - hell of a joke, wasn't it? - and he wouldn't come. We had with us the old sheriff, Jim Peters, a good officer in this county, as you know, before now. We had with us every white voter in this precinct, every tax-payer. We found them, these levee-cutting, house-burning fools, right at their work. We left some of them dead there, and run some into the cane, and we took the balance over to that church of theirs which you saw. The water wasn't so high then as you say it is now. There was a regular fight, and the niggers were plumb desperate. They had guns. Jim Bowles, down below here, was shot pretty bad, though I reckon he'll get well. I was shot, too - not bad, but enough to make me some dizzy. Jim Peters - and I reckon he was the real officer of the law - was shot, too, so bad that he died pretty soon. Now I reckon you can tell what we found to be at the bottom of this, and who it was that's been making all this deviltry here for years."

"Delphine!"

"It was nobody else," said Blount. "You talk about human tigers, and fiends, and all that kind of thing; that woman beat anything I ever did see or hear of. She was brave as a lion. Peters and Bowles and I closed in on her, wanting to take her, but she fought like a man, and a brave one. She had two six-shooters, and she dropped us, all three of us; and then before the others could close in on her, she turned loose on herself, and killed herself dead as hell. She didn't see the finish of the others."

Eddring buried his face in his hands and inwardly thanked Providence that he himself had not been present at such a scene.

Blount resumed presently. "Peters didn't die right away," said he. "He lay there with his head propped on a coat rolled up for a piller, and he talked to us all like we was at home in the parlor. 'Keep on with it, boys,' said he. 'Do this thorough. Make this a white man's country; or if you kain't, don't leave no white men alive in it.' Then after a while he turns to me and says he, 'Colonel, you know I'm not a rich man. Now I've got a couple of mighty fine b'ah-dogs, and I want to give 'em to you; but if you don't mind, I'd like mighty well if you'd send my wife over a good cow. She's going to be left in pretty poor shape, I'm afraid, for you know how things have been going on the plantations,' I told him I would. We was both laying on the ground together. I told him I would take care of his folks, for he was a friend of mine, and the right kind of man. He talked on a while like that, and finally he says, 'Well, boys, I'm not going to live, and you've got a heap to do right now, and I mustn't keep you from it. Jake,' says he, 'you Jake, come here.' - Jake was his nigger boy that he always kept around with him. We had three or four good darkies with us. My boy Bill, out there, was along, and this Jake and some others. 'Jake,' says Jim Peters to this boy, 'come around here an' take this piller out from under my head. Lay me down, and lemme die!' Jake he didn't want to, but Jim says to him again, 'Jake, damn you,' says he,'do like I tell you'; so then Jake he took the piller out, and Jim he just lay back and gasped once, 'Oh!' like that, and he was gone. I call that dying like a gentleman," said Blount.

"The poor fools," presently went on the firm voice of the man who was recounting these commonplaces of the recent savage scenes, "they think, and they told us, some of them, that they've got the North behind them. They think the time is going to come when they won't have to work any more. They want to make all this Delta black, and not white. If we could give it to them and fence them in we would be well rid of the whole proposition, North and South alike. These poor fools say that the North will make another war and set them free again! There'll never be another war between the South and the North. Next time it will be North and South together, against the slaves, white and black. But as to the Delta going black, while we men in here are left alive - well, I want to say we'll never live to see it. If the people up North could only know the trouble they make - could only know that that trouble lands hardest on the niggers, I think maybe they'd change a few of their theories. They don't understand. They think that maybe after a while they can make us people think that black is white, and white is black. Carry that out, and it means extermination, on the one side or the other.

"Law?" he went on bitterly; "I wish you'd tell me what *is* the law. Good God, we white men in this country are anxious enough in our hearts to settle all these things. We want to be law-abiding, but how can we, unless we begin everything all over again? Law? You tell me, what *is* the law!"

CHAPTER XV

CERTAIN MOTIVES

Miss Lady and her stout-hearted friend, Clarisse Delchasse, found abundance at hand to engage their activities. Miss Lady ran from one part to another of the great house which once she had known so familiarly. Everywhere was an unlovely disorder and confusion, which spoke of shiftlessness and lack of care. The touch of woman's hand had long been wanting. Colonel Blount, in the hands of his indifferent servants, had indeed seen all things go to ruin about him. To Miss Lady, concerned with the swift changes in her own life, wondering what the future might presently have in store for her, all this seemed a sorry home-coming. She leaned her head against the door and wept in a sudden sense of loneliness; yet presently she lost in part this feeling in a greater access of pity which she felt for the helpless master of the Big House, who had been living thus abandoned and alone. With this there came the woman-like wish to restore the place to some semblance of a home. Even as she dried her eyes, to her entered presently madame, with her sleeves rolled to the elbow and her face aglow in the noble ardor of housekeeping.

"*Voila*!" she cried. "I have foun' it! I have dig it h'out. Here is the soss-*pan* of copper. It was throw' away. It was disspise'. *Mais oui*, but now I shall cook! This house it is ruin'. Such a place I never have seen since I begin. You and I, Mademoiselle, it is for us to make this a place fit for the to-live - but you, what is it? Ah, Mademoiselle, why you weep? Come, Come to me!" And Miss Lady was indeed fain to lay her head upon the broad shoulders, to feel the comforting embrace of madame's fat arms.

"H'idgit!" cried madame, suddenly, starting back.

"H'idgit congenital! H'ass most tremenjouse! Fool *par excellence!*"

Miss Lady gazed to her in wonder. "Auntie," she cried, "who?"

"Who should it be but the M'sieu Eddrang?" replied madame. "For a time it is like the book. Now it is not like the book. Ah, if I Clarisse Delchasse, were a man, and I take the lady away from one man, I'd h'run away with her myself, me, and I'd keep on the h'run. But M'sieu Eddrang, how is it that he does? Bah! He does not speak t'ree, four word to you the whole time on the boat. You, who have been the idol of the young *gentilhommes* of New Orleans - you, who have been worship'! Now, it is not one man, and it is not another, although *ma 'tite fille*, she is alone, here in this desert *execrable*. Bah! It is for you to disspise that M'sieu Eddrang. He is not *grand homme*. Come. I take you back to New Orleans."

Miss Lady looked at her with a curious shade of perplexity on her face. "You mistake, auntie," said she. "I do not wish to be back at New Orleans. I am done with the stage - I'll never dance again. I am - I'm just lonesome - I don't know why. I have been so troubled. I don't know where I belong. Auntie, it's an awful feeling not to know that you belong somewhere, or to some one."

"You billong to me," said Madame Delchasse, stoutly. "As to that h'idgit, - no, never!"

"But Mr. Eddring brought us safely through the forest," said Miss Lady, arguing now for him. "I don't know what became of Mr. Decherd, or why he left us, but we can't accuse Mr. Eddring of anything ungentlemanly after that time. But why was he so anxious to come? Why was Colonel Blount so anxious? I don't understand all these things. And Mr. Eddring and Colonel Cal seem to want to talk to each other, and not to us."

"Bah! Those men!" said Madame Delchasse. "What can they do but for us? This place, it is horrible neglect'. But come, I show you my soss-*pan.*"

As Miss Lady had said, Blount and Eddring were long and eagerly engaged in conversation. They were rapidly running over the new links in the strange chain of evidence which had now for some time been forging, Eddring being especially curious now as to Blount's discoveries in connection with the girl Delphine.

"It's plain enough," said Blount, finally, "that this thing between Decherd and Delphine had been going on for a long time. Delphine left a good many papers, which we found among her belongings. It's all turned out just about as we figured before you went to New Orleans; but we found one letter from Decherd to Delphine that uncovered his hand completely, and it was this, to my notion, that made Delphine so desperate."

"Let me have that letter, Cal."

"All right, I'll get it for you after a while, along with all the other papers. It gives the whole thing away. He just told her he was through with her, and with Mrs. Ellison, too. Told her he wouldn't send her no more money, and turned her loose to take care of herself the best she could. He allowed that she, and Mrs. Ellison, too, could do what they wanted to. That was when he told Delphine that if she made him any trouble he'd come out and charge her with the train wreck. He was the planner of that wreck. He knew right where that log-pile was at. He wanted another accident on that railroad, and he wanted Delphine mixed up in it, so he could control her after that. She was willing enough, because by that time I reckon she just about hated all the world. And Decherd came down on that very train, and got off at our station just before the smash. There was a little danger in that, but at the same time it was the best way in the world to rid himself of all suspicion. After the wreck he just mixed with the crowd, and nobody thought of him one way or the other. Pretty smooth, wasn't it?

"Oh, he had nerve, too, that fellow did. He wasn't scared, at least not of these two women, although I'm right sure Mrs. Ellison and he might have had reason to be scared of the law in some of their carryings-on before now. It is easy enough to see that Mrs. Ellison never was Miss Lady's mother."

"No," said Eddring, "that couldn't have been. Some day we'll know all about that. A good lawyer might get at the truth, even yet."

"Good lawyer?" said Blount. "How about you?"

Eddring shook his head.

"What do you mean?" asked Blount.

"Well," said Eddring, bitterly, "I told you I'd bring Miss Lady through, and I did. But that ends it. I am neither lawyer nor friend for any young woman who thinks I'm a thief."

"What are you talking about?"

"Well, she told me to my own face that I stole that list of judgment claims from my own railroad. She told me that I was dishonest. She forbade me ever to see her again."

"Seems like you *did* see her again," said Blount, philosophically. "Well now, you just think over both sides of that. You want to forget some of the things women say."

"I'll forget nothing," replied Eddring, "I don't need any advice in such matters as that. No man, and no woman, can accuse me in that way and ever make it right without coming to me voluntarily and making apology and explanation. I say voluntarily, meaning for a woman. If it were a man, I'd take the first steps myself."

"Oh, well, get your feathers up, if you want to," said Blount. "I suppose every fellow is entitled to his own kind of damned foolishness. First thing, let's go on through with this Delphine business. Now, was that girl crazy, or was she just a natural devil? Folks mostly have reasons for doing things."

"I should think this letter you mention would explain everything for Delphine," said Eddring. "She was born a good hater, and she was surely misled and deceived for years - finally thrown over and taunted."

"But where did they first hook up together, and what made 'em?"

"No doubt she and Decherd knew each other before either came to your place. Decherd's main motive was money. Delphine was no doubt his mistress, even here; but he was looking after the legal side of matters all the time. What he promised Delphine no one knows. It looks as though he and Mrs. Ellison were hunting in couple, too. Now, Mrs. Ellison had brains, and she was an attractive woman, too - full of sex, full of love and hate, and full of unscrupulousness as well. Rather a dangerous proposition, I should say, to have right here in your own house. Now, here was Decherd mixed up with two, or perhaps all three of these women at the same time! That took nerve."

"I should say it did," said Blount. "It was the same sort of nerve a fellow has to have when he starts on across a trembling bog. He just keeps on a-running."

"Well, he had to keep running, sure as you're born. A fine situation, all around, wasn't it?"

"Yes," said Blount, tersely. "If I had known all that was going on here, I wouldn't maybe have felt altogether easy about it."

"Well, Miss Lady's going away helped Decherd. By this time he had to lighten cargo somewhere. We don't know about his first relations with Mrs. Ellison, and we don't know just how he got rid of her. Perhaps he didn't quite want to dispense with Mrs. Ellison, since he might need her in legal matters later on. He wanted to get rid of Delphine, but he couldn't kill her outright, and illegally, so he resolved to get her killed legally if he could! I have no doubt in the world, Cal, that Decherd planned the train wreck. Maybe he thought it meant more damage suits; but I think as you do, his main reason was to get rid of Delphine. He probably hid the handkerchief under the log-pile. He probably was glad to see the dogs run the trail right to your door. But Delphine had a nerve of her own. I have no doubt it was she who turned your pack loose, and wiped out the sheriff's trail right there."

"By jinks!" said Blount, rubbing his chin thoughtfully. "Things were happening, right around here."

"They were happening, and they are not done happening yet. Now, I've brought you Miss Lady. You take care of her. Better keep that Frenchwoman here, too, if you can. Decherd may turn up again sometime, or maybe Mrs. Ellison, though I think Decherd's teeth are pretty well pulled, I can't act as Miss Lady's lawyer, but I'll promise to act as your friend."

"And hers?"

"Yes, and hers," said Eddring, hesitatingly. "We are hardly through with all this yet."

"It's been pretty bad down here," said the old planter.

"Yes, and we know now how it happened and who was at the head of the trouble, and what cat's-paws were used in it all. Decherd fails in his first attempt to get rid of Delphine legally, so he stirs her up to still worse acts; tells her there is no profit in law and order, but only in destruction. He tells her how to incite these ignorant niggers; how to bring up all the old talk of their day of deliverance, the time when they won't have to work, the time when they will be not only the equals, but the superiors of the whites. He tells Delphine that she is the naturally appointed Queen of these people. She is savage enough to fit in with all their savagery. She does rule it as a queen. In her soul there are thoughts, wild thoughts which you and I can never understand, because we are white, and all white. Delphine is neither white nor black, neither red, nor white, nor black. She is a product of race amalgamation, a monstrosity, a horror, the germ of a national destruction. She is a queen - a queen of annihilation!

"And so this thing went on," resumed Eddring, after a time, "this plotting which meant war and destruction, not for this household alone, nor this district, nor this state, but for this nation! What prevented it? I'll tell you. It was our Miss Lady. It was the White Woman, the white woman of America. Whatever happens, whatever stands or falls, whatever is the law or is not the law, that is the thing to be cherished always and to be protected at any cost or any risk. This house is no better than the women in it, nor is any home, nor is any nation. Lawless, American men may be, but not so the women; and in them we reverence the law. When the women go, the nation goes. They are the salvation of this nation - the stronghold of its purity. In the commercialization and the corruption of a people the women are the last to go. In the South we have taken care of them always. I'm not preaching. I only say, it was our Miss Lady who, by the Providence of God, acted here as the spirit of all that means progress, all that means development and civilization.

"Cal, you think I'm a visionary, that I'm a dreamer. Perhaps I am. But I think on my honor that the angel of our salvation here was one girl who had no conception of the part she played. I have told you, she is *our* Miss Lady. There's nothing in this for me personally, but at least you and I can take off our hats to her. Maybe sometime the picture will blur and merge, so that, for us two old fellows, Miss Lady will just mean Woman. I reckon all of us old fellows, and all the young ones, can take care of Her."

The two sat looking at each other a moment. Ere their silence
was broken there came the sound of a quick step down the
hall, and a light tap at the door. There appeared, framed in the
doorway, the figure of Miss Lady herself; but not Miss Lady
the dancer of New Orleans, nor yet Miss Lady as recently
garbed for her voyage through the wilderness. In her
rummaging about the once familiar recesses of the Big House,
she had come across a simple gown of lawn, which she had
worn long ago, when scarce more than a child. Now, albeit
rounder, firmer and fuller of figure than when she had
departed in search of that bigger world beyond the rim of the
hedging forest, it was the same Miss Lady of the Big House
once more. She had come back to her old friends, and to a
world which now seemed strangely sweet and strangely dear.
Her sleeves were rolled up; her hair was tumbled about her
brow, and her eyes were dancing with new merriment.

"Please, gentlemen," said she, with a dainty courtesy, "and
would you come out to dinner? You really should see what
Madame Delchasse has done with her new sauce-pan."

Blount and Eddring both arose; there was gravity in the gaze of
either, though the heart of either might have leaped.

"So it is you, child," said Colonel Blount; "it is you again! Just
as you went. You're Miss Lady, come back to us again."
Impulsively forgetting everything but the one thought, he
sprang to her and flung his arm about her shoulders. And Miss
Lady could not find it in her heart to shrink from such a
welcome.

"Oh, I'm glad to see you - glad to see you," repeated Calvin
Blount. "Mr. Eddring, here, was just saying how good it is to
have you back again."

Mute, she turned her eyes toward Eddring. The short upper lip
trembled; in her eyes there was more than half a suspicion

of moisture.

"Yes, we are very glad," said John Eddring, simply. With no word she put out her hand to each, and drew them out into the hall.

CHAPTER XVI

THE NEW SHERIFF

As Eddring and Blount sat engaged in conversation after dinner that same evening, they were interrupted by a sudden disturbance in the hall. "Stan' aside, you-all," cried a pompous voice. "You wanteh hindeh a officah o' de law?"

Hurrying footfalls followed, and presently the face of old Bill, Colonel Blount's faithful bear-hunter, appeared at the door, "Hit's dat fool new sheriff, Mas' Cunnel," he explained, "Mose Taylor. Why, he says he got a wah'nt fo' you. I tol' him like enough you was busy."

"Let him come in, Bill, let him come right along in," said Calvin Blount, suavely. "Mose Taylor, eh? That's our new sheriff," said he to Eddring. "He's our joke. Hell of a joke, ain't it?"

Presently there came to the door the form of the new sheriff, large, portly and pompous. Taylor was a mulatto who long had entertained political ambitions. The realization of one of his ambitions seemed for this present moment to give him no especial happiness. On his face stood beads of sudden perspiration. His office had never before seemed to him quite so serious as it did at this moment. At his waist he wore a belt supporting a pair of heavy revolvers with highly ornamented handles - a present from certain admirers to one who was looked upon as fit to do much for the elevation of his race. The new sheriff did not at that moment seem to think of these revolvers. As Mose Taylor entered the door he cast his glance backward, over his shoulder. It did not encourage him to see his cowardly posse of black followers gathered in a huddle at the edge of the overflowed lawn, beside their boat. They were waiting to see what would happen to their leader; and their leader now heartily wished that he had remained with them.

"Come on in, Mose," said Blount, with honey-like sweetness. "Come in and take a chair." The man sidled in. "Sit down," said Blount, "*sit down!* Sit down on it good; that chair ain't hot;" and the sheriff suddenly obeyed. "I always like to see the sheriff of Tullahoma County feeling easy-like in my house. Now, tell me, damn you, what you want around here?"

"Cunnel Blount, sah - well, I got a papah, a wah'nt from co'te, f-fo' you, sah. I - I - I - didn't think you was quite so well, sah."

"Uh-huh! So that's why you came, eh? I reckon you'd be mighty glad if I was a heap sicker, wouldn't you?"

"I dunno, sah."

"What's your warrant for, Mose?" said Calvin Blount, still quietly. "Stealing hogs this time, or killing somebody's cows, maybe? Out with it. Now, damn you, can't you read your own warrant?"

"Well, sah, you-all know there wuz some killin' - my wah'nt - "

"Yes, we-all *do* know there was some killing, a little of it, the *beginning* of it, a *part* of it. Now, tell me, have you the nerve - are you *fool* enough to come down here and try to arrest any of us white gentlemen for what we did a few days ago? Now talk. Tell me!" Blount's face took on its red fighting-hue.

"Wait!" cried Eddring, speaking to Blount, "this is an officer of the law. This is the law." He rose and stepped between the two, even as the sheriff fumbled in his pocket for the paper which had lately been the bolster of his courage, the warrant which in grim jest had been issued by the court of that county to its duly instituted executive officer.

Blount's face was an evil thing to see. At a grasp he caught from a belt which hung at the head board of the bed a well-worn revolver whitened where long friction on the scabbard had worn away the bluing. "Out of the way, Eddring," he cried. "Get your head out of the way, man!" His pistol sight followed steadily here and there, searching for a clean opening at its victim, now partly protected by Eddring as the latter sprang between them. Blount sat on the edge of the bed, his crippled arm fast at his side, his unshaven face aflame, his red eye burning in an unspeakable rage as it shone down the pistol-barrel, grimly hunting for a vital spot on the body of the man beyond him.

"Get out, quick," cried Eddring, and pushed the man through the door. He sprang to Blount and pushed him in turn back upon the bed.

"It's the law!" he reiterated.

"The law be damned!" cried Calvin Blount. "Let me up! Let me at him! *Him* - to come around here to arrest *me*-that damned nigger! You, Bill!" he called out, raising his voice. "Throw him off my place. Kill him!" He struggled furiously with Eddring in his effort to gain the door.

The new sheriff of Tullahoma County was ashen in color when he emerged into the hall; and then it was only to look into the muzzle of a rifle, held steadily by old Bill. There ambled up to Bill's side, also, Jack, and between them they laid hold of the sheriff of the county and pushed him out of the house and across the lawn, administering meanwhile to his body repeated deliberate and energetic kicks, and thus enthusiastically propelling him into the very presence of his waiting posse, who raised never a hand to resent these indignities to one who had been their chosen representative for the advancement of their race.

"I'll see 'bout dis yer, I will!" cried the sheriff, as at last he got clear and took refuge in the boat which lay waiting at the edge of the lawn. "I'll have you-all up for 'sistin' a officah, dat's whut I will."

"'Sistin' a officah! Who! *You?*" said Bill. The scorn in his voice was infinite. "Say, you low-down scoun'rel, you say very much mo' an' I'll blow yoh head off. You're on our *lan'*, does you know dat? Now you git *off*, right soon."

The officer of the law retreated as far as he could into the boat. "You thought Cunnel Blount was all 'lone in bed, too weak to move, didn't you?" resumed Bill. "Why, blame you, you couldn't 'rest Colonel Calvin Blount, not if he was *daid!* Go 'long dah, now!"

Mose Taylor, the grim jest, the sardonic answer of the whites of Tullahoma County to those who deal fluently with questions of which they know but little, was fain to take Bill's sincere advice. Behind the shelter of the first clump of trees, he folded his arms into a posture as near resembling that of Napoleon as he could assume. He frowned heavily. "Huh!" said he savagely, looking from one to another of the crew who made his "posse." "Huh!" he said again, and yet again, "Huh!" A cloud sat on his soul. It seemed to him that persons like himself, earnestly engaged in settling the race problem, ought not to have such difficulties cast in their way.

Meantime, in the house, Eddring still confronted the rage of Colonel Blount.

"You," panted Blount. "You! I thought you were one of us."

"I am, I am!" cried Eddring. "I was with you in what you did. I tried to get to you. It had to be done. But somewhere, Cal, we must stop. We've got to pull up. We can't fight lawlessness with worse lawlessness. We must begin with the law."

A bitter smile was his answer. "Is that sort of sheriff the foundation that you lay?" said Calvin Blount, panting, as at length he threw his six-shooter upon the bed. "Let me tell you, then, the law is never going to stand. That's no law for the Delta."

Eddring sunk his face between his hands. "Cal," he said, "we've got to begin. This country is being ruined, and perhaps it is partly our own fault. Now, I am guilty as you. are; but I say, we have got to give ourselves up to the law."

"Give myself up? Why, of *course* I will. I was going up directly, soon as I got well, to talk it over with the judge, and arrange for a trial. All this has got to be squared up legally, of course. But that's a heap different from sending a nigger sheriff down here to arrest Cal Blount in his own house. Why, I'm one of the oldest citizens in these here bottoms. I've carried my end of the log for fifty years, with black and white. Why, if I should go in with that fellow, where'd be my reputation? I'd have a heap of show of living down here after that, wouldn't I? Why, my neighbors'd kill me, and do me a kindness at that."

"But we must begin," said Eddring, insistently, once more. "There must be some law. We'll go in and surrender. I'll take your case."

"You mean you'll be my lawyer at the trial?"

"Yes, I'll defend you. But as for you and me, we're for the state, after all. We've got to prosecute this entire system which prevails down here to-day. We're growing more and more lawless all over the South, all over America. Now, we don't want that. We don't believe in it. Then what can we do? How can we get to the bottom of this thing? Cal, I reckon you and I are brave enough to begin."

Even as they were speaking, they heard a knock at the door, and Miss Lady once more stood looking in hesitatingly upon these stern-faced men. Upon her own face there was horror, terror.

"I don't know what to do!" she cried, her hands at her temples. "I don't know where to go. You tell me this is my home, and I have nowhere else to go, but this is a *terrible* place. Why, I have just heard about what happened - about Delphine and those others. Why, sir," - this to Eddring, - "you knew it all the time. You saw. You knew!"

"Yes," said Eddring, "that is why I would not let you walk down that little path on the island. I didn't want you to know - we didn't want you ever to know."

"Yes, Miss Lady," affirmed Blount, "we knew. We didn't want you to know."

"But is there no law?" she cried. "Why do you do these things? The punishment is for the officers, for the courts, and not for you. Why, how can I *look* at you without shivering?"

"What shall we do, Miss Lady?" asked Blount, coldly. "What's the right thing to do? Listen. We've done this thing for *you*. You're a white girl. The white women of this country - if we *didn't* do these things, what chance would you and your like have in this country? Now, we've done it for you, and we'll finish the way you say. You're to decide. Shall we go in and surrender? Shall we be tried? Remember, it is our own lives at stake, then."

"We will go in, and we will meet our trial," said John Eddring, rising and interrupting, even as Miss Lady buried her face in her hands. "We will begin, right here."

CHAPTER XVII

THE LAW OF THE LAND

One morning in the early fall, the little town of Clarksville, county-seat of Tullahoma County, was thronged with people from all the country round about. There was in progress the trial of certain white citizens under indictment for murder, among these some of the most respected men of that region. The case of Colonel Calvin Blount had been chosen as the first of many.

The court-room in the square brick court house was packed with masses of silent men. The halls were crowded. The yard of the court house was full, and the streets were alive with grim-faced men. The hitching racks were lined with saddle horses, and other horses and countless mules were hitched to fences and trees even beyond the outskirts of the town. The hotels had long since abandoned system, and every dwelling house was open and full to overflowing.

Outside of the town, or mingling in the fringes of the crowd at its edges, there huddled even greater numbers of those of the colored race. Some of these were armed. The white men in the streets were armed. None showed hurry or agitation; none shouted or gesticulated; yet the clerk of the court had a pistol in his pocket; each juryman was likewise equipped; the judge on the bench knew there was a pistol in the drawer of the desk before him. This gathering of the people was thoughtfully prepared. It was a crisis, and was so recognized.

The silent audience was packed close up to the rail back of

which was stationed the judge's stand and jury-box. Within the railing there was scanty room; every member of the local bar was there, and many lawyers from counties round about.

Erect in the grave-faced assemblage, there stood one man, pale of face but with burning eyes. It was John Eddring, attorney for the defense in the case of the state against Calvin Blount, charged with murder. His voice, clean-cut, eager, incisive, reached every corner of the room. His gestures were few and downright. He was swept forward by his own convictions of the truth.

Eddring was approaching the conclusion of the argument which he had begun the previous day. The testimony in these cases, known generally as the "lynching cases," had long been in and had passed through examination, cross-examination, rebuttal and surrebuttal.

Eddring knew that he would be followed by an able man, a district attorney conscientious in the discharge of his duty, however unpleasant it might be. He had therefore with the greatest care analyzed the evidence of the state as offered, and had demonstrated the technical impossibility of a conviction. Yet this, he knew, would not upon this occasion suffice. He went on toward the heart of the real case which he felt was then on trial before this jury of the people.

"Your Honor and gentlemen of the jury," he continued, "we all know that we are, in effect, trying today not one man, not one district, not one state, but an entire system. We are trying the South. The life and the liberty of the South are at stake. To prove this, these men have come in and given themselves up as an atonement, as a blood offering like to that of old; seeking to prove that what they continually have coveted is not lawlessness, but the law.

"Now I say this, and I say, also, let each of us have a care lest he lose touch with the eternal pillar of the truth. There it is. It rises before you, gentlemen, that silent, somber shaft. It finds its summit in the sky. I pray God to keep my own hand in touch thereto, and my eyes turned not aside. And my life, with that of these others, is offered freely in proof that we covet not lawlessness, but the law! We are white men, and where the white man has gone, there has he builded ever, first of all, his temple of the law. Upon whatever land the Anglo-Saxon sets his foot, of that land he is the master, or there he finds his grave. First he lays his hearthstone, and upon that foundation he builds his temple of the law. A race which has no hearthstone knows no law.

"Inasmuch as God has made all manner of things diverse, setting no fence even between species and species, creating all blades of grass alike, yet not one the duplicate of another; then neither should we, being human, essay a wisdom greater than that of the eternal compromise of life. No human document, no sum of human wisdom, not even the Deity of all life can or does guarantee a success which means individual equality in the result of effort. The chance, the opportunity - that is the law, and that is all the law. Beyond that did not go the intent of that Divinity which decreed the scheme under which this earth must endure. To war and conflict each creature is foreordained, for so runs the decree of life. But never, in the divine wisdom, was it established that the mouth of the stream should be its source; that inequality should be equality; that failure should be success; that unfitness should mean survival.

"In reading the pages of the great and beloved Constitution of America there have been those who have juggled the import of the word 'success' with the meaning of the *chance to succeed*.

"There was such juggling in those war amendments to that Constitution, which to-day represent the folly of a part of America - not of all of America. Those amendments, if they be not of themselves war measures, were at least consequences of war measures. This Constitution which we call supreme can, of itself, be amended - can, indeed, itself be set aside by its own servants, as was proved in that very war whose memory is still in our minds. The Supreme Court, in the Legal Tender case, admittedly set aside the Constitution. It did so of necessity, and as a measure demanded by the times of war. The supreme letter of the law has not always been respected by this people, nor by its wisest men, by its most august servants.

"It is not the law, gentlemen, vainly to call two blades of grass identical, vainly to call the hare and tiger alike and equal; vainly to call, if you like, black the same as white. The law is that if it be possible for the hare to approach its neighbor in ways desirable, it be given its *chance* to do so. If the black man can grow like to the white in all human attainments, if he can grow and succeed, then let him have the *chance* to do so.

"But that same chance of betterment and advancement, that same selfish chance to prevail and to survive, that chance to succeed given under the divine intent, must be accorded also to that creature known as the white man. If he, the white man, can prevail, can survive, can succeed, he, too, must have his chance. That is the law! But the chance of either white or black man is his own and is not negotiable. That is the law! Not without fitness can there be ultimate success. Not until the fullness of the years can there be attainment for any creature of this earth. That is the law! There is no tree growing in the center of this ordained universe wherefrom the full fruit of survival and of success may be plucked and eaten without effort and without earning. No individual has done it. No one can do it. Bounty and gift do not make success. It must be *won!*

"Is this doctrine difficult? If so, we can not change it. It is the great law, irrevocable and unamendable, and it is no more kind and no more cruel than life itself is kind or cruel. It is the law. That is the law!

"The makers of the Constitution, the amenders of the Constitution - that document subject to change, subject to being ignored, as has been the case - could never, under the enduring law, guarantee success plucked as an apple for each and every man who had not earned it. Gentlemen, talk not to

EMERSON HOUGH

me of the broad charity of this nation, or of its general justice to humanity. Call not this piece-work Constitution of ours, amended and subject to amendment, an approach to divine charity or wisdom. No; for in some of its effects it has proved to be the most cruel and unjust measure ever known in all human laws.

"It was cruel and unjust to whom? To us? To the white man? No, no. It was cruel in that it presented a title to success, to fitness and to survival unto eager, ignorant hands, and then by its own limitations snatched that title away from them again. It sought to do that which can not be done - to establish growth instead of the chance to grow. It was cruel. It was unjust. In the wisdom of a later day its patchwork form must once more be changed. It must be changed as a protection, no more against the former slaves of the South than against the future slaves of the North.

"Gentlemen, if that change could be effected to-morrow by the offering up of this life - of these lives now in your hands - I say these lives would be laid down gladly. Take them if you will. They are our pledge that we covet not lawlessness, but the law; our pledge that, having no law, we have been eager to act lawfully as we might. The reign of lawlessness and terror must end in this country. We must contrive some machinery of the law which shall command respect. We must not continually drag the name of the South - the name of America - in the mire of lawlessness. To do that is to smirch the flag - the one flag of America. But we denounce and will always denounce that false decree which says that black is white; that inequality is equality; that lack of manhood is manhood itself; that the absence of a hearthstone can mean a home; that the absence of the home can mean a permanent society.

"In the future the North, packed and crowded beyond endurance, with imported and herded white slaves who in time will demand the position of masters - as the blacks may legally demand that position here to-day - will pay her price for the right to make this plea. The South has already paid a thousand times for her right to make it to-day. With treasure she has paid for it; with roof-tree and hearth-tree she has paid it dear, and with the sacred tears of women. With the sacrifice of her own future she has paid for that right. But the South and the North belong together, not held apart by politics, but held together in brotherhood. In the name of all justice, let us hope that the South shall not be asked to pay the bitterest of all prices, the misunderstanding and the alienation of those whom she loves and would embrace as her brothers. Let us hope, in the name of mercy, if not of justice, that the South shall be understood as a region having a problem, a problem which is national, and not sectional, and *not political.* Let us in all fairness hope that our northern brothers will understand that the South is honest in her attempt to deal with that problem in her time, which is the time of to-day.

"Your Honor, I do not depart from my argument. I am not here for wild talk regarding the relations of the two races. It is the ages alone which will decide that problem. But I am here to stand for the law and not for lawlessness. I am here to say that our flag, the American flag, is for all men, and for America; not for Africa alone, or for Europe alone, but for America. It is the flag of progress, not the flag of anarchy. It is the banner of civilization and not of savagery. That, and not the banner of Africa or of Europe, must be our ensign to-day.

"Your Honor, and gentlemen, we are not here today to conclude that God set the white man over the black. We are to conclude simply that He set him *apart* from the black man. The divine right of slavery was an impiety, and, worst of all, an absurdity. The South made that mistake, and bitter has been the price of her folly. Yet the South, having sinned, paid the price of her sinning in all ways exacted of her. She accepted the ruling of the North, and, as a distinguished orator once said, surrendered 'bravely and frankly.' But she did not admit, and please God, never will admit, that those fresh from savagery should govern the white men, that they should institute the machinery of the law whereunder the white man must live.

"Gentlemen, you see before you, sardonically done, the fruits of the Black Justice. Is that the Law? If it be, then send us to our graves; for as that Black Justice formally exists to-day, Calvin Blount, and I, and these others, must go back to our fields or to our graves. Do you wish to send us to the latter? If you do, you send these other white men just as lawfully back to take up the hoe of labor, to bend their necks under the black yoke of African ignorance and savagery. Is that the Law? In my heart, gentlemen, I believe that those who say this is the law have not read the history of this country, do not understand the theory of this country, and can not speak for it unselfishly or honestly.

"Yet, gentlemen, that is the dilemma into which our brothers of the North would continually thrust us. Suppose that, casting about for some possible measure to free us from one point or the other of that dilemma, we should seek some legal compromise which would free us from the letter of this oppressive law of our national Constitution. Suppose there should be proposed some general and stern limitation of the franchise? Such an onerous qualification must needs apply to black and white alike. Who would be first to object to it? It would be the politicians of the North, who could not afford to exact even a prepaid poll-tax as a test for a vote. In time the North will need to free her white slaves, already turbulent and rebellious. In time she will have to pay for them, as we of the South have paid. After that great civil war which is yet to come, the men of the North may perhaps understand more fully the meaning of that phrase 'the manhood suffrage' and know that manhood means survival, that good manhood means the product of a good environment, a survival slowly and fitly won. By that time, North and South, perhaps, will know that the franchise should be as the bulwark of the law, not the destroyer of the law. Until that time, we of the South must continue to pay our part of the price of the national lawlessness; and we must continue, each commonwealth for itself as best it may, to enact laws which shall in part lessen the intolerable weight of that which we have set up as the idol of our national laws - that Constitution, which is impossible and not practicable, which is merciless instead of just, which is cruel instead of being kind, and most cruel to those whom it is thought to shelter. Meantime the South feels still the intolerable weight of that Constitution, the intolerable sting of the demand of her northern brothers, that she shall be asked to endure, in the name of this incubus, this body of the law, the continuous burglarizing of her honor and her prosperity - the burglarizing of the house of her society.

"We know that it is the chiefest of cruelty and unkindness, the chiefest of madness, to incite these poor and ignorant people - ever ready to follow the voice of sophistry or selfishness - to believe that their burglary of the house of success is right and reasonable; because it is certain that such burglary will be met in the South by the law, by the White Justice, and that, if need be, until either white or black man shall exist no more in this portion of America. Gentlemen, North and South owe it to America, America owes it to the world, that there be held aloft for our worship an image of the Law more honorable than this. Until that time of a more honorable image for our worship, there must perhaps go on the enormous folly of one portion of this nation asking another portion to destroy itself for the sake of an unworthy race. This demand, gentlemen, I take to be an actual treason to the law and to this country.

"The white man has won his rights - why? Because he was able to do so. He accords to any other race the same privilege. That is the law of survival; it is greater than any law of politics, greater than any statute law.

"But, your Honor, these men can not be acquitted under any plea dealing with generalizations alone. The law of the land must be observed in so far as that law exists.

"Now I ask whether at the time of the acts charged against Calvin Blount there existed any adequate machinery of the law. I have pointed out to you the precedent of the great case handled by Mr. Webster in the city of New York, in which case the statutes were set aside by the greater law of an immediate and overpowering necessity. I submit to you that necessity, the greatest of all laws, and in precedent respected by our courts as such, would have overridden even the regular machinery of our laws had it been in operation. I submit further to you that no law existed in this country at that time; that the service of the law to its citizens had ceased. If the greatest court of the country still tolerates the burglary of the house of society by this so-called manhood suffrage, which should rather be called the per capita suffrage, then at least the lesser courts, wiser than the greater, recognize the fact that some crimes require no warrant for arrest; that sometimes the citizen is court and executive in one and at once.

"As the greatest authorities of the law have written, in the organization of society the individual never surrenders all of his rights. He retains for ever and inalienably, after all his delegations to society and the law, a residuum of power for his own. He retains under the great and supreme law of all life, that sweet, that divine privilege, his *chance* to succeed, his *chance* to survive! No tyranny, no oppression, can overcome that sweetest and strongest of all the Anglo-Saxon's coveted rights. Instead, he has ever risen against the law, when that law has demanded of him this last, this ultimate and inalienable right, this principle under which he has builded the civilization of the world.

"In defiance of statute laws grown weak and impotent, the barons at Runnymede wrested Magna Charta from King John; in defiance of statute laws grown weak and impotent, the free men of England wrested their Habeas Corpus Act from King Charles; in defiance of statute laws grown weak and impotent, the colonists of America wrested a virgin empire from King George.

"And, please God, in defiance of statute laws grown weak and impotent, the white man will wrest from whatsoever hand may hold it, the right to protect the integrity of his race, the safety of his women, the sanctity of his two-fold temple of the law!

"I therefore submit to you that a sacred exigency demanded the action of this prisoner, of these prisoners; and I submit that this prisoner at the bar is innocent before the law. But beyond that I add my plea, with that of this honorable court, and of these gentlemen, that one day we may have given to us an image of the Law which we may venerate in letter and in spirit, and a law capable of its own enforcement.

"As I stand before you, gentlemen, this prisoner, this cause, its feeble advocate, seem small and inconsiderable. But at my side I see arising the eternal pillars of the temple of the White Justice. Do you not see them, rising solemn and stately before you, those pillars, their heads taking hold upon the heavens? If that temple has been defiled, if it has been cast down, then let us hope that South and North will restore it again in its full majesty. And when, finally, aided, as we hope, by our brothers of the North, we, as citizens of an ofttimes mistaken, yet eventually to be united America, shall have builded this renewed temple of the law, then the lives of the white men of this state will be - like ours joined in this trial before you - free pledge that the men of this country, so long charged with lawlessness, shall come and bow in that temple in reverence of that law which they have always coveted and which they covet here to-day. Your Honor, and gentlemen of the jury, in the face of that statement, I say that not Calvin Blount - nor any one of these prisoners - has violated the law. And so I close with the words of the ancient form of pleading: Of this we do indeed put ourselves upon the country."

In the silence which fell upon the room as Eddring closed, the district attorney arose to present the case of the state. He began slowly, gravely, logically. He presented the printed page of the statutes, called attention to the formal accuracy of the proceedings, the overwhelming nature of the evidence; he explained that without law, nothing remained but anarchy. He pointed out to the jury that here was the law, plain and unmistakable; here were the facts, obvious and uncontroverted, the convicting facts. He spoke of the infamy which had been cast upon the name of the South by reason of just such deeds as these. He urged the necessity for an absolute and unyielding observance of the letter of the law, those statutes from which they dared not depart. They were statutes which could not be overswept by any glittering speciousness, or set aside by fine spun theories as to what might or might not be a more desirable order of affairs. He reminded them of their oath, their sworn promise to enforce the law - *this* law, the law of the printed page.

He spoke for two hours, and he did his duty; but he addressed himself to men of stone, and he knew it even as he spoke. Not to be moved by his words were these set and solemn faces. Concluding with a passionate appeal that they should protect the fair name of their country from the stigma of lawlessness, he resumed his seat, knowing then the verdict which would follow.

The judge, an old man with silvery hair, turned to the jury.

"Retire, gentlemen, to consider of your verdict."

The door to the jury-room closed behind them, and left a thousand eyes fixed anxiously upon it.

They had scarcely disappeared when the knock of the foreman was heard at the door.

"Bring in the jury, Mr. Sheriff," the judge ordered.

The foreman of the jury, an unknown man, tall and stooped, with scraggly hair and beard, handed a folded paper to the clerk.

"Mr. Clerk, read the verdict," the judge ordered; and the clerk read: "We, the jury, find the defendant not guilty."

The words were received in utter silence.

Presently all, jury and bar and spectators, filed from the

court-room, quietly, not with oaths or threats of violence for those others who at the outskirts of the town were waiting for their answer. And they, the waiting ones, found their answer in this silence, and so now slipped out into the forest. The crowds of white men in the town also quietly melted away.

That night at the hotel the judge and certain citizens were engaged in quiet conversation.

"I think," said the judge, "that this young gentleman, Mr. Eddring, belongs somewhere in a position of trust. I believe that he can be depended upon to think, and not merely to play politics for the sake of office holding. We have had too much politics in the South, and too much in America. It's time now we did a little thinking."

"You're right about that, Judge," broke in the voice of Calvin Blount. "But it's just as he says, we've got to begin. We've got to have some kind of law to begin under."

The judge sighed. "It is humiliating to have to resort to any sort of subterfuge," said he. "Of course, in law, the rule must apply to black and white alike. I see that one of our sister states has passed a law allowing no one to vote who can not read, or who can not write on dictation any section of the Constitution; or who has not paid state and county taxes for two preceding years. This test is not applied to any one who was entitled to vote in any one of the states of the Union on January first, 1867, or at some time prior thereto. It does not apply to any legitimate lineal descendant of persons entitled to vote prior to that time. That is an evasion. Yet, as this young gentleman said, we can not submit to the burglarizing of the house of our society. Until we may legally repel, we must legally evade."

"Why, see here, men," broke in Blount, again, "if you'll let me say so, Judge, there ain't no law higher than the law of poker. Now we've let Mr. Nigger into the game with us; or, anyhow, he's here, and somebody gives him a few chips. He don't buy 'em for himself, and he don't know the value of 'em. His chips ought to be good as far as they last. The trouble with Mr. Nigger is, he's wanting to get into every jack-pot with less'n a pair of deuces, and wanting to play on the ground that his white chips are as good as the other fellow's blue ones. Now, that ain't *poker!*"

"It Shirley ain't," said the tall foreman, wagging a scraggly beard.

The judge smiled softly and gravely. "No," said he. "There should be justice to the white man as well as the black. You will notice the order in which I place those terms."

Calvin Blount hitched his chair closer up to the table. "But now you were saying, Judge, that we ought to do something for this young fellow, Eddring. I have known him a long time, from the time he was claim agent on the railroad. I want to say he's a man and a gentleman, not afraid of anything, and he wants to do what's right. I don't think he puts money ahead of everything else in the world. For my part, if he was my representative in the Legislature, or in Congress either, I'd feel right sure he'd represent me strictly according to the legitimate rules of *poker;* and that's a blamed sight more than a whole lot of politicians are doing to-day, *North* or South."

"It Shirley is!" again said the foreman, wagging his scraggly beard.

CHAPTER XVIII

MISS LADY AT THE BIG HOUSE

The days wore on not ungentle at the Big House, until the mild southern winter had taken the place of mellow fall, and until presently all the land was again full of the warm, sweet smell of spring. Softness and gentleness rested on all the world, and upon every side were tokens that calm had come again to a land late distraught. Slowly the signs of wreck and ruin disappeared about the plantation. The track of the receding waters was covered with a swift verdure. The cabins, late half-submerged and deserted, again found, at least in part, a tenantry. Songs were heard once more as the plowmen resumed their labors in the fields. Green and white and pink colors appeared, and gracious odors, and kindly sights filled now all the horizon. Peace, and content, and hope seemed now at hand once more. The master of the Big House saw about him his accustomed kingdom, and once more his subjects felt the hand of a master, if as firm, perhaps more kindly than ever before.

As for Miss Lady, she dropped back into the life of the place as though she had been gone but for a day. Care and responsibility sat upon the brow of Madame Delchasse, but Miss Lady, not less useful in the household economy, went about her employment as if she had never been away. Of those who welcomed her back to the Big House there was none more thankful and adoring than the old bear-dog, Hec. At the first sight of his divinity, not forgotten in all these long months, Hec, himself grown very old and gray, well-nigh wriggled his rheumatic frame apart, and lifted up his voice in a very wail of thanksgiving. From that time on he rarely allowed Miss Lady out of his sight, but pursued her about the place, hobbling and whimpering when her feet grew too swift; nor did his homage know any change save when Miss Lady deserted him to bestow her attentions elsewhere, whether upon little yellow chickens, or upon some of the toddling puppies which filled the yard about the Big House.

Of all little helpless things, Miss Lady could not find too many for her attention. Upon one certain morning in the spring, some time after the late trial at the Clarksville court, Miss Lady was sitting out on the board-pile beneath the evergreen trees in the front yard of the Big House. Her wide hat, confined loosely by its strings, had fallen back on her shoulders, so that the sun and the warm wind had their way of the brown hair, and the cheeks now flushed with tender solicitude for the three puppies she held in her lap. Yet other puppies scrambled at a pan of milk close by her feet, while at a distance old Hec, too dignified to engage in such procedures, lay in the shade and gazed at her with reproachful eyes. Calvin Blount, coming about the corner of the house, stood for a while and gazed at this picture in silence before he approached and interrupted.

"Miss Lady," said he, "you never did know how glad I am to have you back here again. Why, a while ago I didn't care what became of me, or of anything else. I wasn't even half-training my pack of dogs. Now I have got more'n fifty of the best hounds that ever run a trail, and with you to take care of the cripples and the puppies, it certainly looks like the old pack is going to last a while yet. Yes, you surely are right useful on the place."

"You are not any gladder than I am," said Miss Lady. "I've every reason in the world to be glad."

"Well," said Blount, seating himself apart on the end of the board-pile, "I've got a few, myself. This here is a heap better than being in jail, or maybe getting hung."

"Don't talk about it," said Miss Lady, shuddering.

"I don't want to think -"

"Well, it was Jack Eddring got us out of it all, I reckon," said Blount, breaking off a splinter from the board. "Did you ever stop to think, Miss Lady, that he's a powerful fine young man?"

"Why do you always talk about him?" said Miss Lady, turning, to the sudden discomfort of one of the puppies. "Every time anything comes up -"

"Now, hold on," said Blount, "you don't say a word against that young man while I'm around. I want to tell you that fellow has showed me a heap. He's a square, hard-working man, as honest as the day is long, straight as a string, square as they make 'em, and not afraid of nothing on earth. I ask him to come down here and go b'ah hunting. He always says he has to work - works harder than any nigger I ever had on the place. Now that's what he done showed me. I reckon he'd be a good sort of model for this whole southern country to-day. He's proof enough to my mind that a man can work, and do his own work, and still be a gentleman. I've been right lazy in my time, I reckon, b'ah hunting and that sort of thing, but now I come to think it all over, I don't know but what Jack Eddring is as near right as anybody I know of. He allows he's got something to *do* in this world, and he's starting out to do it. He sort of showed me that maybe that's about the best thing a man can do with himself - just work.

"Besides, Miss Lady," - and here Blount turned upon her suddenly, "that man's done a heap for you."

"Oh, well -" began Miss Lady.

"And he thinks a heap of you. That is," - and here Blount undertook to save himself from what he swiftly fancied might be indiscretion - "he's like all of us people down in here, you know. Now they tell me that up North, in the big cities where I've never been at, there's so many women that folks think they're right common. I don't believe that, nohow, for it don't stand to reason. Now we-all know that a woman is something a good ways off, and high up and hard to reach. That's the way we-all feel. But now even if we allow it that way, I want to say that Jack Eddring has done a heap for you, Miss Lady, that maybe you don't know about. He didn't have to do it, either."

"I never asked him to do anything - I never told him."

"No, you didn't," said Cal Blount, gravely. "You sort of allowed that he was a meddling sneak-thief, Miss Lady. I want to say right here that I allow a lot different from that. Now, if I know that man at all, he ain't going to come around you and make any sort of talk. You'll have to go to *him*."

"I'll not!" said Miss Lady, again eliciting a yelp from one of the puppies in her lap.

"There, there, now," said Blount, gently. "Just you hold on a minute. Don't say you will or you won't. I just want to ask you one thing, Miss Lady. Who do you reckon you are? *I* know you're Miss Lady, and that's all I want to know. But who do *you* think you are?"

The kindness of the keen gray eye disarmed Miss Lady. In the sheer instinct of youth and vitality she spread out her arms wide, her face turned up halfway toward the sky, her lips half-parted: "Oh, don't ask me, Colonel Cal," said she. "I'm alive, and it's spring. I danced in the big room this morning, Colonel Cal! Isn't it enough, just to be alive?" Thus she evaded that question, which she had so long shunned as impossible of answer.

"Yes, it's enough, Miss Lady," said the old planter, gravely. "It's enough for you. But now, we men who are your friends have got to take *care* of you. We've got to do the thinking. Now, I'm saying that Jack Eddring has done a heap of thinking for you that you don't know anything about."

"Oh, I know he sort of took charge of things down there at New Orleans. He told me a lot. And then - about Mr. Decherd -"

"Yes, about Mr. Decherd. I've never talked much to you about that, because the time hadn't come. Now I want to say that Jack Eddring had more right to throw that man Decherd off the boat than ever you understood. I'd have done it the same way, only maybe rougher. We're friends of yours. You're ours, you know. You haven't got any mother. Thank God, you haven't got any husband. You haven't got any father. Now tell me, Miss Lady, who do you reckon Henry Decherd is, and what do you think he wanted to do?"

Miss Lady, suddenly sober, turned toward him a face grave and thoughtful. A certain portion of the old morbidness returned to her. "It's not kind of you, Colonel Cal," said she, "to remind me that I'm nobody. I'm worse than an orphan. I'm worse than a foundling. How I endure staying here is more than I can tell. Shall I go away again?"

"There, there, none of that," said Blount, sharply. "I'll have none of that; and you'll understand that right away. You're here, and you belong here. You don't go out beyond the edge of this yard and get tangled up with any more Henry Decherds, I'll tell you *that*. Now, there's certain things people are fitted for. There's Mrs. Delchasse, a-stewing and a-kicking all the time because she wants to go back to New Orleans. I tell her she can't go, because she's got to stay here and take care of you. Now I'm fit to hunt b'ah. I can tell by looking at a b'ah's track which way he's going to run. Same way with Mrs. Delchasse. She can just look at a cook stove and tell what it's going to do. You can run the rest of this house, and do it easy. We're all right, just the way we are. Now it's going to be that way for a while, and no other way, and I don't want no orphan talk from you. For the time being I'm your daddy - and nothing else.

"But now," he went on, presently, "Jack Eddring is fit to do other things. He's been digging around, like he maybe told you part way, for all I know, and he's found out a heap of things about you that you didn't know, and I didn't know. Miss Lady, as far as I know, you may be richer than I am before long. If you think I've missed the corn-bread you've done eat at my place, why, maybe some day we can negotiate for you to pay for it. Now I ask you once more, *who* are you? and you can't tell. How ought you to feel toward the man who *can* tell you what you are, and who you are? And him a man who can do that, not for pay, but just because you are Miss Lady. How ought you to feel in a case like that?"

Miss Lady said nothing. She only looked anxious and ill at ease.

"Now listen. I'm going to tell you what we know about you, or think we know.

"We think your real name is Louise Loisson, just the name you picked out for yourself. We think that was the name of your mother, and of your grandmother, too, for that matter. If all that is so, then you're rich, if you can prove your title; and we think you can. Tell me, what do you know about Mrs. Ellison? And what do you know about Henry Decherd? Were they ever married?"

A deep flush of shame sprang to Miss Lady's face as she turned about at this. "Colonel Cal," she began, and her voice trembled; "you hurt. All this hurts me so."

"Now hold on, child," said Blount, quickly. "None of that, either. This is strictly business. I know you are not the child of Mrs. Ellison. You are somebody else's daughter. You were in her company or her possession for a long time; just why, we can't prove yet a while. But there was something right mysterious between that fellow Decherd and Mrs. Ellison. Did you ever see them much together, as long as you were living with Mrs. Ellison?"

"No," said Miss Lady, "never, except as they met occasionally here or there. Mrs. Ellison traveled a great deal from time to time, when I was little, before we went to New Orleans, where I went to school with the Sisters. She, my mother - that is, Mrs. Ellison - had money from somewhere, not always very much. Mr. Decherd told me often that he simply was an old friend of hers. I always thought he was a lawyer somewhere in this state. Sometimes he went to St. Louis. We went to New Orleans; and that was the last I saw of him for some years until we came here to the Big House."

"That's all you know?" asked Blount. "You don't remember any mother of your own?"

"Not in the least." Tears welled from her eyes, and this time Blount did not protest.

"Miss Lady," said he, "there are some things we can't clear up yet. We can't prove just yet who was your own mother, but I want to tell you, you were born as far above that sort of life as that there sun is above the earth. No matter how much Decherd loved you, or how much right he had to love you, he couldn't do you anything but wrong and harm, and injury, and shame. As near as we can find out, he was about as bad, and about as sharp a man as ever struck this country. We couldn't hardly believe at first how smooth he was. Miss Lady, we can't tell just what his relations to Mrs. Ellison were. We know they had some kind of an understanding. We know that he was mixed up with Delphine down here on some sort of a basis. We know that he was robbing the railroad here with a list of judgment claims against the road, which he stole in some way. We know he was underneath a heap of this trouble with the niggers down here, and that he used Delphine as a cat's-paw in that. It was his scheme to have other people stir up all the trouble they could, so he could carry on his own devilment behind the smoke. Now we know he was mixed up with those two women somehow. I won't ask you any questions, and won't try to understand why you could have been so blind as not to know your own friends. - No, Miss

Lady, come back here, and sit right down. You've got to take your own medicine, and some day you've got to know your own friends. Now sit down, and hold on till I tell you what I know about this."

And so, to a Miss Lady alternately shocked and ashamed, he went on to tell in his own fashion, and to the best of his knowledge, the facts of the strange story which had been canvassed between himself and Eddring long before. The sun was still farther up in the heavens when he had concluded, and when finally he rose to his feet and stood erect before her.

"So there you are, Miss Lady," said he. "You couldn't be any better than we knew you were all along. I don't think any more of you now than I ever did; and I don't believe Jack Eddring does either. Now, we don't know where this man Decherd will turn up again. You've got to stay here until we find out about that. But this thing can't run along this way, and it's got to be settled on a business basis. We've got to find Mrs. Ellison and make her tell what she knows. As to Decherd, his own rope'll hang him before long. Now, I'm going to be your agent, your attorney-in-fact. That's what we'd call a 'next friend' in law, maybe, though you don't need any guardian now. If you've got any better friend, you name him, but I know you haven't. Then we'll start suit to get possession of that property, which is yours. Jack Eddring will be your attorney. I'll appoint him myself, right now. He's just a little too good for you, Miss Lady, for you didn't think he was honest; but he'll handle this case. The only promise I want of you is this: if you get plumb rich and independent, and able to go where you like, and marry anybody you want to, you won't get up and go right away at once and leave us all. You won't do that right away, now will you, Miss Lady?"

Tears still stood in Miss Lady's eyes, as she put both her hands in the big one extended to her. "Colonel Cal," said she, "it's a wonder that I can know my friends, or tell the truth, or do anything that's right. It's been deceit, and treachery, and wrong about me all the time. I have hardly heard a true word, it seems to me, except when I was with the Sisters. But I think that she, Mrs. Ellison, told me one true thing, although she didn't mean it that way. She said, 'There's nothing in the world for a woman except the men.' That's the truth. It's been the truth for me. They're not all bad; I know now I've met two good ones, at least."

"You said two?" asked Blount.

Miss Lady hesitated. "Yes - two," she said, "I'm so sorry."

Blount caught the penitence of her tone and the meaning of her unfinished speech, and was content to leave his friend's case as it was. "Miss Lady," said he, sternly, "what do you mean idling around here all the morning? Can't you hear my dogs hollering? Them puppies will just naturally starve to death, and here you are a-visiting around in the shade, not tending to business."

It was a sober and thoughtful young woman who looked up at him. "All my life, Colonel Cal," said she, "there has been a sort of cloud before my eyes. I could not see clearly. Tell me, do you think I'll ever understand, and see everything clearly, and be my real self?"

"Yes, girl," said Calvin Blount, "you'll see it all clear, some day; and I hope it won't be long. Now, I said, go feed them puppies. And look at old Hec, there, wanting to talk to you."

CHAPTER XIX

THREE LADIES LOUISE

In the city, as well as in the country, spring came with a sensible charm. John Eddring, as he gazed out of his office one morning at the slow life of the southern city and felt the breath of the warm wind at the casement, abandoned himself for the time to the relaxation of the season. Peace and content seemed to abide here also, and Eddring, looking out of his window, sighed not altogether in sadness that his world was proving so endurable; that it might even, in time, prove comforting. With a man's exultation, he found happiness in the certainty that he could do his work, and that there was work for him to do - work perhaps in some sort higher than that which he had recently assigned to himself. Before him on his desk there lay a communication which meant his nomination as candidate at the next election for the state Legislature. It was pointed out to him that in all likelihood greater honors might await him at the hands of his district, as of the county. He found in this not so much personal pride as a sense of responsibility. Yet there remained comfort in the fact that he was growing, that he was in some measure attaining. As with any man truly great, this left him no more selfish, no more egotistic, than is the stringed instrument which, under the miracle of a higher power, finds itself capable of music.

Upon Eddring's desk at that moment there lay close beside the opened letter certain papers, none other than the brief in the case of Louise Loisson against Henry Decherd, in ejectment, defendant charged with holding certain properties without legal title thereto. For years now Eddring had followed the curious and intricate question of the Loisson estate, and little by little he had seen the tangled skein unravel beneath his hand. There were necessary links of the evidence yet to be supplied.

As against all adverse title, there needed to be urged for his client descent for three generations, carried in each generation by a single child, who in each case bore the name of Louise Loisson - certainly a strange and singular legal contingency. There needed to be three ladies Louise; and of these he had found but two. There was no great difficulty in establishing the fact that the grandmother of Louise Loisson was the daughter of the Comte de Loisson; that she returned to Paris early in the nineteenth century; that in spite of her noble birth she figured for some years as a danseuse in leading Continental cities, - a dancer of strange dances. This Louise Loisson, as he discovered, had some years later, after declining all manner of titled suitors, married a distant cousin, by name Raoul de Loisson, of Favreuil-Chantry, France; a young nobleman of democratic tendencies, who later removed to New Orleans, in the state of Louisiana. So much for the first Louise Loisson.

Records showed that to Raoul and Louise Loisson was born one daughter, Louise, who married one Robert Fanning, a planter and cattle dealer. But the confusion of records brought about by the Civil War left it impossible to tell what became of this Louise Loisson-Fanning, or of either of her parents. The trail ended abruptly; nor could Eddring find any means of pursuing it further, certain as he was that, in the person of Miss Lady, he had found the third Louise Loisson and the rightful heiress of the Loisson properties in the mountains below St. Louis. Again he looked at his uncompleted papers, and again he sighed.

It was well toward noon, and Eddring was busying himself about other matters, when he heard the knock of his faithful henchman, Jack, and bade him enter.

"Lady done sent me over fom de hotel, sah," said Jack. "I

brung her trunk up f'om de de-pot. Heah's her kyard. She's over to the hotel, an' wants you to come oveh dah."

Eddring started to his feet as he saw the name upon the card. "Tell the lady," said he, "to come here to my own office. Tell her to come at once, and say that I will wait for her." And thus, a half-hour later, there appeared at his door the figure of Alice Ellison, sometime adventurous, yet not always happy, woman of fortune.

Eddring gazed at her sharply. She seemed older. Traces of dissipation showed upon her face. Her eye, a trifle more furtive, glanced from side to side as though she felt herself pursued. Yet in spite of all, Alice Ellison, even at her years, was a woman not wholly without charm. She stood now, hesitating, her hand still upon the knob of the door, her face not altogether confident as she gazed at the man before her.

"Come in, Madam, and be seated," said Eddring. "I am very glad to see you."

His tone reassured her, and she entered, half-extending to him her hand.

"I - I know you are a good lawyer, Mr. Eddring," said she, "and I - well, I'm in trouble. I've a case, a very interesting one, which means a great deal of money to some one. I thought that perhaps you'd like to take my case. I have always had so much respect for you, Mr. Eddring."

She turned upon him eyes which might have been compelling enough under certain circumstances, but whose glance was lost upon the man before her. Eddring stepped quietly to the door, closed it and sprung the lock. "Madam," said he, "are you alone in this case? Do you not really mean that you and Mr. Henry Decherd are partners in this enterprise?"

She started up. "Open the door!" she cried. "Let me out!"

"No," said Eddring; "you can not go. In one way it is effrontery for you to come here. But in another, it was the best thing you could do. The case of yourself and this man Decherd might be taken without retainer by the prosecuting attorney of any of a half-dozen localities. You may know that I'm acquainted with many of the details of this case in the past; but still you have done well to come here."

"You'll not tell him - " she began.

"You mean Decherd?" She nodded, her hand at her throat. "I'm afraid of him," she said. "He'll kill me. He'll kill me some day, surely. I wanted you - I wanted you to take care of me. I - I've always thought so much of you, Mr. Eddring."

She reached out to him a pitiful hand, and on her face was the horrible mask of a woman endeavoring feminine arts while upon her soul there sat naught but horror and personal concern. Eddring looked at her in simple pity. "Be seated here, Madam," said he. "Be quiet, and make yourself at ease. The safest thing you can do is to tell me the whole truth. I want your story, and I must have it. That will be the safest thing for you."

"But I don't want - I don't want any one to hear us."

"No one need hear us. We shall not need even a notary or a clerk. Talk to me freely, and afterward I will make a memorandum, which you can attest. In the case of a contested land title, that can later be introduced under a bill for the perpetuation of the evidence. You must simply tell me the truth, now, and in your own way."

The face of Alice Ellison grew more haggard. Suddenly all the weakness of her sex swept over her - all the weakness also of the wrong-doer. The comfort of the confessional seemed the sole happiness possible for her. And so it was that she gave to Eddring the first direct confirmation of that which he had by piece-work reasoning convinced himself to be the truth. He first rapidly ran over the salient features of the Loisson story, explaining to her fully his interest In the same, and pointing out to her the certainty of his success as well as the hopelessness of any contest on the part of herself or Decherd. Thereafter his questions induced the other to speak definitely.

"You were right about the book," said Alice Ellison. "It was found in the Congressional Library by that man, by Mr. Decherd. I took it from there myself, and I always kept it. The first Louise Loisson married her cousin, I think, in about 1841, and she and her husband came to New Orleans not long after that. Louise Loisson the second was born in 1848 at New Orleans, and she married, as you say, this Mr. Fanning. She was not known as Louise Loisson. Raoul de Loisson turned a very ardent democrat. He was known in New Orleans, or at least publicly known, under the name of Ellison, which form of his name he thought was more American.

"Louise, his daughter, was also known under the name of Ellison. She was not married until 1874. Before her marriage she was an orphan, and you might have found, had you been lucky enough, proof of the fact that she was known on the stage of the old French Opera House, even after the close of the Civil War. Her mother died while Louise, the second Louise, was in her youth. Her father, then a major in a Louisiana regiment, was killed during the war, in the fighting near Atlanta.

"Louise Ellison was thus, like all the other unfortunate girls of that family, left alone early in life. The first Louise perhaps learned her strange dancing in a school of her own somewhere in the West. Louise Ellison the second also had her own methods. She danced in New Orleans for a time, but went from there to Paris. They all danced - they could not help it. It was heredity, I suppose. The second one danced, like her mother - and then married."

"I thought you said she was married in New Orleans."

"Not in New Orleans, but in Paris. You know, at one time, the rich planters of Louisiana spent half the year regularly in Paris. It was so with Robert Fanning. The story is that he met her first in Paris, dancing at one of the theaters, and creating a furore, as her mother had before her. He learned that she was American and from New Orleans, and year after year he urged her to marry him. She must have been late in her twenties before she finally did so, for that was in 1874. They probably lived in Paris for a time, for it was not until 1877 that they came back to Fanning's plantation, where her baby was born."

The hand of John Eddring, lying upon the table before him, twitched and trembled. "And that child," said he, "was Miss Lady Ellison? Tell me, tell me at once!"

"Yes," whispered Alice Ellison, her eyes turned aside from his gaze. Eddring drew a long sigh of relief. "Thank God!" said he. "So that was our Miss Lady Ellison, and she was not your child. Now, tell me, as soon as you can, how did it all happen? Tell me, where did you meet Decherd? Who was he? Was he your husband? Tell me now, as fast as you can."

Mrs. Ellison paled before his vehemence, and her voice broke a bit tremulously. "Well, then, wait," said she. "I'm going to tell you. You must know all this is hard - awfully hard. If I told you this you could put me in prison. You could do anything. Promise me that you will not take any action."

"I promise you," said Eddring, sharply. "Tell me the truth, and help me to put this girl where she belongs, and I'll see that you are not prosecuted. But now tell me about yourself and this man Decherd. Were you married? Where did you meet him?"

"I was born in the North," she went on, hesitating. "I won't tell you my name. My family was good enough. I may have been wild when I was a girl. I won't say as to that. I was a good deal older than Henry Decherd when I first met him at New York. He attended a law school there. He told me he came of good family, and he seemed able and well-bred enough. He was infatuated with me. We - well, we left New York together."

"Were you married?"

"You need not know. At least we were engaged then to be married, and God knows our lives were tangled closely enough from that time on. We were not very old, either of us. I presume we cared for each other - you know how that is. The trouble with him was he was following off after all the women in the world. Some think that is strength. Any woman who knows how to love knows it is weakness, and not strength. At any rate, it was that which made our first trouble. Meantime, he was not regularly taking up the practice of the law. I found him practically disowned by his family, who were Shreveport people originally. In one way or another he found a bit to do. He knew Robert Fanning and his wife through the fact that he had done legal work of some sort for Fanning. He knew also an old lawyer, or sort of notary, who used to do business for Eaoul de Loisson, or Ralph Ellison, as he called himself, years before. I can't tell you the name of that old lawyer, but Decherd could if he wanted to. He was somewhere down on Baronne Street in those days.

"At that time Mr. Decherd used to talk to me more freely. He told me that the old lawyer had told him that the Loissons were legal heirs to considerable lands somewhere up the river, not far from St. Louis. He said that Raoul de Loisson always laughed at that when he brought it up, and declared that any good American ought to be able to make his own living by himself, without counting upon his wife's fortune. Robert Fanning felt the same way. He thought he could make a living for his wife, without looking up the old estate, which at that time was not known to be of any great value."

"But go on, tell me about Fanning," broke in Eddring, impatiently.

"I am going to, as well as I can. You must remember that Mr.

Decherd was then still a very young man indeed. I myself was older, as I said. This old notary, or lawyer, or whatever he was, had never seen me, and I do not know whether he was well acquainted or not with the Louise Ellison who was Fanning's wife. I only know that we went out to Fanning's plantation sometime about the year 1877. Mr. Fanning was away in Texas, and there came news of his death somewhere down in the Rio Grande country, where he had gone to purchase cattle. I don't think his wife ever knew of his fate. Henry Decherd and I were there together at the plantation.

"If I told you the truth now you would not believe it. But what I am telling you is the truth, and I will swear to it. Louise Fanning died two days after her baby was born. I lay there in their house at that time, and they told me that my baby had died. There was no one then acting as the head of the house. The servants were all distracted. One day some one came and put this live baby, the daughter of Louise Fanning, in my arms. Oh! you don't know, but I longed so for my baby! My arms fairly ached. So then I took this one and loved it. Sir, I was a mother to her, a sort of mother - as good, I suppose, as I could have been at all - for a long time."

Eddring sat looking at her, his fingers pressed closely to his lips. "What you tell me, Madam, is very, very strange," said he. "It might perhaps have been true."

"Believe it or not," said Alice Ellison, "it is the truth, as I have told you. There was no head to that household. There was no place to leave that little child. I took it for my own. I did not at that time intend any wrong. I don't know whether Decherd did at that time or not. It was there at the Fannings' that we met the girl Delphine, who had come in there from some-where in the Indian Nations. She was then in her early teens, and was good-looking. I don't want to talk much about it, but it was then, I think, that Henry Decherd got - got interested in her. What he told her I don't know. He found out in some way that her name was Loise. In some way then and later he got to looking up the name of Loise in St. Louis, where the girl said her people originally lived. He assumed the management of her case, along with some other lawyers to whom he carried it."

"But did he think she was the heiress of the Loisson estates?"

"You, as a lawyer, can tell that better than I can. In some ways he had a good mind. He never told me much after that, except that he said if this case was ever decided he could not lose, no matter which way it went. We waited, years and years, for the case to get through the Supreme Court."

"How did you live in the meantime, and where did you go?"

"Don't ask me that. We lived the best way we could. Decherd got money now and again, and for reasons of his own he sent some money, once in a while, to keep me and the child, although he practically abandoned me, and, as I think, associated the more with this girl Delphine. He claimed to me all the time that it was necessary for him to live in this part of the country, in order to handle the lawsuit for her. She moved up here from New Orleans, I suppose to some town not far from Colonel Blount's plantation. I think he got us in there at Blount's place because he thought it would be less expense to him. In the meantime, I had educated the girl the best I could. Sir, I loved her in a way, until I thought other men were noticing her; and then I could not stand it."

"But you have not told me all of your story up to that time," said Eddring. "It is not easy for one absolutely to steal a child, and never be detected and punished for it. Moreover, you have not explained to me how you came by the name under which you were known to all of us. You say you were not Mrs. Decherd. Then who were you?"

The woman's lip half-curled in scorn. "Henry Decherd would have guessed that long ago," said she. "Who was to detect us? What was there to hinder? The Fanning family was wiped out. After the war he had no relatives remaining. I have just told you his wife was unknown in this country. This was her first visit after her marriage in Paris. When Henry Decherd and I took the baby back to New Orleans, what was there to hinder my being Louise Ellison-Fanning, the widow of Robert Fanning? Decherd was my attorney. The old notary helped these supposed descendants of his friend. It was he who helped us find the lead lands in St. Francois County. The old notary was as much a lover of the old nobility as Raoul de Loisson was a flouter of it."

"Ah, I begin to see," said Eddring. "I can see it unwinding now!"

"Yes, it was not difficult, but on the contrary, very simple. A criminal, if you please, may be bold, and boldness means success. Now, it was this old notary who, through friends of his in the Louisiana Legislature, had the Ellison name changed back legally to Loisson, as the records of that state show to-day, although you have not discovered those facts. As for me, it made little difference. The name of Ellison was established in the state of Louisiana. I simply took it, and wore it because I had no better. I did as many another woman has done; got on as best I could. But I tell you, I loved the girl for a long time. She was sweet and good. I felt she was my own, until the time when she began to dance; and then I knew perfectly well that sometime the truth would come out. I could feel it. Blood and breeding - I tell you, you can't escape that. It's all bound to come out. I might have known - I did know. I dreaded it, all along. I always knew the truth would come out some day."

The two sat looking at each other in silence for a time. "Tell me the rest," said Eddring, at length.

"The old lawyer died in 1879 or 1880," she went on, "but by that time Mr. Decherd knew all that he cared to learn. As I said, he was less confidential with me after that. That was the time when he was infatuated with Delphine. Everything was to his liking. He was fond of intrigue, and the more intricate it was, the better for him. He was not afraid - when he had only

EMERSON HOUGH

women to be afraid of. With Delphine and me he did as he pleased, passing from one to the other. Delphine knew a part of the story, I do not know just how much. I never dared talk too much with Delphine, for fear I might learn too much, or she might learn too much. I was afraid of her, and I was more afraid of him. When Miss Lady grew up, then I got jealous of her - oh! I could not help it. I'm a woman, you know, and a woman likes to be loved by some one. I got to comparing Decherd with Colonel Blount; and then I - well, never mind. I need only say I was frightened, and I needed a friend, and I knew the Big House was the best home we were apt to have, and the safest place. It was a terrible situation down there, and only three of us knew. Of the three, Decherd was the only one who knew all the facts."

"I'll say for him," said Eddring, "that his boldness was startling enough. He was a dangerous man."

"Yes, he was dangerous. But when he got started in this he could not turn back."

"Exactly what Colonel Blount said to me one time," said Eddring. "He was on a trembling bog, and he had to keep on running."

"Did Colonel Blount say that? Does he know everything?"

"As much as I know, or presently he will do so; I shall tell him all of this in due time."

"Where is the girl? Where is Lady now?"

"At the Big House, and safe."

"And where is Henry Decherd?"

"That I do not know. We'll hear from him some day, no doubt."

The woman looked about her, as though still in fear. "Tell me, Mr. Eddring," said she, "did you - did you ever - I mean, do you love that girl yourself?"

"Very much, Madam," said John Eddring, quietly,

"Are you going to marry her?"

"No."

"Then why did she give you her case?"

"I was chosen by her friend, Colonel Blount, as the lawyer best acquainted with these facts."

"Ah! sir," said Mrs. Ellison, turning again upon him the full glance of her dark eyes. "Why? Can you not see - do you not know? Why trouble with a half-baked chit like her? Drop it all, sir. You are lawyer enough to know that my case is as good as hers, if handled well. If I knew one man upon whom I could depend - ah! you do not know, you will not see!"

One hand, white, thick-palmed, shapely, approached his upon the table. He could feel its warmth before it touched his own. Then swiftly he caught the hand in a hard and stern grasp, looking straight into the eyes of its owner. "Madam," said he, "none of this! I have asked you to tell me the truth. I have told you the truth. The truth leaves us very far apart. You are safe; but you must understand." Her eyes sank, and on her cheek the dull flush reappeared.

"Now I want you to go on and answer a few more questions," said Eddring, finally. "I suppose that while you were all there at the Big House you were partners, after a fashion. How much did you know of Delphine's stirring up the negroes in that neighborhood?"

"I did not know much of it. I only guessed. I put nothing beyond Decherd."

"Did you know anything about the levee-cutting?"

"Nothing whatever. They didn't tell me anything of that. I presume it didn't suit Henry Decherd to tell me everything he was doing."

"I can imagine that," said Eddring. "There was a time for Decherd to lighten ship, and, as you say, he had only women to fear."

"I knew myself when the time came for me to leave him," said the woman, now apathetically. "I went over to St. Louis soon after Miss Lady first left the Big House, and after Decherd followed her. I knew that he was smitten with Miss Lady, and that there would be trouble, and that neither Delphine nor myself would be safe. I hid as best I could, and lived as best I could. Lately I have been frightened. I thought I would come to see you. I hoped you might help me. I don't know what I did think."

"You don't know where Decherd is at present?"

"No, I do not."

"Do you have any hope that he will ever care for you in any way?"

"Yes," said the woman, slowly and dully, "he cares for me. He'll care for me. He'll find me some day, now that you've taken Miss Lady from him."

"And you will go back to him?"

"Never! God forbid. Love him? No!"

"Yet you think he will look you up again. Why? To get help in this lawsuit?"

"You do not know him. He knows that all his hope in this

lawsuit was gone long ago. He's not a fool. But he is going to hunt me up some day. He's going to find me; and then - he's going to kill me. He's killed Delphine, and he's going to kill me."

The two white hands, trembling now as though with a palsy, fell on the table in front of her. Her eyes, not seeing Eddring, gazed staring straight in front of her. The horror of her soul was written upon her face. Remorse, repentance, fear for the atonement - these had their way with her who was lately known as Alice Ellison, woman of fortune, and now served ill by fortune's hand.

All at once she broke from her half-stupor, her overstrung nerves giving way. A cry of terror burst from her lips. "You!" she cried, "you will not love me, you will not save me! Oh, Lady, girl - oh, is there no one, is there no one in all the world?"

John Eddring took her firmly by the shoulders, and after a time half-quieted her.

"Wine," she sobbed; "brandy - give me something."

Eddring threw open the door. "Jack," he cried; "Jack, come here. Run across the street for me. When you come back order a carriage. This lady is ill."

She sat for a time, trembling. Eddring, himself agitated, completed his hurried writing. She signed. He called a notary, and she made oath with a hand that shook as she uplifted it.

John Eddring, possessed at length of the last thread of his mystery, helped down the stairs the trembling and terror-stricken woman who had been the final agent of a justice long deferred. "Madam," he said, as he assisted her into the carriage, "I thank you for Miss Lady. If you ever have any need, address me; and meantime, keep careful watch. Take care of yourself, and be sure this knowledge will never be used against you. We shall not see you want."

She seemed not to hear him. Her eyes still stared straight in front of her. "He's coming," she whispered. "It will be the end!"

CHAPTER XX

THE LID OF THE GRAVE

In a little room of a poor hotel situated on a back street of the city of New Orleans, a man bent over an old trunk which had that day been unearthed from a long-time hiding-place. It had for years been left unopened. It was like opening a grave now to raise its cover. The man almost shuddered as he bent over and looked in, curious as though these things had never before met his gaze. There was a dull odor of dead flowers long boxed up. A faint rustling as of intangible things became half audible, as though spirits passed out at this contact with the outer air.

"Twelve years ago - and this is the sort of luggage I carried then," he mused. "What taste! What a foolish boy! Dear me. Well - what?" His bravado failed him. He started, fearing something. Yet presently he peered in.

It was like a grave, yet one where some beneficent or some cruel process of nature had resisted the way of death and change. "Foolish boy!" he muttered, as he peered in and saw Life as it had been for him when he had shut down the lid. "God! it's strange. There ought to be a picture or so near the top." He touched the tray, and the dead flowers and dry papers rustled again until he started back. His face, tired, dissipated, deeply lined, went all the paler, but presently he delved in again.

"Pictures of myself, eh? the first thing. I was always first thing to myself. Nice, clean boy, wasn't I? Wouldn't have known it was myself. Might have been a parson, almost. Here's another.

Militia uniform, all that. Might have been a major, almost. Uh-hum! High school diploma here - very important. Eighteen - great God, was it so long ago as that? University diploma - Latin. Can't read it now. Might have been a professor, mightn't I? Diploma of law school; also Latin. Certificate of admission to the bar of - . Might have been a lawyer. Might have been a judge, mightn't I? Might have a home now; white, green blinds, brick walk up to the door, paling fence - that kind of thing. Might have had a home - wife and babies - eh! Baby? Children? What? Well, I couldn't call this much of a home, could I, now?"

He unfolded some old newspapers and periodicals of a departed period, bearing proof of certain of his own handi- craft. "Might have been a writer - poet - that sort of thing!" He smiled quizzically. "Not so bad. Not so bad. I couldn't do as well to-day, I'm afraid. Seem to have lost it - let go somewhere. I never could depend on myself - never could depend - ah, what's this? Yes, here are the ladies, God bless them - la-ladies - God bless 'em!"

The lower tray was filled with pictures of girls or women of all types, some of them beautiful, some of them coarse, most of them attractive from a certain point of view. "God! what a lot!" he murmured. "How did I do it? By asking, I reckon. Six - six - six of one - six of another. Women and men alike, eh? Well, I don't know. Ask 'em, you win. Or, don't ask 'em, you win."

His hand fell upon the frame of a little mirror laid away in the old trunk. He picked it up and gazed steadily at what it revealed. "Changed," he said, "changed a lot. Must have gone a pace, eh? Lawyer. Judge. Writer-man. Poet. I thought these beat all of that," - and he looked down again at the smiling faces. He picked them up one at a time and laid them on the bed beside him. "Alice, Nora, Clara, Kate, Margaret - I'll guess at the names, and guess at some of the faces now. It's the same, all alike, the hunting of love: the hunting - the hunt - ing - of - love! Great thing. But of course we never do find it, do we?

Ladies, good night." This he said in half-mocking solemnity.

He bowed ironically; yet his face was more uneasy now than wholly mocking. He looked once more at the trunk-tray, and found what he apparently half-feared to see. "Madam!" he whispered. "Madam! Alice!" He gazed at a face strong and full, with deep curved lips, and wide jaw, and large dark eyes, deeply browed and striking, the face of a woman to beckon to a man, to make him forget, for a time - and that was Alice Ellison as he had known her years ago, before - before - He turned away and would not look at this. He tried to laugh, to mock. "Bless you, ladies," he said, "I've often said I would like to see you all together in the same room. Eh - but the finding of it - oh, we never do find it, do we? Not love. I never could depend on myself.

"What! What's this!" he exclaimed, as his hand now touched something else, a hard object in the bottom of the trunk, beneath the tray. "Why, here's my old pistol. Twelve years old. I thought I'd lost it. Loaded! My faith, loaded for twelve years. Wonder if it would go off."

He sat on the edge of the bed, looking into the trunk, the revolver in his hand. Slowly, slowly, as though against his will, his face turned, and he found himself looking down at the pictured smiling faces that stared up at him. The last picture seemed to frighten him with its smile. All the pictures smiled. "Alice!" he whispered.

"My God!" cried Henry Decherd, suddenly. "They're alive! They're coming to life!"

They stood about him now in the little room, smiling, beckoning; Alice, Nora, Kate, Jane, Margaret, all the rest, as he addressed them. They smiled and beckoned; but he could not reply, whether to those honest or not honest, to those deceived or undeceived.

The face of Alice Ellison, strong-jawed, dark-browed,

large-eyed, stared at him steadily from behind a certain chair. He could see that her hair was wet. It hung down on her neck, on her shoulders. It clung to her temples. Her eyes gazed at him stonily now. He saw it all again - the struggle! He heard his own accusations, and hers. He heard her pleading, her cry for mercy; and then her cry of terror. He saw her face, staring up at him from the water. As he gazed, the other faces faded away into the darkness. He stood, staring, Henry Decherd, murderer of the woman whom he once had loved.

The porter of the hotel said on the next day that he remembered hearing late in the night a sort of crash, which sounded like the dropping of a trunk lid. He did not know what it was. The lid of the grave had fallen again for Henry Decherd!

CHAPTER XXI

THE RED RIOT OF YOUTH

The rim of the ancient forest still made the boundary of the little world of Miss Lady. Still she looked out beyond it in query, yearningly, longingly, though now she found herself more content than ever in her life before.

It was the daily habit of Miss Lady to ride for a time the big chestnut saddler which Colonel Blount had devoted to her special use. Mounted thus on Cherry, she cantered each day over the fields, where a renewed industry had now set on again. The simple field hands looked upon her as a higher being, and as their special messenger. If a baby was sick at a distant cabin, Miss Lady knew of it, and had the proper aid despatched. If the daughter of this or the other laborer needed shoes and could not wait until Christmas accounting time, it was Miss Lady who interceded with the master of the Big House.

"I couldn't get along here without you now," said that stern soul to her gruffly. "But I reckon you'd better run away again, for I'm afraid of people that I can't get along without. Besides, you're spoiling all my dogs, a-honeying of 'em up the way you do."

Miss Lady only laughed at that; though each day she looked out at the edge of her world.

Sometimes so wistfully did Miss Lady look out beyond the rim of the forest that she felt interest in the railway trains which carried her now and then to the cities north or south of her. Sometimes, even, girl-like she would mount Cherry, jump the front fence in violation of Colonel Blount's imperative orders, and scurry down to the station to have a look at the incoming trains. The conductors of all these trains knew her well, and often the brakeman or the conductor would hand out to her some package from the city as she rode up close to the car step, after the train had paused. The picture of Miss Lady and Cherry was a pleasant one, and more than one passenger peered out of a car window to see the tall girl who rode so well and who seemed so sure that all the world meant well and kindly toward her.

Miss Lady was now fully worthy to be called beautiful. She rarely rode otherwise than bare-headed, and the high-rolled masses of her hair had grown tawnier and redder for that reason. Her figure gave perfect lines to the scarlet jacket which so well became her. Her gauntlets fitted well the small, firm hands, and her foot was ever well-shod. Ah, indeed, in those days, when Miss Lady for the time forgot her past unhappiness, almost at times ceased to wonder what lay out beyond the forest, almost resigned herself to the mere happiness of a glorious young womanhood - she did indeed seem well-named as Lady, thoroughbred, titled as by right. Her eyes were wide and trustful, her lips high-curved, her cheeks pink with the rush of the air when Cherry galloped hard; her head was high, her gaze direct. And if, now and again, when the train had departed, Miss Lady, having come swiftly, she knew not why, rode back again slowly, she knew not why; if at times her eyes grew pensive as she listened to the mockers gurgling in the dogwood or on the honeysuckle, her spirits rose again, and her face was sure to brighten when she came near to the house and hurried Cherry up to the mounting block. She was the high-light in all the picture, unconsciously first in the gaze and thought of all. No woman ever was more worshiped; no, nor was ever one more fit for worship. Again, as old Jules once had said, she had become a religion!

One morning Miss Lady, her hair in its usual riot of tawny

brown, her face flushed, her lips laughing as she urged Cherry's nose up to the car side, was met by the conductor at the step, who called out to her gaily, "Company to-day." Miss Lady did not fully understand, and so waited, looking excellently well turned out in the bright jacket and the dainty gloves which lay on Cherry's tugging rein, as she sat easily, with the grace of a born horsewoman. And so, before she understood this speech, the train passed on; and as it passed it showed to these newly arrived passengers upon the platform this picture of Miss Lady, one not easily to be surpassed in any land, fit long to linger in any eye.

It was John Eddring who now gazed at this picture, and who felt rise to his lips the swift salutation of his soul, tenderer than ever now in its instantaneous homage. He had not dreamed that she could grow so beautiful. He had not known that love could mean so much - that it could mean more than every-thing - that it could outweigh every human interest and every human resolve! His heart, long suppressed by an iron determination; his whole nature, gone a-hunger in the long fight for success, now at once rebelled and broke all shackles in one swift instant of its mutiny. He knew now how unjust he had been to himself, for that he had worked and had not lived. The years broke from him, and he was young. For with him youth had not been lost, but set aside, unspent. Now it came to him all at once - the red riot of youth and love. It must have shone in his eyes, must have trembled in his touch, as he hurried over the rails at which Cherry's dainty forefeet now were pausing, and reached up his arms to her, murmuring he knew not what.

He helped her dismount, and caught then her gaze directed behind him. John Eddring had forgotten that his mother was with him. She came forward now, reaching out her hand, then reaching out her arms.

"Child," said the white-haired old lady, "I've heard it all, all your strange story. My son has come to tell you that you have succeeded at last. Your case is won!"

She touched Miss Lady's tumbled tawny hair with her own gentle hand. "My girl," said she, "my dear girl; and you never knew your own mother? You never knew what that was? My dear, it is very sweet to have a mother."

Miss Lady, knowing no better thing, kissed her impulsively, and the older lady drew her close, in such communion as only women may understand. Mrs. Eddring again touched lightly the red-brown hair. "I never had a daughter," said she. "I've only a boy. That's my boy there."

Eddring, who had meantime taken Cherry's bridle rein, was now walking on in advance toward the lane that led to the house. The girl caught the old lady's hands in her own, and then threw her arms about the thin figure in a swift embrace. So, arm in arm, they also turned toward the lane; and which was then welcoming the other home neither could have said.

CHAPTER XXII

AMENDE HONORABLE

"Well, what do you want, boy?" Blount gruffly asked of Eddring on the morning after his arrival. "Are you on a still hunt for that Congressional nomination?"

"No, it's of a heap more importance than that," said Eddring.

"Humph! Maybe. Bill, oh, *Bill!* Here, you go and get the big glass mug, and a bunch of mint. Come out here, Eddring. Sit down on the board-pile in the shade - I've been going to build a roof on my doghouse with these boards as long as I can remember."

They had just seated themselves upon the board-pile, and were waiting for Bill with the mint when Eddring looked up and smiled. "Who's that coming?" he asked, pointing down the lane.

"That? Why, I reckon that's Jim Bowles and his wife, Sar' Ann. They come up once in a while to get a little milk, when they ain't too durn tired. Their cow - why, say, it was a good many years ago your blamed railroad killed that cow. They never did get another one since. And that reminds me, Mr. John Eddring - that reminds *me* -"

He fumbled in the wallet which he drew from his pocket, and produced an old and well-creased bit of paper. "Look here," said he, "you owe me for that filly of mine yet. That old railroad never did settle at all. Here it is. Fifty dollars."

"I thought it was fifteen," said Eddring, with twinkling eyes.

"That's what I said," replied Blount, solemnly, as he tore the paper in bits and dropped them at his feet. "I said fifteen! Anyway I'm in no humor to be a-quarreling about a little thing like that. Why, man, I'm just beginning to enjoy life. We're going to make a big crop of cotton this year, I've got the best pack of b'ah-dogs I ever did have yet, and there's more b'ah out in the woods than you ever did see."

"I suppose your ladies leave you once in a while, to go down to New Orleans?" inquired Eddring.

"No, *sir!* New Orleans no more," said Blount. "Why, you know, just as a business precaution, I bought that house down there that Madame Delchasse used to own. It's sort of in the family now. Shut off that running down to New Orleans."

"Well, how does Madame Delchasse like that?" asked Eddring.

"Man," said Blount, earnestly, "there's some things that seem to be sort of settled by fate - couldn't come out no other way. Do you suppose for one minute that I'm going to allow to get away from me the only woman I ever did see that could cook b'ah meat fit to eat? Well, I reckon not! Besides, what she can do to most anything is simply enough to scare you. She can take common crawfish, like the niggers catch all around here - and a shell off of a mussel, and out of them two things she makes what she calls a 'kokeeyon of eckriveese,' and - *say, man!* You bet your bottom dollar Madame Delchasse ain't going to get away from here. Don't matter a damn if she *ain't* got over putting hair-oil in her cocktails, like they do at New Orleans - we won't fall out about that, either. I don't have to drink 'em. Only thing, she calls a cussed old catfish a 'poisson.' That's when we begin to tangle some. But taking it all in all - up one side and down the other - I never did know before what *good* cooking meant. Why she's *got* to cook - she'd die if she didn't cook. Her go back to New Orleans? - well, I reckon not!

"Why, say," continued Blount, "don't it sometimes seem that luck sort of runs in streaks in this world? All cloudy, then out comes the sun - lovely world! Now, for one while it looked like things were pretty cloudy down here. But the sun's done come out again. Everything's all right, here at the Big House, now, sure's you're born. We'll go out and get a b'ah to-morrow. Come on, let's go see the dogs."

"Well, you know, I must be getting back to business before long," began Eddring.

"Business, what business?" protested Colonel Blount. "Say, have you asked that girl yet?" He was fumbling at the gate latch as he spoke, or he might have seen Eddring's face suddenly flush red.

"Whom do you mean?" he managed to stammer.

Blount whirled and looked him full in the eye. "You know mighty well who I mean."

Eddring turned away. "I told you, Cal," - he began.

"Oh, you *told* me! Well I could have told *you* a long time ago that Miss Lady had this whole thing straightened out in her head. Do you reckon she's a fool? I don't reckon she thinks you're a thief any more. I reckon like enough she thinks you're just a supreme damned *fool*. I know *I* do."

"Turn 'em loose, Cal!" cried Eddring, suddenly. "Open the gates! Let 'em out! I want to hear 'em holler!" The pack poured out, motley, vociferous, eager for the chase, filling the air with their wild music, with a riot of primeval, savage life. "Get me a horse saddled, Cal, quick," cried Eddring. "I want to feel leather under me again. I want to feel the air in my ears. I've got to ride, to move! Man, I'm going to *live*!"

"Now," said Blount, rubbing his chin, "you're beginning to *talk*. The man that don't like a good b'ah chase once in a while is no earthly use to me."

But Eddring did not ride to the far forest that day. A good horseman, and now well mounted, he made a handsome figure as he galloped off across the field. As he rode, his eye searched here and there, till it caught sight of the flash of a scarlet jacket beyond a distant screen of high green brier. He put his horse over the rail fence and pulled up at her side.

"You ride well," said Miss Lady, critically. "I didn't know that. Why didn't you tell me?"

"There have been a good many things about me that you didn't know," said Eddring, "and there's a heap of things I haven't told you."

Knowing in the instant now that a time of accounting had come, she looked at him miserably, her eyes downcast, her hands fiddling with the reins.

"But then, Miss Lady, you didn't know; it wasn't your fault," he added quickly.

"Oh," said the girl, impulsively taming toward him, her face very red, "I am so sorry, I am so *sorry*! To think of all you have done for us, for me. Why, every bit of safety and happiness in my life has come through you. I have felt that, and wanted *so* long to tell you and to thank you. You - you didn't come!"

"Never mind, never mind," said Eddring, wishing now nothing in the world so much as that he might have spared her this confession. "I've come now - oh, my girl, I've come now."

"All this time," said she, evading as long as she might, "you were trying, you were working, all alone. Mr. Eddring, it was not merely kind of you, it was noble!" And now poor Miss Lady flushed even more hotly than ever, though her heart was lighter for the truth thus told.

Eddring looked straight on down the road ahead of them, the road which broke the rim of the forest toward which they had now unconsciously faced. At length he turned toward her.

"Miss Lady," said he, simply, "I have loved you so much, so very much. I've always loved you. I didn't dare admit it to myself for a long time; but it's run away with me now, absolutely and for ever. I can't look at life - I can't turn any way - I can't think of *anything* in which I don't see you. It's been this way a long time, but now I'm gone. I can't pull up. Miss Lady, I *couldn't* go back now and begin life over again alone. I couldn't do that now. I wouldn't want to make you unhappy, ever. Do you think, oh, *don't* you think that you could depend on me? Don't you think you could love me?"

Miss Lady's eyes were cast down, and her hands were busy at the reins which she shifted between her fingers. Cherry walked slowly and still more slowly, until at length Eddring laid his hand upon the bridle, and Cherry turned about an inquiring eye. He reached out his hand and took in it the small, gray-gloved one which had half-loosed its grasp upon the rein.

"Miss Lady," he whispered. And then slowly the girl lifted her eyes and looked full at him - her eyes now grown soft and gentle.

"Yes," said she, "I can depend," Her voice was very low. Yet the woman-whisper reached to the edge of all the universe - a universe robbed of its last secret by the woman-soul. "I can see you clearly," said Miss Lady, softly. "I see your heart. Yes. I am sure. I understand - I know now who I am. And I know - I know it all. All!"

"But do you love me!" he demanded; and now Cherry's nose was drawn quite over the neck of Jerry. Miss Lady would not answer that, but turned away her face, which was now very pink. "Tell me," he demanded, frowning in his own earnest-ness, and catching the bridle hand in a stern clasp, "may I depend? Tell me, girl. I can not wait."

There was a gentle breeze among the tree-tops. A mocker near by trilled and gurgled. Eddring leaned forward. It seemed to him he heard a whisper which told him that he might be sure.

Choose from Thousands of 1stWorldLibrary Classics By

Adolphus WilliamWard
Aesop
Agatha Christie
Alexander Aaronsohn
Alexander Kielland
Alexandre Dumas
Alfred Gatty
Alfred Ollivant
Alice Duer Miller
Alice Turner Curtis
Alice Dunbar
Ambrose Bierce
Amelia E. Barr
Andrew Lang
Andrew McFarland Davis
Anna Sewell
Annie Besant
Annie Hamilton Donnell
Annie Payson Call
Anton Chekhov
Arnold Bennett
Arthur Conan Doyle
Arthur Ransome
Atticus
B. M. Bower
Basil King
Bayard Taylor
Ben Macomber
Booth Tarkington
Bram Stoker
C. Collodi
C. E. Orr
C. M. Ingleby
Carolyn Wells
Catherine Parr Traill
Charles A. Eastman
Charles Dickens
Charles Dudley Warner
Charles Farrar Browne
Charles Ives
Charles Kingsley
Charles Lathrop Pack
Charles Whibley
Charles Willing Beale
Charlotte M. Braeme
Charlotte M.Yonge
Clair W. Hayes
Clarence Day Jr.
Clarence E. Mulford

Clemence Housman
Confucius
Cornelis DeWitt Wilcox
Cyril Burleigh
D. H. Lawrence
Daniel Defoe
David Garnett
Don Carlos Janes
Donald Keyhole
Dorothy Kilner
Dougan Clark
E. Nesbit
E.P.Roe
E. Phillips Oppenheim
Edgar Allan Poe
Edgar Rice Burroughs
Edith Wharton
Edward J. O'Biren
John Cournos
Edwin L. Arnold
Eleanor Atkins
Elizabeth Cleghorn
Gaskell
Elizabeth Von Arnim
Ellem Key
Emily Dickinson
Erasmus W. Jones
Ernie Howard Pie
Ethel Turner
Ethel Watts Mumford
Eugenie Foa
Eugene Wood
Evelyn Everett-Green
Everard Cotes
F. J. Cross
Federick Austin Ogg
Ferdinand Ossendowski
Francis Bacon
Francis Darwin
Frances Hodgson Burnett
Frank Gee Patchin
Frank Harris
Frank Jewett Mather
Frank L. Packard
Frederick Trevor Hill
Frederick Winslow Taylor
Friedrich Kerst
Friedrich Nietzsche
Fyodor Dostoyevsky

Gabrielle E. Jackson
Garrett P. Serviss
Gaston Leroux
George Ade
Geroge Bernard Shaw
George Ebers
George Eliot
George MacDonald
George Orwell
George Tucker
George W. Cable
George Wharton James
Gertrude Atherton
Grace E. King
Grant Allen
Guillermo A. Sherwell
Gulielma Zollinger
Gustav Flaubert
H. A. Cody
H. B. Irving
H. G. Wells
H. H. Munro
H. Irving Hancock
H. Rider Haggard
H. W. C. Davis
Hamilton Wright Mabie
Hans Christian Andersen
Harold Avery
Harold McGrath
Harriet Beecher Stowe
Harry Houidini
Helent Hunt Jackson
Helen Nicolay
Hendy David Thoreau
Henrik Ibsen
Henry Adams
Henry Ford
Henry Frost
Henry James
Henry Jones Ford
Henry Seton Merriman
Henry Wadsworth
Longfellow
Henry W Longfellow
Herbert A. Giles
Herbert N. Casson
Herman Hesse
Homer
Honore De Balzac

Horace Walpole	Laurence Housman	Robert Lansing
Horatio Alger, Jr.	Leo Tolstoy	Robert Michael Ballantyne
Howard Pyle	Leonid Andreyev	Robert W. Chambers
Howard R. Garis	Lewis Carroll	Rosa Nouchette Carey
Hugh Lofting	Lilian Bell	Ross Kay
Hugh Walpole	Lloyd Osbourne	Rudyard Kipling
Humphry Ward	Louis Tracy	Samuel B. Allison
Ian Maclaren	Louisa May Alcott	Samuel Hopkins Adams
Israel Abrahams	Lucy Fitch Perkins	Sarah Bernhardt
J.G.Austin	Lucy Maud Montgomery	Selma Lagerlof
J. Henri Fabre	Lydia Miller Middleton	Sherwood Anderson
J. M. Barrie	Lyndon Orr	Sigmund Freud
J. Macdonald Oxley	M. H. Adams	Standish O'Grady
J. S. Knowles	Margaret E. Sangster	Stanley Weyman
J. Storer Clouston	Margaret Vandercook	Stella Benson
Jack London	Maria Edgeworth	Stephen Crane
Jacob Abbott	Maria Thompson Daviess	Stewart Edward White
James Allen	Mariano Azuela	Stijn Streuvels
James Lane Allen	Marion Polk Angellotti	Swami Abhedananda
James Andrews	Mark Overton	Swami Parmananda
James Baldwin	Mark Twain	T. S. Ackland
James DeMille	Mary Austin	The Princess Der Ling
James Joyce	Mary Cole	Thomas A. Janvier
James Oliver Curwood	Mary Rowlandson	Thomas A Kempis
James Oppenheim	Mary Wollstonecraft	Thomas Anderton
James Otis	Shelley	Thomas Bailey Aldrich
Jane Austen	Max Beerbohm	Thomas Bulfinch
Jens Peter Jacobsen	Myra Kelly	Thomas De Quincey
Jerome K. Jerome	Nathaniel Hawthrone	Thomas H. Huxley
John Burroughs	O. F. Walton	Thomas Hardy
John F. Kennedy	Oscar Wilde	Thomas More
John Gay	Owen Johnson	Thornton W. Burgess
John Glasworthy	P.G.Wodehouse	U. S. Grant
John Habberton	Paul and Mable Thorn	Valentine Williams
John Joy Bell	Paul G. Tomlinson	Victor Appleton
John Milton	Paul Severing	Virginia Woolf
John Philip Sousa	Peter B. Kyne	Walter Scott
Jonathan Swift	Plato	Washington Irving
Joseph Carey	R. Derby Holmes	Wilbur Lawton
Joseph Conrad	R. L. Stevenson	Wilkie Collins
Joseph Jacobs	Rabindranath Tagore	Willa Cather
Julian Hawthrone	Rahul Alvares	Willard F. Baker
Julies Vernes	Ralph Waldo Emmerson	William Makepeace
Justin Huntly McCarthy	Rene Descartes	Thackeray
Kakuzo Okakura	Rex E. Beach	William W. Walter
Kenneth Grahame	Richard Harding Davis	Winston Churchill
Kate Langley Bosher	Richard Jefferies	Yei Theodora Ozaki
L. A. Abbot	Robert Barr	Young E. Allison
L. T. Meade	Robert Frost	Zane Grey
L. Frank Baum	Robert Gordon Anderson	
Laura Lee Hope	Robert L. Drake	

www.ingramcontent.com/pod-product-compliance
Lightning Source LLC
Chambersburg PA
CBHW021330250626
47155CB00002B/665